M000223084

THE DECOY

CHLOÉ ARCHAMBAULT

To Sylvain, Christophe and Victor

CHAPTER 1

I heard the footsteps down the hall and froze. Slow and steady. I knew that walk and its monotonous pace. I recognized it immediately. And I knew who it belonged to. I glanced at the time in the corner of the computer screen. Eleven thirty-two. The watchman was almost twenty minutes ahead of schedule. *What the hell?*

The soft squeaking of his rubber soles slowed down and stopped. How close was he behind the door of the office? I couldn't tell. Nothing moved in the thin ray of light that filtered along the door sill inside the darkened room. I held my breath and listened, as I imagined he did too on the other side of the door. The light whiz of a computer fan was the only sound I heard.

At this time of night the office of Gaëlle Pinard, one of McGill's most distinguished computer science scholars, was always empty. Dr. Pinard was an early riser. Her office hours started at seven thirty in the morning. So why the stop? I looked again at the glowing screen on the professor's desk. About half the files I wanted to copy had been downloaded on my portable hard disk. I needed more time.

A set of keys jingled behind the door.

Shit.

My heart jumped inside my chest. I reached out for the switch on the side of the monitor, which turned black and died instantaneously, and lowered myself behind the desk and underneath it as the watchman inserted a key in the door lock. The blinding light of the ceiling fixtures came on in a flash and saturated the office in a white, fluorescent glow that illuminated the disorderly books and shelves. The photographs and the trinkets. The piles of papers. *What was the watchman doing?*

Professor Pinard's desk was a stately piece of furniture made of solid oak with a front panel that hid the sitter's legs. I heard the watchman take a step inside the office, then stop.

Breathe slow. Relax.

There was a slight shuffle closer to my wooden niche and I suddenly thought about the portable hard disk I had left on the desk, plugged into the desktop with its pin light blinking. Surely the watchman had seen it.

Shit.

There was movement again, this time towards the door. The watchman was leaving. He hadn't touched anything, hadn't stayed longer than was necessary. He never did. He never poked around, never stole, never lied. For weeks I had kept watch over Ibrahim Bencherif, the night watchman with the grey hair, and had failed to find anything that could be used as leverage. I had surreptitiously snooped on the Internet into the different spheres of his private life like a pickpocket into the various compartments of a handbag. To no avail. The man was happily married with two grown daughters. One a dental hygienist, the other a security guard in the Metro. A community man but all within reason. A moderate.

The office went dark again, and I heard the door being shut. I came out of my hiding place and listened to the fading sound of the watchman's footsteps. As expected, heading to the glass-enclosed staircase at the end of the hall, on his way to another deserted hallway one floor up. Which meant I had no more than five minutes to get back upstairs.

"Shit."

I turned the monitor back on and waited, my fingers ready to pounce on the keyboard.

"Come on, goddammit."

The download was still incomplete. I closed all the files and the applications before disconnecting the portable disk. I pulled at it, wrapped the cord around its flat black core and squeezed it against my belly into the waistband of my jeans.

Don't mess it up.

I took one last look around and pulled the chair closer to the desk, exactly as it was when I had entered the room. I hadn't touched anything else. That was the rule. Never touch anything unless you had to. The less you moved things around the easier it was to put them back in their place before leaving. I opened the office door and stepped into the hallway.

At such late hour, the lights in all the common areas of the building, including the corridors, were dimmed. The Trottier Building, like the rest of the McGill campus, reduced its energy consumption at night as much as it possibly could. The place was deserted and quiet, almost church-like. There was no one around except the watchman, one floor up making his round. I walked past a series of closed office doors and headed for the glowing exit sign at the opposite end of the hall.

Ten more minutes. That was all I needed to finish the job. Also, the time it would have taken me to run away from this place and never come back. Go down the stairwell and leave. But I couldn't do that. Not tonight. Perhaps never. I had to go back upstairs and do as was planned. Quickly get to the grad-uate students' study room and sit down with my notes and laptop. All of it waiting for me on the third floor. Sit down and be a student again. A nice studious girl, straightforward. Smart and cheery.

I climbed the emergency stairwell two by two, carefully

landing my feet noiselessly on the metal panes. On the third floor landing I opened the emergency door and slipped sideways into the hallway just as Ibrahim's head appeared inside the glass enclosure at its opposite end. I quickly turned left into the ladies' room and went into a stall, waited for a few seconds, flushed the toilet and stopped at the sink to turn on the tap. I counted to three, walked out of the washroom and came face to face with the watchman.

"Good evening miss Nina," he said.

He greeted me with a smile and the kind expression he used for that twenty-five-year-old graduate student he knew. The one who often stayed late and said good evening and good night.

"Good evening Ibrahim."

"Working late again?"

"Yeah. Lots of work, as always. But I'm leaving now. Good night."

"Good night."

Ibrahim was a gentle soul, always polite and respectful. His unexpected visit to professor Pinard's office had obviously been a coincidence, nothing more. The watchman had probably been asked by his supervisor to add a few random office checks when making his rounds. And tonight, of all the offices of the Trottier Building, he'd chosen the one I was in. Chance played a part in everything and this evening, it had thrown me a curveball.

In the graduate students' study room all the desks were empty except mine. I walked to it and started to collect my things. I pulled the portable hard disk from inside my jeans and caught my reflection in one of the windows, a tall rectangle of blackness. I stood up straight, dropped my shoulders and let out a deep breath. Everything was fine.

Downloading Professor Pinard's most recent research in homomorphic encryption, the most secure way to share and store sensitive data, was my latest assignment. And to complete it would require another nighttime visit to her first-floor office. That didn't bother me. Breaking into offices, and into personal files kept off the networks, was the sort of thing I had been doing on a regular basis since the start of the school year, when someone at the Foreign Intelligence Service of the Russian Federation, the *Sluzhba Vneshney Razvedki*, commonly known as the SVR, or simply the Service, had decided I needed more hands-on experience. Apparently, managing troll accounts on the Internet and hacking into power grids wasn't enough of a challenge anymore. They wanted me 'on the ground'. But were they even useful, those files I had been stealing? Professor Pinard's research was undoubtedly cutting edge, but some of the work by the other teaching staff was by no means unique.

I supposed it didn't really matter. The few of us left had to be kept busy. The Service wanted me to steal the data and so I did, and I was good at it. Any near-miss or close encounter was part of my training. "Nerves of steal", as Dmitry used to say, beaming with pride. "Better than the *amerikanskiy* and their Special Ops, hey?" I thought of Dmitry and how he used to tell me stories after we finished training. As a young man, he had been a sailor on the Pacific Fleet. Based in Vladivostok, where the fleet's headquarters used to be. One night, I had asked him about my becoming a naval officer. But that hadn't been part of the plan. Also, little girls weren't allowed to join the Russian navy, Dmitry had said.

I closed my bag and lifted my coat from the back of my chair. Nina Palester, the graduate student in computer science, was going home.

CHAPTER 2

Out on the street, a handful of students quickly passed by on the sidewalks. The end of term exam period made the McGill Ghetto unusually quiet, even on a Thursday night. I crossed University Street and headed east on Milton, a narrow one-way lane. A gust of wind ruffled the branches of a flimsy tree above my head and sent a shiver down my neck. We were almost at the end of April and there was still no hint of the balmier weather the meteorologists insisted was just around the corner. The air remained chilly, like the breath of the North pole. I pulled up the collar of my pea coat, a midnight blue garment that resembled those worn by sailors, and in my right pocket felt the vibrations of my mobile telephone.

A missed call from Irina. At this late hour, it was unusual.

Irina, known as Marie Lacoste Palester, was my handler and my fictitious mother. I didn't have a mother, but Irina was the closest thing to it. She and Dmitry, known as Jérome Palester, were my fictitious parents. They lived in Saint-Lambert, a tony south shore suburb directly across the Saint Lawrence River from downtown Montreal. We had a house there. A family home.

I was named Ekaterina Yegorova at the time I had been

introduced to Irina and Dmitry, after having been selected at Orphanage Number Two to live with them based on my exceptional mastery of the French language and my natural talents in swimming, judo and advanced mathematics. An eleven-year-old girl, slightly apprehensive. All packed-up and ready to move in their apartment in the Belyaevo district of Moscow.

A little *rebenok*, that's what I was. A kid. Born to unknown parents and to whom the director of the orphanage had, upon my arrival there and as was her usual habit, given the family name of one of the motherland's celebrated war heroes. To bear the name of Anna Yegorova, a brave pilot of the Red Army, a hero of the Second World War, was "infinitely better than bearing the name of your natural parents, whoever they might be," the director often said, as she looked me in the eyes. "You must feel *inspired* Katyusha, by the name the state has given to you." She was a short, older woman. No taller than I was, with owlish eyebrows and half-moon glasses. I didn't feel inspired when she spoke to me. I didn't feel much of anything.

The Palesters were real estate agents. A husband-and-wife power team who owned a small, independent agency. But that was only for cover. More importantly, my family was part of the Illegals Program, as it was called in the United States. My parents supervised the other Illegals. They operated a home base for Russian agents on their way to *Amerika*, those who were first sent to its northern neighbour for a few years to acquire a Canadian passport, blend in with the locals then move south. Irina and Dmitry would fix things for them. They would help them secure an apartment. They would act as their mailbox with Central Control and handle their counterfeited identity documents.

Our family home had also been used on a couple of occasions as a safehouse where agents, no longer secure in the U.S., had taken shelter. Twice in the past ten years a fugitive had driven up the country roads of Northern Vermont and crossed into the Province of Quebec at one of the sleepy ports of entry scattered along the Canadian border. My parents had hidden each of them, a man the first time, then a woman, and successfully sent them off the North American continent in less than twenty-four hours. As efficient as a Fedex service for live human beings.

These rescue operations had taken place shortly after the FBI had arrested ten Russian agents in the United States, in June 2010. Since then, the Program had been greatly reduced by Moscow. The few of us left didn't have much to do anymore. But we were still here.

I held the telephone to my frozen ear and called Irina.

"Good evening *chérie*."

My mother's voice was soft and affectionate.

"*Allo maman*. Is everything alright?"

"Everything is fine. But guess who called us this evening?" she said.

"Who?"

"Hans. He said you weren't picking up your calls. He came back this afternoon. He said he wanted to surprise you."

I stopped for a moment and smiled. That was what the late phone call was about. Yuri had returned. Yuri Fedorov, known to all as Hans Meier from Germany, my official boyfriend selected by the Service. A strapping young man, caring, considerate, sometimes even funny. A twenty-six-year-old, six feet four inches tall giant with blond hair and a chiseled jawline who made love like an athlete doing his daily round of push-ups. An orphan just like me, plucked from Orphanage Number Four. I hadn't expected to see him again so soon.

Yuri was an excellent agent, highly trained. He'd landed in Montreal three years earlier on a student visa and shortly thereafter he and I had been paired by the Service to operate as a couple. The two of us worked out together. We went for long runs on Mount Royal and practiced martial arts and hand to hand combat. We got along fine most of the time although at the beginning of our relationship, I hadn't been so certain we would. "I'm not so sure he's my type," I had confided to Irina shortly after Yuri and I had been introduced, as I vaguely resented feeling like a promised bride in an arranged marriage. "But of course he is," my mother had said. "The two of you have been selected to work together by *algorithm*."

I'd grown attached to Yuri more than I knew I should, even though on some occasions he did get on my nerves. It was alright to have feelings, Irina said, but those had to be secondary. Any of us could be reassigned at a moment's notice and in the grand scheme of things my feelings towards him were of no importance. And now after having been gone for eight weeks, courtesy of the Service, Yuri had returned, and my solo existence just ended.

"*Chérie?*"

"Sorry *maman*. I was at McGill, studying late," I said.

"That's what I thought. By the way, why don't you and Hans come over for dinner tomorrow night? We haven't seen you in a while. And it would be really nice to see Hans."

That was Irina's way of asking if I wanted to deliver some files.

"Tomorrow? I don't think so. Too much work."

"Really? Oh, come on. Just for a quick dinner, nothing fancy. You and Hans will have a nice meal then the two of you can drive back to Montreal as soon as you're done. *Papa* would be so happy to see you."

It sounded like something was up and we were being summoned to a meeting.

"Alright. I'll speak to Hans."

"Great. So, we'll see you tomorrow at around five thirty, okay? I love you Nini."

A cat scurried across the street and disappeared under a

parked car. And there it was again, this feeling of wanting to vanish. To fall off the radar. Instead of heading back to my apartment I turned left on Lorne, a quiet side street. I suddenly wanted to roam. To walk around without anyone knowing my whereabouts. It was a new kind of yearning this thirst for freedom, something that had happened for the first time a couple of weeks after Yuri had left. One night in March, when the weather had been abnormally mild and a soft breeze had blown in from the south, I had gone out walking, alone, along the eastern side of Mount Royal Park. I had walked north on Avenue du Parc all the way to Outremont then back to the Ghetto, along Parc Jeanne-Mance. The wind full of humidity had cooled my cheeks and I had experienced the most intoxicating sensation. The feeling of being free.

I followed the street as it curved to the right in a crescent before crossing another side street and ending in a cul-de-sac. On both sides century-old brick and greystone houses stood still in a deep slumber. I filled my lungs with cold air as my mind started to wander, back to Russia and to those grainy memories of my youth.

"Ekaterina, my sweet child". Nothing had ever been the same following the utterance of these words, unforgettable, by the chief recruiting officer of the Youth Division of the Service. Words that were to this day etched in the mind of the little girl I had been at the time, spoken by Ivan Iegorovitch, known as Uncle Ivan to the children of the orphanage.

Uncle Ivan. A name that exuded kindness and bonhomie, given to a clone of Stalin as he liked to appear in those staged black and white photographs from the 1930s, smiling and surrounded by children. An imposing figure with a dark mustache who wore a military uniform on his occasional visits to the orphanage. Me, standing in front of him in my blue uniform, my arms straight at my sides as the director had instructed us to do. Him, seated behind the desk of the director, which she had lent him for the occasion with much bowing and reverential curtsies. "Ekaterina, my sweet child, there are certain people who believe you may not be a good candidate for the Service because of your parents". *My what?*

It was the first time anyone had referred in any way to my birth parents. My *parents?* What parents? The one thing the children of the orphanage knew with any certainty was that they *didn't have* any parents. They were the children of the state. A state that knew how to find the brightest and most talented among them through the agency of Uncle Ivan. And on that day Uncle Ivan, with his eyes black as coal and his enormous mustache, had confirmed in the office of the director that I was an exceptional child. A gifted little girl for whom there would be no better outlet for the development of her superior talents than the Foreign Intelligence Service. Who cared about the reservations some people had expressed in relation to my family tree? It wasn't like I had anything to do with it. These words, spoken by Uncle Ivan, had made him laugh almost hysterically. And when he had finally finished appreciating his own sense of humour, he had declared, solemnly, that the Russian Federation was proud to welcome the young and talented Ekaterina Yegorova among the newer recruits of the Service.

I heard footsteps behind me and glanced over my shoulder. A man in a short winter coat had followed me into the cul-de-sac. I looked to my left and right and realized I was caught in a trap. The houses in the dead end were built in a row, stacked against one another with no passageways from the front to the rear of the buildings. The only available escape route was over a small wooden fence I had passed a moment ago to my right, which was now behind the man following me, who incidentally had slowed down his walk, just as I had.

Was my mind playing tricks? I climbed the stairs to one of the houses and pretended to ring the doorbell. The man stopped next to a parked car and started to look for his key inside his coat pockets. I pretended to ring the doorbell a second time and waited, while he stood by the car, a small SUV model with a 'baby on board' sign in its rear window and continued looking for his missing car key.

The man was tailing me, I was certain of it. My heart started to beat faster. I wasn't sure what to do next.

I climbed down the stairs and walked towards him, then pretended to notice him for the first time. He turned around, also pretended to realize my presence and smiled the sheepish smile of someone in need of a helping hand.

"Hi," he said.

"Hi."

Neither of us would have won an Oscar. My stalker had a short dark beard that covered the lower half of his face and wore a baseball cap pulled over his eyes. His clothes were unremarkable. A black, no-name ski jacket and a pair of jeans. A bystander would have been at a loss to try to describe him in greater details.

"I'm sorry and I really don't mean to bother you in any way whatsoever, but I think I've lost my car keys and my cell phone battery is dead. Do you think I could use your phone to make a quick call?" he said.

The perfect way to get me close enough to him to put myself at risk.

"Sure," I said.

"Thanks. That's really nice of you."

I took a couple of steps forward and put my hand inside my coat pocket. I needed to take a good swing at him and at less than a meter away, I threw my foot forward as hard as I could. The man bent in two and let out a cry, but he'd somehow been able to avoid the full impact of my boot against his groin at the very last second. He was in pain, no doubt about it, but still managed to lunge at me and grab the back of my coat as I tried to run. I tumbled on the pavement and my assailant fell on top of me.

The man was heavy and tried to pin me to the ground. I reached for his face and pushed my thumbs into his eyes as he wrapped his fingers around my neck and tried to strangle me. I couldn't breathe. The pressure on my throat was unbearable and I felt my larynx on the brink of collapse. I pushed my thumbs harder towards the inside of his eye sockets and felt something recede under my right finger. The man let out a scream and rolled off me while holding his left hand to his face as air finally filled my chest. I felt dizzy but knew I had to get out of there as fast as I could. I stumbled upright but was immediately projected forward to the ground once again, this time by the impact of another man who jumped on my attacker, who was back on his feet, and started to throw violent punches at his face.

From around the corner I heard the screeching tires of a speeding car. I put a foot on the ground, then another, and managed to pull myself up. Flashing red and blue lights appeared out of the darkness and washed over the brick walls, turning the blind alley into a silent discotheque. The head-lights of the police car blinded me, and I momentarily closed my eyes as the cruiser squealed to a halt next to me. Two policemen jumped out of the car, a short blond one, youthful but prematurely bald with what remained of his hair neatly cropped, and a tall lanky one a few years older who looked like a Cuban musician I had seen on the cover of a magazine. My left hip was sore, as was my left arm. I suddenly felt dizzy, lost my balance, and took a step forward.

The bald policeman approached me and blinded me even further by directing his torch light to my face.

"Êtes-vous blessée?"

"Non, non. Ça va."

We continued speaking in French.

"D'you need to sit down?" he said.

"No. I think I'm okay."

The tall policeman shouted at the man who had attacked

me a moment earlier as he jumped over the wood fence, his only way out, and ran. The other man, the one who had punched my assailant in the face with no lack of enthusiasm, was nowhere to be seen. The Cuban instantly started chasing after my aggressor and jumped over the fence as if running a hurdle race. He was quite athletic and quickly disappeared after his prey in the darkness of a back alley. The radio of his partner, strapped to his shoulder, started to speak to him in the special dialect of the SPVM, the *Service de police de la ville de Montréal*.

"10-6. *Votre position s'il vous plaît.*"

The blond policeman pressed his transmitter with his left fingers and spoke to the dispatch. I could see that he was nervous, probably new on the job. But the return of the Cuban athlete put him out of his misery.

"You lost him?"

"Yeah," the tall policeman said. "Bastard."

He was hot and visibly ticked off.

"*Mademoiselle* here says that she's not injured."

His superior nodded and turned to me.

"We'd like you to sit in the car for a few minutes. So you can tell us what happened," he said.

Agreeing was the better option.

"Are you from France?" the blond one said.

"Yes," I said, "from Lyons. But my family's originally from Poland."

Even after living in Montreal for more than a decade there was no way I could pass off as a *Québécoise*. My accent, as light as it was, or so I thought, was instantaneously detectable by the French-speaking natives. While French is spoken in France with the front of the mouth, and English pretty much every-where in the world generally spoken with the back of it, the French spoken in *Québec* originates from a mysterious spot midway between the two. It is one of the hardest accents to replicate and getting the right intonation, as I did, and using colloquial expressions, as I also did, was by no means sufficient to allow me to blend in. To all who knew them, the Palesters were French from *la France*. That was part of our cover story.

The Cuban opened a rear door of the police car and I fell more than I sat on its thick vinyl seat. I thought about Irina and felt my shoulders stiffen. What had just taken place made certain I would have to confess to a couple of recent incidents I had so far avoided mentioning to my parents. Some recent events I had decided not to share. I had misread a situation and was now in for a chat I wasn't looking forward to.

CHAPTER 3

"**C**an you describe them, the two men?"

From the passenger seat at the front of the car the rookie, who had introduced himself as David a moment earlier, waited with his pen and paper.

"Not really. It was dark."

I wanted to downplay my involvement into what had happened as much as possible. Make myself small. An open and shut case was what this incident had to be. Minimal interaction with the authorities was another rule of the Program.

Constable David looked at me, then wrote something on his pad. Then looked at me again. The dark brown eyes of his partner, whose name I had been told was Manuel, briefly crossed my own in the rear-view mirror.

"Is this your street? The one you live on?" constable Manuel said.

His eyes scrutinized my face for any reaction. There was little doubt he was the one in charge.

"No. I live on Durocher. Between Prince-Arthur and Milton."

"So why were you here? In the cul-de-sac?"

Constable Manuel knew something wasn't right. His instincts told him so.

"I was just walking. I thought I'd go to the end of the street then turn back and go home," I said. "When I stay late at the university to do some work, I like to take a short walk before going back to my apartment. To get some fresh air."

The truth has a certain ring to it. The tall policeman heard it and had nothing further to say. Constable David understood the interview was over. He reached into a front compartment and handed me his card.

"Alright. I think we're done. Thank you very much for your help. We're going to add your report and your personal information to our database. The *service de police* is starting a program of community policing in the Milton-Park sector. If you can give us your full address and phone number, that will be all. We can also offer you a lift home if you're interested," he said.

Constable David was something of a charmer. A moment later he was out of the car and opening the rear door of the cruiser to let me out, right in front of my apartment, with the solicitude of a valet manning the red-carpet. A car door that could only be opened from the outside.

"*Merci.*"

"*Bonne soirée,*" he said.

My name and address in a police database. Just what I needed to end this shit show of an evening on a high note. I climbed the twenty stairs to the front door of my apartment as the white and blue car disappeared around the corner. I lived on the first floor of an old stone house, a once stately home that had been divided into separate dwellings. Inside, there were high ceilings with plaster moldings and wooden doors with ancient fixtures. The place had a lot of charm and belonged to that category of student accommodation easily identifiable as 'paid-for-by-mom-and-dad'. I opened the door and slammed it shut behind me.

I slipped off my boots and dropped my navy coat over the back of the couch in the living room. It was quiet inside my apartment, and I didn't bother to turn on the lights. I was relieved to be home, and very tired. I was shaken, too. It was my first time being involved in a fight with a stranger and the experience had deeply rumpled my core. I felt pain in my left arm, and I sat for a moment in the living room, holding it and flexing it slowly.

I should have known that sort of thing was going to happen. It had been a little more than two weeks since I had sensed for the first time that I was being followed. And then it had happened again, on and off. A feeling of being watched as I walked down the street, of being spied on, as if the eyes of an unknown person would sometimes glue themselves on the back of my neck. I had tried in vain to catch the person I thought was out there, watching me. Once, as I was leaving the McGill campus, I had turned around abruptly and walked back as fast as I could, as if I had forgotten something. But none of the people I had encountered on my way back had tripped any of my inner wires. Yet after each of these incidents, I had, once back at my apartment, realized I had narrowly missed this one silhouette that hovered in the background. A presence I could feel but couldn't single out, as if it had been made of sand or water, constantly slipping through my fingers. Someone only my subconscious could see.

I pulled out my phone and stared at it. It was almost one in the morning. Should I call Irina? I hesitated. I hadn't told any of this to my parents. I had decided to handle the situation on my own. To be an Illegal meant I was expected to be independent and able to resolve issues single-handedly. And at twenty-five, I no longer reported back to my parents every single thing that happened even though they were, factually, my superiors in the hierarchy of the Service.

But being in the Program also meant being part of a team and after tonight, I no longer had a choice. Even if the man who had attacked me turned out to be nothing more than a vile city predator, which was still a possibility, I couldn't keep to myself the fact that I was being followed. But I would tell my parents in person. Tomorrow. At the house.

It was time to call it a day. In the bathroom, I rubbed some medicated gel on my left arm and examined my neck. I brushed my teeth, washed my face and went straight to bed. As soon as I lay down darkness engulfed me and I fell unconscious on my pillow, exhausted.

All around me the beds in the dormitory were empty. I stood up and walked to the hallway. No one was there. There was no one in the other rooms. One was full of old beds and blankets, piled on top of one another. Was the orphanage closing? My heart started to beat faster. I ran downstairs and into a corridor that led to a deserted kitchen. "Hello?" I called out but no one answered. I was alone but at the same time felt as if someone was watching me. All of a sudden, the high-pitched shriek of a fire alarm pierced the air. I ran down another corridor. The alarm grew louder. I tried to open a door, but it was locked.

I woke up with a start. The doorbell in my apartment, an old mechanical thing with a tiny hammer that beat on a metal cloche, exploded in a series of frenzied bursts. I put on a pair of sweatpants and walked down the passage towards the entry. A familiar silhouette with salt and pepper hair stood behind the tall rectangular window of the front door and I immediately recognized my next-door neighbour, Markus.

Markus was a writer who lived in the house immediately next to mine with his cat, Dickens, and his flight attendant husband, Jacques. The front door of his property, one of the few remaining ones in the McGill Ghetto that hadn't been divided up in separate flats, was less than two meters away from my own, with our respective outdoor staircases separated by a void no larger than the length of my arm. By swinging my legs over the guardrail and taking a giant step, I could cross over to his place without having to climb down to the sidewalk.

Officially sixty but looking ten years younger, my neighbour almost always dressed the same, with a black turtleneck or t-shirt, depending on the weather, and heavy glasses mounted on thick black frames that made him look like a newsroom journalist from the early 1960s. In the beginning, he and I had exchanged a multitude of insignificant comments, some micro-discussions that never lasted more than thirty seconds. "How are you Markus?" "It's still cold today, isn't it?" "How's Jacques? Still flying to Europe this week?" A slow-moving introduction that had taken place over a period of almost two years. And then, one day, he had invited me over for some tea and I had sat for the first time in his living room while Jacques, jetlagged, dozed off with Dickens on his lap on a nearby couch. I liked them both very much and tried not to remember that Irina had vetted them with the Service before I had moved in my apartment.

I opened the door to let him in.

"Hi. Oh, *merde*! Nina, were you asleep? I'm so sorry if I woke you up."

Markus' French was impeccable, spoken with the elongated vowels of the anglophones and those "r" they so lightly pronounce.

"Don't worry about it. I had to get up anyway."

It was a quarter past nine.

"Apologies for the early intrusion but there's something I really wanted to tell you. Something strange that I think you should know," he said.

"What is it?"

"Last night when I was sitting in my living room, I saw a man across the street who stopped, right in front of your apartment, and looked at your windows. He didn't do it for long, no more than a couple of seconds, but what's really bizarre is that it was the second time I was seeing that man doing it. Five days ago, I saw the same man doing the exact same thing."

I was fully awake by then.

"Really?"

"Yeah."

"What kind of man?"

"Normal looking. He was wearing a winter jacket and a baseball cap. Nothing unusual or weird about him."

"The same guy, twice? Are you sure?"

"A hundred percent."

"Maybe he's just someone looking to buy a place around here or something."

"At night? I don't think so. And that's really not what he seemed to be doing."

"And you're sure he was looking specifically at my windows?"

"Positive. Especially after last night. I was sitting at my desk in the living room, with a perfect view of the street and the sidewalk."

"Do you remember what time it was?"

"Around eleven thirty. I was about to go to bed. I'm not sure I remember what time it was the first time I saw him, but I know it was dark outside. Why do you ask?"

"I was wondering if I was home at the time you saw him."

"Why? D'you think he could be a burglar checking to see if you were there?"

"Could be. What did he look like, physically?"

"About six feet tall. Short hair. Normal size. I mean, not particularly thin or overweight either. He was across the street so I couldn't really see the details of his face. Like I said, he was wearing a baseball cap and a winter jacket. The same jacket he wore the first time I saw him."

"Did you notice if he had a beard?"

"I don't think so but if he did, I'd say it was more like a stubble. Do you know who he is?"

27

"No. But I came across this guy with a beard a couple of times recently and I thought he looked kind of weird."

"You mean close to here?"

"Yeah, on Milton. But he kind of looked like he was homeless."

Markus shook his head.

"The man I saw didn't look like a homeless person."

"Wow. I'm not sure what to make of this. It's a little unnerving, to tell you honestly. Thanks for letting me know. I guess I'll have to be careful when I come home at night. Do you think I should report this to the police?"

"You could try. But also make sure your door and your windows are locked."

"I will. Hey, do you want to come in for a cup of coffee? I was just about to make some."

"Oh no, my dear. Thank you but I've already had my morning *capu*. I have a shitload of things to do this morning and then I have to go to the grocery store."

Markus had already placed his hand over the doorknob. He was a man of impeccable manners who never overstayed his welcome.

"I'll see you later," he said.

In the kitchen I made myself an *allongé* with a little milk. A man looking at my windows? He was probably the same man who had attacked me the night before. And the fact that Markus had seen him scouting my apartment twice in the past few days made it less likely that he was a freak roaming the Ghetto for a random girl to stalk. Whoever he was, this man had come around to see if I was home, then, figuring I wasn't, had waited for me. It seemed obvious he knew I was a McGill student and had rightfully assumed I would be leaving campus through the Milton gates, then walk towards my apartment.

But what about the second man, the one who had attacked *him*? Had he been following the man who was following me? There was always the possibility that the second man was a passerby, a good Samaritan who had come to my rescue. But then, why disappear before the arrival of the police? It was a good thing Yuri was back. Having him around would reduce my chances of being caught flat-footed as I had been the night before.

And speaking of the devil. I picked up my telephone on the floor of the bedroom and saw that my official boyfriend had sent me a message. *Coming to ur place at ten :)*. The news put a smile on my face, and I momentarily forgot about the night before. I put my phone down, peeled off my clothes and headed to the bathroom. I was happy Yuri was coming over. I had missed him, even though I had tried hard not too. But I also knew I had changed while he was gone. Under the steaming jet of the shower, I wondered how I would feel upon seeing him.

Standing in front of the mirror, I examined my face. No wonder Markus hadn't said anything. I was lucky. My neck showed no marks of my attempted strangulation and that was a very good thing. I wasn't sure how or when I should tell Yuri about what had happened. I started to brush my teeth and heard the front door open.

Yuri had a key to my apartment, and I had one to his. His place was on the west side of the McGill campus, in one of those tall residential towers that stood over the heart of the city on the steep southern flank of Mount Royal. I heard the old wood flooring of my apartment crack under his feet as he made his way towards the back, where I was, still in the bathroom. I turned my head and saw him, filling the doorframe. He smiled.

"*Privyet.*"

His lips had moved in a whisper. It was strictly forbidden for agents to speak Russian among themselves, to avoid developing a bad habit. But we still did it, Yuri and I, in secret.

"*Dobroye utro.*"

"How are you, Katyusha?"

"Not bad. When did you get back?"

"Yesterday."

My boyfriend was a good-looking man and that morning, after not having seen him for almost two months, I found him particularly attractive. He wore a pair of jeans, a t-shirt and his old leather jacket, the one that looked like it belonged in an old D-Day war movie. His dark blond hair was still damp, as mine was.

"Well, fancy that," I said. "I wasn't even sure we would ever see each other again."

"Of course, we would."

"How so?"

His smile grew wider.

"Because I will always come back for you. No matter what."

His eyes left my face and travelled down my back to the curve of my ass, loosely wrapped in a towel. My hair wasn't very long, it was cut above the shoulders, but Yuri leaned forward and lifted it to kiss the back of my neck.

"So, you're saying that you would always come back for me? No matter the circumstances?" I said.

"Uh-huh."

"Even after a long period of time?"

I wanted to tease him.

"Even after the longest time."

I turned around and kissed him.

"And where were you, exactly?"

He lifted his eyebrows.

"Some interesting places."

I am not a short person. I am one meter and seventy centimeters tall, almost five feet eight inches in *amerikanskiy* measurement. But next to Yuri, I always felt tiny. That was part of his charm. And when I was in the mood for it, I got a big kick from being lifted in the air, naked, without the least bit of effort on his part. He and I made love regularly, pretty much all over my apartment. On the kitchen counter, on my desk, against the wall. Yuri was an athlete, a real beast when it came to sex. Of course, he wasn't without flaws. For one thing, he wasn't particularly subtle. His interests, other than serving the Russian motherland and being a good agent, veered towards the superficial. He liked to talk about sports and the nice things he wished he could buy. He also liked to try different colognes, some more pleasant than others, and the switching around between the different scents sometimes bothered me.

But that morning things flowed between Yuri and me. I came closer and wrapped my arms around his waist. His hands slid down my back and disappeared under the towel and a second later, our mouths were glued together as we both seemed to want to devour each other alive. Yuri wriggled out of his jeans and lifted me with one hand placed under my butt. We stepped into the corridor and he pushed my back against the wall while his underwear travelled down his legs towards the floor. We moved to my bed a few minutes later, where we lay afterwards, naked. My room faced an alley and was the quietest place in the apartment. Through the sheer fabric of the curtains the morning sun shone on the old wooden floor. I closed my eyes. It felt good to have Yuri lying next to me.

My partner's fingers brushed against my skin and I opened my eyes. His hand followed the contour of my hips as he lay on his back.

"Admit it. You missed me," he said, smiling.

I turned on my side and examined my partner's profile.

"Maybe," I said. "What about you. Did you miss me?"

"Of course I did."

I knew this wasn't entirely true. But that was Yuri.

"So where exactly did they send you, for two months?"

"You know I can't tell you that."

I knew that was what he would say. It was one of the

golden rules of the Service. Never tell the agents more than what was necessary for them to know. What Yuri did during those eight weeks I would probably never find out.

"I think Irina and Dmitry have something important to tell us tonight," I said.

He looked at me.

"I know. That's the reason I was sent back. I have no idea what it's about. No one told me anything."

Yuri turned on his side to face me and lowered his eyes to my hip bone. I looked down and noticed a nice purple bruise on my left side, the size of a hockey puck.

"What's this?" he said.

I suddenly had no choice but to spill some of the beans about the night before.

"I was followed by a man last night."

The steely blue eyes of my partner scrutinized my own.

"What do you mean? What happened?"

"I left McGill at around eleven thirty and this weirdo started following me on Milton and I didn't want to lead him back here, so I turned on Lorne to see what he would do. That's when he ran after me and grabbed me, and I defended myself."

"Did he hurt you?" he said.

"No, not really. He grabbed me and pushed me into a parked car, so I kneed him hard in the balls and hit him a couple of times and pushed him away, and he let go of me. There was also this other guy, a passerby, who started to yell at him. And then a police car showed up and he just ran."

I had lied naturally without a moment's hesitation, and I wasn't certain why. Was it because I hadn't yet told Irina and Dmitry about being followed? Or because I knew I had miscalculated the seriousness of a situation and was embarrassed by it? I didn't think I knew the answer. And now it was too late to backtrack and tell Yuri the truth.

"Have you told Irina and Dmitry about this?"

"Not yet. The whole thing lasted no more than fifteen seconds."

Yuri drilled his eyes into mine. I placed my hand on his chest, large and flat and almost hairless.

"It's no big deal, really," I said. "These things happen. The guy was obviously some kind of pervert. Lots of girls have reported being followed by strange men in the Ghetto."

"Being followed is one thing. Being attacked is entirely different. Did you talk to the police?"

I nodded yes, slowly.

"And?"

"They took my statement. They needed my name and address for some kind of database."

"Ouch. That's not good."

"I know. Irina's not going to like it."

I thought about telling Yuri what Markus had said to me earlier in the day but decided not to. A man looking at my windows wouldn't have made any sense after telling him I had been attacked by an incidental pervert. And I also knew I should report back to Irina and Dmitry before I told anyone else. It wouldn't absolve me, but it might help my case.

CHAPTER 4

At around noon I stepped out of my apartment with Yuri and saw Markus on the sidewalk with his shopping trolley. He lifted it awkwardly and was about to carry it down the short cement staircase that led to the half-basement entrance of his house.

"Hello Markus. Hey, wait a second. Let me help you with that," Yuri said.

My partner was being a gentleman. He knew the drill. Illegals had to be found likeable by the people they interacted with.

"Oh, hello Hans. How so very nice of you. Thank you."

Yuri picked up the trolley and brought it down to the windowless staff service door, a relic of the past. As he climbed back up the service door opened and Jacques appeared, clad in a Bedouin robe.

"There you are," Markus said. "Always a minute late."

"Hello Nina. Hello Hans."

"Hi Jacques. I love your robe," I said.

"Thank you. It's from Morocco."

"You know, that's where Jacques and I met," Markus said.

"In Morocco?" Yuri said.

"Well, actually, on a plane to Casablanca," Markus said.

"Oh my God. Please don't remind me. I didn't know what the hell was wrong with that passenger. I mean, he kept asking for things. A glass of water. A drink. A blanket. An extra pillow. Another drink," Jacques said. "And he did this for seven hours."

"I wanted to speak to you! You're such a grumpy flight attendant."

"Cabin service director," Jacques said.

Markus rolled his eyes.

"That's what they call you when you start to get old."

He turned to Yuri.

"Hans, before I forget, I wanted to tell you how sorry I am about what happened to your father."

"Thanks Markus. It's been hard but according to the doctors he's finally on the mend."

"The same from me," Jacques said.

Eight weeks earlier, I had told Markus and Jacques that Hans, my boyfriend, had left Montreal in a hurry and flown to Berlin, where his father had suffered a violent heart attack. Yuri spoke German fluently, as well as English, and some French. Having a fictitious family in Berlin was part of his cover. As the story went, his father, a lawyer, had spent weeks in intensive care due to some complications while Hans, his only son, had chosen to remain in Berlin with his mother. An agreed-upon explanation for Yuri's sudden disappearance and prolonged absence from my daily life. And now, Yuri was back.

"Alright children, we'll see you later," Markus said.

"*Ba-bye vous deux*," Jacques said before he closed the door.

"I'll pick you up at five," Yuri said.

He kissed me on the forehead and left. It was a beautiful day. I could feel my cheeks burning under the midday sun, a first since winter had officially ended. I closed my eyes for a moment and stood still. I didn't have any lectures to attend that afternoon. I had thought of going to one of the computer labs at the Trottier to do some work but decided I wouldn't.

And besides, I could afford to be a slacker. I had excellent grades. And Central Control didn't give a damn about my grade point average. My masters' thesis in machine learning with an emphasis on generative adversarial networks, those algorithmic models that generate deep fakes, was no doubt a crowd pleaser among my superiors at the Service, but nothing more. What Central Control apparently cared about, at least officially, was the sensitive research files I copied and stole at McGill and the roster of Internet accounts I managed on a daily basis. And even those didn't seem to excite them that much. As for the hacking work, it was intermittent at best. No matter what Dmitry and Irina said, the purpose we served was questionable.

I unbuttoned my navy coat and walked to Avenue du Parc to try to find an opened *terrasse*. There was some outdoor seating at Milton B, a students' restaurant at the corner of Milton and I took a chair at one of their rickety tables. I ordered a latte and took my laptop out of my bag. It was trolling time. I logged into Facebook and started to type.

Hi everyone I wanted to let you know that the little boy I told you about three weeks ago isn't doing any better. He came to the clinic yesterday and seemed withdrawn and didn't make eye contact. It all started after he got his first HepA shot. I saw it happen with my own eyes. No one is supposed to say anything about it and if the clinic knew I was posting about this I would lose my job but BEWARE OF VACCINES. Big pharma is LYING about the side effects.

That was my California pediatric nurse burner account I would be closing the following week. The Service wanted me to fan the flames of the most common conspiracy theories that proliferated on the Internet. The anti-vaccine movement was an easy target with plenty of chat groups. On my other accounts I wrote about the 'deep state' and offered 'proof' that FEMA was secretly building concentration camps.

I checked to see if I was being asked to coordinate any of my day's postings with my fellow trolls. According to Irina, most were employed by the Internet Research Agency in Saint Petersburg, "a known troll farm operation", as the American press called it. The Agency recruited its bloggers in orphanages and social service agencies, just as I had been recruited by the Service, and paid them wages, Irina had said. I hoped they were decently paid. The work was boring and dumbfoundedly repetitive.

I visited my other accounts and surfed the Net for a short while, then finished my coffee, packed my bag and went inside the restaurant to pay. On my way to the washroom I came across the waitress, a diminutive brunette with short, pale blue fingernails, and asked for the check.

When I came back, she stood behind the counter and handed it to me with a standard-size white envelope.

"The man that was sitting over there in the corner asked me to give this to you," she said.

A man? I quickly scanned the inside of the restaurant, which was empty.

"He said that he knew you but didn't want to bother you. I thought it was kind of weird the way he said it, but I took it anyway. He left a minute ago. I hope there's nothing creepy inside. And if there is, I'm really sorry."

A shot of adrenaline travelled up my spine.

"What did he look like?"

"Nothing special," she said.

I added a tip to my bill on the debit machine and tapped it with my credit card under the watchful eyes of the waitress.

"Nothing at all?"

She raised her eyebrows and seemed to try hard to remember.

"Around fifty, I guess. It's hard to say at that age. There was some grey in his hair but not a lot. Mostly here."

She brushed her temples with her blue painted nails.

"How tall was he?" I said.

She filled her cheeks with air and closed her mouth. It made her look like a discouraged little frog, one who couldn't believe she was being asked to recall how many waterlilies floated in her pond.

"Like, average? I couldn't really see. He was sitting down."

"Did he have a beard?" I said.

"No. He didn't."

I looked around to see if there were any surveillance cameras inside the restaurant. There was only one. Right there in front of me, over the counter.

"Did he give you the envelope here, at the counter, or at his table?"

"At the table. He left it with his money. He paid cash."

Of course he did.

Outside the restaurant, I ripped open the envelope and found a single folded page of paper in it, a photocopy of an article from The New York Times. It was an older piece of writing from the look of it, taken from a past edition of the newspaper. *Spy Ring Broken Off in Bethesda* was the title of it. *On November 6, the FBI arrested a man in Washington suspected of being a Russian agent.* I kept on reading. The Bureau had also been investigating a couple in Bethesda, a suburb of Washington D.C. A man and a woman they believed were members of the same network. The woman had been killed and her body had been found in a multi-storey parking garage. The man had disappeared. According to a neighbour, the couple lived quietly in a nice house and had a young child. The FBI wouldn't comment any further as the investigation was ongoing.

Why had this article been given to me? Was it a warning? A notification that something similar was about to happen to me and my parents? According to Irina, the Program had started years before the arrests of 2010. Where these people Illegals as well? There was also the possibility that the article was somehow personally connected to me. But how? I didn't know what to think.

I thought about the description the waitress had given me of the man in the restaurant. Being beardless, he couldn't be the man who had attacked me the night before, unless he had shaved. But even then, I had a gut feeling he was a different person. My assailant had been a younger man, not someone middle-aged. He didn't have any grey hair, that I remembered clearly. And why would he now give me a newspaper article after having tried to strangle me? I folded the page back inside the envelope, slipped it in the left pocket of my coat and walked home.

At five o'clock sharp Yuri waited for me in front of my apartment in his car, a grey Jetta in need of a paint job. I opened the car door and immediately saw that he was in a sour mood.

"Central Control has confirmed they want me to stay here for the next three months," he said.

"So?"

"So, it sucks. I thought I was being sent back for something specific, but it looks like they also want me to stay for another tour of duty. I mean, seriously. What are we *really* doing over here?"

"I don't know."

"Exactly."

"Three months is not a big deal."

"Maybe not for you but I'm getting really tired of this place."

My heart twisted sideways for a second. Wherever he would go Yuri wouldn't miss me at all. It was a simple fact.

We drove south in silence, passing through downtown on streets that gently rolled downhill towards the older part of town. Then through the Griffintown neighbourhood with its mix of old industrial brick buildings and swanky new condos, on our way to the Victoria Bridge. At a red light a brand-new BMW stopped next to Yuri's car, and he glanced at it with envy. My partner hated his old car. He felt like a loser driving it. What he wanted was a flashy car, something that cost money. An Audi, perhaps even a Porsche. Yuri had expensive tastes.

"Do your three months then ask Central Control for a transfer," I said.

He let out an exasperated sigh.

"Sure. But why wait that long before sending me to a place where I can actually do some work? It has nothing to do with you Katyusha, but I'm really fed up with being here waiting for God knows what to happen. When nothing ever happens."

It was the first time I was seeing Yuri being so dissatisfied. The good soldier suddenly wanted more than what was being offered to him by the Service. While he was away, my partner had developed an appetite for life. Perhaps the changes that had started to affect me while he was gone weren't so uncommon after all. But his affliction was different from mine. I didn't care about the so-called good life. He did. And he wanted it badly.

"That thing Irina and Dmitry want to tell us about, tonight? It better be good," he said.

I put my hand in my coat pocket and felt the contour of the envelope with the copy of The New York Times article in it. Should I mention it to my parents during our meeting with Yuri or in private at a later time? I hesitated. Along with being followed, being scouted, being attacked *and* my interview with the police, it was a lot to confess to in a single sitting. One thing I knew was that I didn't want to talk about any of this with Yuri alone. After not telling him what had really happened the night before, my sudden change of heart would likely seem odd, even suspicious, and I didn't want Yuri to be wary of me. Not after being separated from him for such a long time. Besides, Irina was the one I really needed to speak to.

We left the bridge and drove into Saint-Lambert, an attractive suburb with nice parks, mature trees, quaint little stores and cozy restaurants. The dream come true landing pad for those with uncomplicated ambitions and an enviable balance sheet. Yuri made a left turn at the first traffic light and continued towards the town center. A few more minutes of driving took us to a leafy lane with spacious early twentieth century houses. He slowed the Jetta and stopped in front of a well-to-do brick cottage, the Palester family home.

I was eleven when I had arrived with my parents on Pine Street. Months before, we had boarded a plane at Moscow's Domodedovo Airport on a cold winter morning and flown to Cyprus, where we had stayed for six weeks and ceased to be Russian to the outside world. The Service had given us European Union passports issued by the *République Française* and I became Nina, the French girl with the ponytail who read *Les aventures de Harry Potter*. At the end of our stay, we had left for Morocco where we'd played tourists for a few days, then crossed the Mediterranean on a ferry to Gibraltar like a happy family returning home to the continent after an adventurous holiday in *Maroc*. In Spain, we had rented a house with a breathtaking view of the Southern coast and taken lots of pictures. Finally, in August, we had flown to Canada and moved into our new home, in Saint-Lambert.

In the beginning, Uncle Ivan would call me without fail once a month and Irina and Dmitry would take me to the secret room in the basement of our house, a small, sound-proofed cabin behind the water-heater, to speak to him. They would place a pair of heavy headphones over my ears before Uncle Ivan greeted me with joy, live from Moscow. He would start the call by asking about my school and about my new friends. He would crack a few jokes and laugh loudly into the apparatus he was using to speak to me. He would always mention how proud he was of me and how I was cited as an example to the newer recruits of the Service. Our conversation ended in the same way almost every time. Uncle Ivan would suddenly turn serious and would wish me good luck for my future missions. "Ekaterina Yegorova, the future of our motherland rests in part on your brave little shoulders," he would say in a deep voice. Later, his calls became irregular. "Ivan Iegorovitch is an important man," Irina and Dmitry would say to me, "he hasn't forgotten about you. You're very special to him." And when I was sixteen years old, they had ceased completely.

Dmitry opened the door of my parents' house and came out on the porch to greet us. With his greyish hair neatly combed to the side and his long-sleeved polo shirt in soft merino wool, my fictitious father was as usual very stylish. Jérome Palester was everyone's favourite neighbour, especially among the women. He was chic and sexy, falsely bohemian. The embodiment of what people must have imagined was a typical family man from the *sixième arrondissement*, especially if they knew little or nothing about the place.

"Hello beautiful. Hello Hans."

As Dmitry and I kissed each other on the cheek Irina slipped through the door and snuggled by my side.

"Hello, Hans. What a joy to see you again. And my Nini. Hello sweetheart. Look at you, so pale. You've been working too hard, *chérie*."

We stepped inside the house, past Dmitry who closed the door behind us, and ceased our role-playing on the spot. Like well-trained actors, we stepped out of character as soon as we exited the stage.

"All good?" Irina said as she ushered us in.

"Business as usual," Yuri said.

"Glad to see you're back in one piece. I wasn't told what you did but I heard it went well." she said.

We followed my mother through the white Modernist

living room of my parents' house and headed for the kitchen. It was Dmitry who had decorated our home. Irina couldn't have cared less about the sofas and the chairs, but her imprint was all over the house, nonetheless. With Irina, nothing was ever out of place. There were no pieces of paper lying about, no invoices or scribbled notes of any kind. Whatever was left on display was intentional. Some photographs meant to document our fictitious past. Some books, mostly generic best-sellers as mainstream as the Palesters wanted themselves to be.

"I know it's a bit early but are you two hungry?" Irina said.

In the kitchen a large pot of borscht was being kept warm over the stove. Had Irina cooked us something? Yuri bent his neck over the cooking range like a big blond bear anxious to fill its stomach.

"That soup looks amazing," he said.

Irina glanced at him with a half-smile.

"Dmitry made it, of course."

My mother, for all I knew, was a lieutenant-colonel in the North American Intelligence Division of the Service and was Dmitry's direct superior. She and Dmitry were lovers and had been living as a couple for as far as I could remember. My father was her confidant, her right-hand man. They trusted each other completely. Together, they were the ultimate team. They never fought, never argued, at least not in front of me. A pair of true professionals. In terms of false parents, I could have done much worse. And they also loved me, even though we weren't normal people.

Irina sat down at the kitchen island and Yuri and I did the same. She had wavy brown hair cut straight at the chin and thin, slightly arched eyebrows that curved over a pair of almond-shaped green eyes. My mother was confident, cool and level-headed. She saw everything, knew everything and guessed everything with remarkable accuracy. Officially, she was forty-eight years old, but I didn't know what her real date of birth was. In fact, I knew very little about her life before she became my mother except for her professional training. I knew she had been a brilliant recruit in the KGB and had received advanced training in behavioural psychology.

Dmitry was the complete opposite. I could never figure out what he knew and what he didn't know. He was amiable, calm, comforting. When he spoke to someone a glint would appear in his eyes, as if his pupils smiled at you. He was an attentive father, the favourite dad of all my little friends. Underneath this apparent congeniality I suspected Dmitry had nerves of the hardest steel. In this respect, he and I were the same. If required to do so, he could have shot someone without loosing his Mister Rogers demeanour. A little swiping of the blood splattered on his pants with a damp cloth, a little combing of his salt and pepper hair and *voilà*. Ready for a glass of Chablis.

Irina waited until Yuri and I had settled onto our seats. There was a tightness in her smile I had rarely seen before, something I could tell Yuri had failed to notice. Dmitry, meanwhile, took four bowls out of a cupboard and filled them up with soup.

"The time has come for both of you to take part in an important mission," she said.

I was surprised by the announcement. Irina's green eyes darted from Yuri's to mine.

"Central Control has informed us that an American, a political attaché, has agreed to deliver some highly confidential information to one of our agents, next week, at the G7. You will be sent there to meet with him and bring us back the info."

The G7. Renamed the G8 between 1997 and 2014 for the duration of that period during which Russia had been invited to join the party, to be later excluded, in 2015, following the reintegration of Crimea into the motherland. The rich nations' private club. Decried on the left by the alter-globalists and more recently on the right by the populists.

From Russia's perspective, the G7 was a self-congratulatory clique of the supposedly right-minded guardians of the civilized world, an aging crew of paternalistic hypocrites. But for the Service, it was a yearly occasion to steal, listen, bribe and mingle, unseen, among the hundreds of participants, employees and security forces who huddled together for a few days behind metal fences and barbed wire.

A butterfly took off inside my stomach. I shot a glance at Yuri, who seemed to be pleased as punch. At last, we were doing something.

"It won't be Yuri's first assignment, Katyusha, but it will be yours. Also, you should know that Ivan Iegorovitch has been told about your upcoming mission and he wishes you the best of luck," Irina said.

Uncle Ivan? My heart skipped a beat. After all these years. What a pleasant surprise.

She continued.

"As I'm sure you already know, the G7 is taking place next week in Charlevoix, an hour and a half north of Quebec City. In a hotel called the *Manoir du Cap*," Irina said.

Dmitry placed our bowls of borscht in front of us and a cup of sour cream in the center of the kitchen island. He opened a cupboard, pulled out a manila folder and handed it to Irina, then took a seat and gave Yuri and me a wink to let us know that everything would be fine.

"It's a three-day mission," he said.

Irina nodded approvingly but her smile was gone. Evidently, we were about to discuss some serious business. The lieutenant-colonel took out a large photograph from the folder and placed it in front of us. The shot, taken outdoors, showed in its center a well-dressed young man with neatly trimmed black hair standing among a small group of people behind another man Yuri and I immediately recognized as the U.S.

Secretary of State. Jacket and tie. The young man with the black hair appeared to be part of the Secretary's entourage.

"Brett Alford. Twenty-eight. Currently employed by a branch of the State Department called the Executive Secretariat. The Secretariat is a multi-function office. Among other things, it coordinates communications between the State Department and the White House, to make sure everyone's on the same page about the international issues important people are expected to comment upon. Alford's job is to draft and review public statements to be made by the Secretary of State, including statements issued by the Secretary while he's travelling abroad. As such, Alford's part of the Secretary's so-called mobile office, which explains his presence at the G7."

The White House. Yuri and I listened in silence with our bowls of red soup untouched. I looked at Irina and tried to decipher her thoughts, but I couldn't. Heavy shades had been drawn. My mother was a wall of inscrutable blankness, and I felt my chest tighten in anticipation of what would come next.

"Brett Alford's father is a well-known political organizer in the state of Alabama. That's how his son got a job in Washington. Alford went to Auburn University and graduated three years ago. He was never particularly brilliant and that's one of the reasons the Secretariat's not a good place for him. He lacks the skills for it. And because his family is not part of any wealthy donor set either, he doesn't really fit in among the bright young things working at the State Department."

She paused and Dmitry took over.

"Substantial political donations are often rewarded by giving a donor's kid a low-level job in the administration," he said. "That's how many not-so-talented young people find work in D.C. But even among that particular crowd, Alford's kind of the odd man out."

Yuri dipped his spoon in the sour cream and dropped a lump of it in his soup. I tasted mine. It was delicious. Borscht was always one of my favourite meals. Irina, meanwhile, still wasn't touching hers.

"Alford is also a drinker," Dmitry said. "He had three DUI arrests during his time at Auburn, all resolved out of court, thanks to his father's connections. But his real problem is online gambling. He places bets on gambling websites almost compulsively. Six months ago, he was practically bankrupt and had to borrow money from a not-so-nice person who specializes in lending money to drug-addicted kids from respectable families. We were alerted to it by one of our contacts. One of our agents in Washington befriended Alford at a bar and offered to help him out. In return for a favour."

"So, Alford's a mole?" Yuri said.

A spoonful of borscht was suspended in midair between his bowl and his closely shaven chin. Irina rewarded his enthusiasm with a fleeting half-smile.

"Yes. But a reluctant one," she said. "As expected, he tried to wriggle his way out of the arrangement once he fully understood what he'd gotten himself into. But our agent convinced him that keeping us happy was a much better choice than spending ten years in a federal prison for violating the Espionage Act."

My parents exchanged a complicit look and Irina opened the folder again. This time she took out a photograph of a grand property, obviously the *Manoir du Cap*, and a large-scale map the size of an oversized tablemat. She placed them side by side in front of us over Alford's photograph.

The *Manoir du Cap* was a fantasy, one of those century-old medieval castles built at a time the wealthy would travel up the Saint Lawrence River for a vacation of fresh air and panoramic water views. I thought about Russia for a fleeting moment, where during that same period war, famine and social upheaval had begun their unstoppable carnage. The world was a brutal place, but more so for certain people.

I examined the map. The hotel and its surrounding

grounds had been highlighted in yellow. I could tell the building itself stood at the top of a steep cliff that overlooked the Saint Lawrence River. Set in a sparsely developed area, on an elongated piece of land stuck alongside the river, it was connected by a private lane to a provincial thruway which appeared to be the only road access to the entire region.

"Brett Alford will arrive at the hotel on Monday and will depart on Friday," Irina said. "Your assignment is to bring back a USB key you will receive from him. The two of you will leave Montreal on Wednesday morning and will come back on Friday afternoon, which gives you four days to prepare for the mission. False identities have been prepared for each of you and have already been reinforced digitally on the Internet. Pictures, transcripts and Instagram posts already exist under your new names and are linked to your photographs. All of it will be taken down once the mission is completed. You will also receive special identification documents that will allow you to access the site."

Something bothered me about the plan.

"Irina," I said, "why is the USB key not given to our agent in Washington? Wouldn't that be a lot easier?"

Yuri shot me a sideway glance. He hadn't picked up on this simple fact, as conspicuous as a white elephant sitting among us with a bowl of borscht and was rattled by his failure to do so.

"Good question, Katyusha. Yes, that would have been a lot easier. But unfortunately, that option is no longer available. A few weeks ago the FBI started doing surveillance on Alford. According to our sources, the Americans have become suspicious that someone within the administration is feeding us inside information. They're not certain of it and they still don't know who that person is, but Alford's on their list of potential suspects. He's being watched, and we can't take the risk of having someone getting caught."

"And he won't be under surveillance while he's at the G7?"

Irina smiled at me warmly as Yuri crossed and uncrossed his legs. He was growing restless and waiting for his chance to come up with something brilliant to say.

"That's right," she said. "Once inside the secured perimeter at the G7, Alford will no longer be watched. The security at the site, as well as the monitoring of anyone getting in and out of the secured premises will be so tight that the FBI has assumed constant surveillance wouldn't be necessary. There's also the question of who's in charge of doing what at the G7. The Secret Service will have the run of the place for the American delegation. And those guys don't like to share with the other agencies."

She paused and looked at Yuri and me.

"We absolutely need this key. And this may be our only chance to get it."

Dmitry wiped the corners of his mouth with a napkin.

"Between now and Wednesday morning we want the two of you to keep a low profile. No speeding ticket, no getting drunk, no dancing naked at someone's birthday party," he said.

My fictitious papa was trying to inject a shot of levity in our very serious meeting, but his smiling remark felt to me like a jab to the stomach. I saw the dark brown eyes of the Cuban-looking policeman peering at me in the rear-view mirror of his car. My name and address were on a database kept by the police. It was time I told my parents what had happened the night before.

"Irina, there's something I have to tell you and Dmitry. I was attacked by a man last night, while I was walking home."

Irina locked her eyes into mine. She didn't say a word.

"A police car showed up two seconds later and the man fled. I had no choice but to talk to the police. They took my statement, and my personal information."

My mother's eyes turned into dark green marbles, as dead and as hard as a pair of small rocks. She was upset, although I knew her anger wasn't directed at me. I looked at Dmitry who said nothing and shot me back the quick look of sorrow of someone with no other choice than to let me wallow in my predicament. My father silently sat on his chair like a sad rescue dog. A brave K-9 who knew it wouldn't be able to dig me out from under such a monstrous avalanche of bad circumstances.

"I was going to tell you everything," I said.

CHAPTER 5

As we drove home Yuri tried to cheer me up.

"It's not your fault, Katyusha. That guy who followed you last night was probably just a sicko. But Irina has a point. We can't afford to take any risks. Next week is too important. If the police decide to follow up on what happened last night, there's no way we can have you connected to the mission."

It was funny to see how Captain Russia had all of a sudden regained his confidence. I, on the other hand, couldn't believe the ocean of shit I had fallen into. I was being excluded from my first real assignment, by far the most important work I had ever been asked by the Service to carry out. The Program was finally being brought back to life, and I was about to miss all of it.

And while Yuri and some girl who was supposed to take my place would be preparing for the mission over the next four days, I had been told to do nothing. I had been instructed go to class, meet some friends, go out and have some fun. There would be no nightly visit to professor Pinard's office, no contact with my parents. There wouldn't be any meetings with Yuri either. Not even for a quick run on the mountain or an hour of judo. As the story went, poor Hans would be hard at work trying to catch up on his lectures after coming back from Berlin and would have zero time to see me.

As we drove back to town on the Victoria Bridge, I looked down at the river underneath us as it churned violently towards a rocky cliff I now knew existed, hundreds of kilometers away. A precipitous wall at the top of which sat the *Manoir du Cap* like the Parthenon at the summit of the Acropolis, ready to welcome the Gods of the G7. But why even think about the summit? I wouldn't be near the place when it happened the following week.

"This really pisses me off," I said.

Yuri squeezed my thigh with his right hand but let it go almost immediately to change gear. We left behind the grey waters of the Saint Lawrence and drove into the city, cruising through downtown on our way to the McGill Ghetto. The city was alive that night with plenty of people out on the street. A buzz of activity floated in the air as dusk descended on a pleasantly mild Friday evening.

"Alright," my partner said "I'll drive you home. I'm meeting with the new girl later tonight on *St-Laurent*."

So much for watching the Stanley cup playoffs, as he would have normally done. I hadn't been told about that meeting in what I imagined would be a trendy bar. As soon as I had finished telling Irina about being assaulted and about my conversation with the police, she had asked me to go down to the basement and turn on the TV. If I wasn't going to take part in the mission, I wasn't going to know anything about it. I'd stayed alone in the basement for almost an hour, curled up with a half-eaten bowl of borscht in a corner of our basement sofa, an old friend from my teenage years. Dmitry eventually came downstairs on his way to the secret room behind the water-heater. Following his discussion with the Service, of which I couldn't hear a thing, I understood that they had found someone to replace me. A girl, probably my age, so that the false identities created for me could still be useful. And now I knew that she was meeting with Yuri later that night.

But something else had happened while I had waited in the basement of our family home. When Irina had finally come downstairs to put an end to my banishment, I hadn't yet told my parents the entire story of what had happened. They knew nothing about my being followed over the past two weeks and about the man in the restaurant and the newspaper article he had left me in an envelope. I had told them the same story I had given Yuri earlier in the morning, nothing more. I couldn't bring myself to add the rest of it, at least not immediately. Not after the sternness with which they had reacted to my abbreviated confession. But I knew I had to tell Irina, and I wanted to speak to her alone.

"Irina, can you come and sit down for a minute? I need to tell you something else."

My mother had sat on the sofa and looked at me. I didn't feel good about what I was about to say.

"I'm really sorry but there's more to the story than what I told you earlier. What happened last night wasn't something random. I think the man who attacked me has been following me for a couple of weeks. And earlier today when I was in a coffee shop, someone left me an envelope with an article of The New York Times in it. About three Russian agents who were caught in Washington D.C. It said in the article that one of the agents died, a woman."

"Stop."

"I'm not…"

She'd gestured for me to stop talking immediately, then taken one of my hands and stared at me intensely.

"Listen to me Katyusha. You must never, ever, tell anyone about what you just told me. About the man following you or the newspaper article. Not Yuri. Not Dmitry. Not anyone."

"But..."

"When the mission is over you and I will go for a drive. Or a walk. Anywhere you want. And we'll talk about it. I will tell you what I know. But until then you must act as if none of this has ever happened. Understood?"

Irina was dead serious as she spoke to me. Whatever this thing was, it was of great concern to her.

"Alright," I'd said.

To my surprise a softness had briefly washed over her face. She had stared at me intently, then squeezed my hand and gestured for me to follow her upstairs. We had gone back to the kitchen and soon after Yuri and I had picked up our coats and left. Later, in the car, I realized I had forgotten to give her the portable hard disk with professor Pinard's files. But at that point, no one seemed to care.

Yuri stopped his car in front of my apartment. The wooden stairs that climbed to my front door waited for me like the gangplank of a ship ready to take me into exile.

"I'll see you later," I said.

My partner kissed me distractedly on the cheek. His mind had already left for a more exciting destination, somewhere I wasn't. I closed the door of the Jetta and stood on the sidewalk as he sped away without wasting a look back.

To be set aside by the Service had wiped away any desire I could have had for a secret walk. I had nothing to do that evening except watch some television and try to digest my disappointment. Across the street, a group of students was heading to a party with two cases of beer, ready to laugh, drink and get physical with anyone willing. I, on the other hand, was Nina Palester, the well-behaved graduate student in computer science who would stay home that night like a good little soldier. They could screw themselves at the Service and shove their mission up their asses.

At eleven I turned off the TV in the living room and reached for the switch of the table lamp. The envelope the waitress had given me at the restaurant lay next to me on the sofa. I had read and reread the article of The New York Times I had found inside of it. I had searched the Internet and found out it had been written in November 1995, which made the story of the arrest in Bethesda almost as old as I was. Vladimir Politchev, Nikolaï Belinski and Marina Serov. Those were the names of the three Russian spies. Marina Serov was the woman who had died.

Although the arrests of the ten Illegals in 2010 had been widely publicized, the events of 1995 hadn't received the same amount of media coverage. In 2010 a swap of agents had taken place. The Bezrukov-Vavilovas, who Irina and Dmitry knew quite well and who had been arrested with their two sons, had been deported to Russia in exchange for Russians who'd been accused of spying for America and the United Kingdom. The same had happened with the others. But no information was available concerning the fate of those arrested in 1995. Where were they and what had happened to them?

There was something else about the article. A possibility that overwhelmed me. Something I knew I wouldn't be able to let go. Aside from trying to warn me of something, I saw no reason for giving me a copy of the newspaper article. Except for one thing. Marina Serov had a young child at the time she was killed. And that child would today be the same age as me. Was it possible I was Maria Serov's child? I'd searched for Serov on the Internet. There was no mention of her anywhere in the Russian press and I couldn't find her name on any web sites. On the Russian side of things, it was as if Maria Serov had never existed. In the North American and European press, she'd been mentioned a few times in 1995, and then never referred to again. I also couldn't find any photograph of her other than the black and white headshot initially used by

The Times. I'd looked at it carefully. I didn't think she and I were very much alike.

I pulled myself out of the sofa and readied myself for bed. In my darkened room I stared at the ceiling, as smooth as a piece of paper and as white as a frozen plain in the dead of winter. I tried to close my eyes but couldn't fall asleep.

If the man who had attacked me wasn't the one who had left me the envelope at the restaurant, I also no longer thought he was the one who had been following me. He really couldn't be. My attacker in the cul-de-sac was young and brutish, almost certainly a professional, highly skilled. He had moved in a series of violent bursts. There had been no fluidity to his movements. The man who was following me, presumably the same person who had left me the envelope, was an older man. A fleeting shadow. A silhouette who floated in the air and vanished like a puff of smoke. And if he was the man who had come to my rescue in the cul-de-sac, he was also someone who wanted to protect me. I needed to find out who he was.

I thought about Irina again. She'd known immediately about that man the moment I had mentioned him in the basement of our family house. She knew who he was. I was desperate to know more but there was nothing I could do about it over the next few days. I wasn't allowed to speak to my mother until the G7 was over.

I opened my eyes and held my breath for a few seconds. In the kitchen the refrigerator hummed, then stopped. I could hear the slightest noises coming from various corners of my apartment, as if my senses had shifted into overdrive. A faint thud. The muffled buzzing of an electrical device. I pushed my duvet aside and got up, then walked in the dark to the living room without making the old flooring crack a single time.

I placed myself to the side of the windows, careful not to be seen from the outside, and looked out on the deserted street. There was no one there. The sidewalks were empty.

Nothing moved along the ribbons of parked cars that stretched on both sides of the street from one corner to the next. Under the dim light of the streetlamps, I saw nothing but cracked cement and the dirt of winter waiting for rainfall.

Go to bed Nina. You're imagining things.

CHAPTER 6

On Saturday morning, I sent a text message to my friend Stacey. Stacey was my best friend at McGill. Or more accurately, Nina Palester's best friend. She was a neuroscience major, and now, like me, a first-year graduate student.

Hi there what are you up to today?

She called me back minutes later.

"Hey."

"Hey."

"Haven't heard from you in a while," she said.

A grand total of three days.

"I know. Hans came back."

"No way. He's back?"

"Uh-huh. He's up to his neck trying to catch up. What's up?"

"Not much. Remember the guy I told you about the last time we spoke?"

Stacey was a little fairy with black hair, a free spirit who made it her mission to jump in as many beds as she cared to visit. There was always a backstory to her various romps, something that made each of them momentarily special. She didn't do one-night stands. She was a romantic. A swashbuckling dater who happened to enjoy having sex. A speleologist tunnelling for love. Sometimes, when she felt tired of it all, she would go back to Nick, her on-and-off boyfriend who had moved to Ottawa the year before. Even the boldest adventurer needed to sail back to port once in a while, to get some rest.

"Yeah, I remember. So, what about him?" I said.

We spent the next twenty minutes analysing this new guy she had met the week before.

"He's a law student," she said.

"Oh yeah?"

Stacey had gone out with a med student in the fall but never someone studying law.

"He's got a great body. I love his hands."

She laughed. My friend was a wayward elf. She was a ton and a half of fun. I envied her freedom. Stacey pushed aside any rule she didn't consider worthy of following.

"He's taking me to a party tonight. Not a *real* party but more like a get-together. The law students still have exams next week. His friends are calling it a 'six to ten'."

She laughed again. In Montreal, people refer to happy hour as a '*cinq à sept*', a 'five to seven'.

"A little drinking party to unwind, you know? You should come. It'll be fun," she said.

You bet. I badly needed a change of air. Too much had happened in too little time, and I couldn't stop thinking about the mission I was no longer a part of and about the man and the newspaper article. The past forty-eight hours weighted on me, and I was looking forward to feeling almost normal again for an evening. Also, my instructions had been crystal clear. I was required to live the life of a student for the next few days. Whoop it up. Go out and party. I agreed to meet Stacey at six. Meanwhile, I would try to work on my master's thesis, which I hoped would keep my mind busy. As for my daily *séance* of postings on my Facebook accounts, the Service could shove it.

At quarter past six I waited for Stacey at the corner of

Durocher and Prince-Arthur, a short stroll up the street from my apartment. It had been a warm and sunny day and tiny green leaves had started to appear on the scrawny trees the city had planted along the sidewalk the year before. The cold seemed to have left us for good and I stood waiting for Stacey in a thick cotton hoodie without the slightest shiver. She finally appeared, crossing the street on her way to meet me with the self-assurance of someone whose primal needs are fully satisfied.

"Holy cow," she said.

She made a face and pretended to look me up and down.

"Going some place?"

She was teasing me, of course. But it was true I almost never wore a little black dress to a party. Except tonight. Tonight, Nina the Student was on a mission to have some fun. And that dress also really fit me. It was short but not overly tight. Layered below the waist, it floated around my hips like a mini flamenco skirt. Paired with a hoodie, and a pair of sneakers, it looked pretty damn cool. Besides, my friend wasn't in any position to say anything about my clothes.

"What about you?" I said. "Have you looked in the mirror?"

She laughed. Under her Burberry-style raincoat my philandering friend sported a see-through Indian white shirt with a pair of denim hot pants worn over black tights. Stacey had little round thighs and the derriere of a chubby child but was the least self-conscious person I knew. She had been born to have a good time.

The party was on the third floor of an old walk-up apartment building and had already started when we arrived. A small crowd congregated in the kitchen where a large sash window had been left opened to let in some fresh air.

"Hey, Nina."

It was Lee, a friend of mine in computer science. I hadn't expected to see him there. Lee was Vietnamese and wore tortoise shell-rimmed glasses. He kissed me on the cheek and introduced me to his friend, some blond guy who drank beer from an enormous mug and looked like the perfect casting for an Oktoberfest advertisement. It seemed most people had opted for an early start. I supposed they all needed a break from studying but one from which they could leave early, go home and get some rest.

"D'you want a beer?" Lee said.

"Sure. That would be great."

Music was playing in the living room at the end of a hallway, where a couple of old couches had been pushed aside. The apartment was a typical student home, with white walls and minimal furniture. Some posters decorated the place, including one of Steve Carrell clad in a business suit, who said he understood nothing.

"Jules, this is my friend Nina."

Stacey's new research subject was called Jules. He took my hand and kissed me on the cheek than gave Stacey a luscious kiss on the mouth. Jules had frizzy black hair and seemed just as lustful as my friend. And yes, he did have a great body. Nick was done for. I didn't know what he was up to in Ottawa that night, but I wouldn't have bet a dollar on him and Stacey making it through to Labour Day.

"D'you want another beer?" Jules said.

Why not. I had finished the first one in less than ten minutes. I thought about Yuri and my replacement, Miss X, and felt as if I had swallowed a small rock. These two would be leaving for Charlevoix in three days and I suspected my partner wouldn't pass on the opportunity to spend some private time with her if she looked the part. That was Yuri. I felt bad thinking about it. I knew better than to allow these feelings to creep up but the thought of him with another girl had me burning with a low blue flame. I took the bottle Jules held over his shoulder and twisted it open.

"Hey gang!"

A red-haired bloke with glasses walked into the kitchen with two girls, one of whom I knew from an elective class. Her name was Marianne and she was on the McGill women's soccer team. She was a big girl, strong as a horse.

"Hey everyone!" she said as she lifted her right arm and showed the plastic bag she was carrying. "Who wants to play beer-pong?"

Fun and games with alcohol. And why the hell not? I kind of liked that silly drinking game where teams competed against one another in successive rounds. All you had to do was throw a little plastic ball in a plastic cup and drink beer. I raised my hand.

"I'm playing," I said.

Stacey looked at me with her eyes wide opened. Her usually quiet pal playing beer-pong? That was something new. Poor Stacey hadn't seen anything yet. Nina was about to let loose. When we Russians make up our mind about something, whoever is on the other side of the fence had better pray for mercy. The West didn't defeat the Germans. The Soviet Union did. After being cut to pieces in Stalingrad, the remaining Nazi boys had run back to Berlin to save the skin on their asses. The end game had been a piece of cake.

"Alright Nina. You'll be playing with Aaron."

I was matched with the red-haired bloke with glasses for the first round. He wasn't very good.

"Shit," he said, as the little white ball bounced off the table and rolled under the fridge. Thankfully, Marianne had a bag full of them.

The redhead and I finished our beer as another team moved in to take our place against Marianne and her team-mate, a short barrel-chested guy with legs as thick as tree trunks. In the living room Lizzo sang about her juice and some people started to dance. I did too, with a freshly opened *pivo*, a nice cold beer to get down and boogie. *A good night to you, Yuri. And also to you, Miss X.*

"Nina! It's our turn."

Aaron my red-headed friend was calling me from the kitchen. I made eye contact with him from the end of the hallway.

"Again?"

"It's the final round. The grand finale for the losing teams."

I managed to squeak past a group of six who had just arrived in the apartment with a bottle of vodka. I wouldn't have minded a nice shot of ice cold *Stoli Elit* but theirs was a sad excuse for a vodka and it wasn't even Russian.

In the kitchen, I caught a glimpse of Stacey and Jules through the opened window as they stood outside on the fire escape. These two seemed overly interested in each other's lips and couldn't have cared less about anything else. Standing next to the kitchen table, my beer-pong partner was waiting for me.

"I'm coming," I said.

I put my empty beer bottle on the windowsill, as Aaron gave me a newly opened one. The enemy had better be ready.

Eyes the colour of steel greeted me from across the table. A fringe of brown hair, a bit too long, falling to the side of a pale face. My adversary had a strong but attractive nose set over medium-size lips and a well-defined jaw. He was shorter than Yuri but still taller than average, a little under six feet tall. He wore an old pair of jeans and a wrinkled shirt of white cotton. A bit of the beach bum look, which suited him. He didn't say anything.

"Should we start?" I said.

A slight smile lifted the corners of his mouth. This guy was sexy.

"Definitely," he said.

I turned towards my teammate. Enough with the amateur. This mission was mine.

"Give me the ball," I said.

My redheaded friend opened his mouth, surprised by this new tone of mine. But like a good boy he placed the plastic ball into the opened hand I held in front of his nose. I threw the ball and it landed into the plastic cup across the table without a hitch.

"Yessss!" my teammate said.

We howled and high-fived. Across the table my opponent and his teammate, a tall skinny guy with wavy brown hair, stared at us, nonplussed.

"Go for it, Theo," the guy with the wavy hair said.

He gave my opponent a little white ball which he threw straight into the plastic cup.

"Yeah baby!"

It was their turn to celebrate with back slaps and a couple of hoots. I took the ball and threw it again. Into the plastic cup it went.

"Haha!" Aaron said.

We did a couple of synchronized disco moves.

"Go for it, dude," wavy hair said.

My adversary threw the ball in the cup once more. And I did too, another time. And he did it again. And I did too. My teammate drifted away, bored with the game, and started a conversation with a red-headed pixie who had just appeared in the kitchen. Theo's teammate vanished into the living room.

"D'you want a beer?" my opponent said.

The colour of his eyes reminded me of granite. Soft and smooth under the opened hand but almost impossible to break.

"Sure."

We took a couple of beer bottles from the fridge. I followed him into the living room where a crowd was hopping under little multicolored Christmas lights hanging from the ceiling. I imagined the ceiling below was about to fall on the neighbours' head, but no one seemed to care. People were listening to Young MC's instructions and busting moves as best they could, with or without much rhythm. The music was loud. We joined the crowd and started to dance. I felt happily tipsy.

"My name is Theo," he yelled into my ear.

"I know."

That curl of the lips again, at the corners of his mouth. He was very attractive, this Theo guy. Laid-back, with a touch of nonchalance. The kind who doesn't seem to care but charms you anyway. I liked being with him.

"I'm Nina."

Theo and I danced some more. We stopped when a boring song came on and retreated to a corner of the room. He said something funny. I laughed. We talked for a while. He placed one arm around my waist. His hand fitted perfectly over my hip and for a second, I imagined us kissing. The Beastie Boys started telling us there would be no sleep 'till Brooklyn and we started to dance again. The living room was full of people. One hell of a spirited fiesta was going on, and it wasn't ten o'clock yet.

"I have to go to the washroom," I said. "I'll be right back."

I made my way down the hall and found the toilet. But when I came out of it two minutes later, the sight I caught stopped me dead in my tracks. At the end of the hallway a tall man in a black shirt and a bulletproof vest, the standard patrol uniform of the SPVM, stood at the entrance of the living room. I only saw his back, but I recognized the shoulders, the long athletic body and the dark brown hair. The music stopped, and it became immediately clear that the neighbours had had enough after all and that the party had been sent to an early grave. Constable David suddenly came into view at the end of the hall, and I took a step back. He said something to his partner Manuel and gestured with his hand towards the kitchen.

It was time I made a quick exit. I didn't want the

policemen to see me at the party. I wanted them to forget about ever meeting me, not to be reminded of my existence. I picked up my hoodie in the kitchen and climbed through the opened window onto the fire escape. Stacey and Jules were long gone. I looked down at the old metal structure that clung to the side of the wall. The staircase hung over an alley at the back of the building. I went down the rusty steps, holding the railing so I wouldn't fall over, and reached the end of the staircase two floors down. The emergency stairs ended with a short vertical ladder, the last rung of which floated three meters above the pavement. I let myself dangle from the lowest rung and fell to the ground like a bag of laundry. Certainly not one of my best landings. Five beers could do that to you. I looked up and saw Constable David's head bopping out of the window like a little wooden bird out of a cuckoo clock. He didn't see me.

There was no one else in the semi-darkness of the back alley. No jokers pretending to have lost their keys. I walked briskly towards the street and passed by a racoon sitting on a garbage can. The critter looked at me calmly with unblinking eyes, as if savoring the weather and enjoying the show. I stopped and wished him good night in Russian on behalf of Putin, Lenin, Dostoevsky, and the whole of the motherland. He scratched his ear and promised me he wouldn't say a thing.

CHAPTER 7

I woke up the next morning to brilliant sunshine that lit the inside of my bedroom like spotlights in a photographer's studio. I was thirsty. Also, I could barely open my eyes. Wasn't there a switch somewhere I could use to turn off this giant lightbulb? I would have gladly signed on for a rainy day, one during which all things would have moved slowly under a ceiling of grey cotton balls. I wanted to stay in bed until noon and listen to the gentle trickle of rain falling against my window.

I turned to my side and opened my eyelids a crack. My dress lay on the floor, as did my sneakers, and my underwear, peeled off during last night's off-loading manoeuvres before I had fallen into bed. I had slept completely naked, with the carelessness of a wildling on a plush bed of ferns. I hadn't even closed the curtains.

I heard the ringing of my telephone somewhere in the bedroom and sat up to listen. My head started to spin, and I closed my eyes for a second and took a deep breath. The ringing came from somewhere at the foot of the bed. I sprung forward and picked up my hoodie from the floor. My phone was inside the front pocket and as I retrieved it, it rang again, for the fourth time. It was Irina calling me. Something was happening.

"*Allo maman?*"

"Hello *chérie*. Everything okay?"

"Yeah. And you?"

Irina was calm but I immediately knew there was trouble.

"Yes, everything's fine. Except that you know Claudine, our neighbour who was supposed to go to Charlevoix in a few days? Well, she had an accident."

An accident? Had something happened to the girl who was supposed to replace me?

"Really? What happened?"

"I don't really know but it sounded pretty bad. She was going with a friend and that friend now has to go with someone else. Anyway, when you see Hans later today tell him it was great to see him. You two should come back and have dinner again in a few days."

"Sure. That sounds great."

"Alright Nini. I'll talk to you later, okay? I have to go. I love you."

Irina had just informed me that Yuri and I would be meeting later in the day. I closed my eyes and fell backward on the mattress. As I nestled my head into one of my pillows, I heard the front door being shut. A moment later, Yuri was there.

"What are you doing?"

My partner stared at me from the doorway of my bedroom as I lay in bed, naked.

"What do you mean, what am I doing? Today's Sunday. And in case you don't remember, I was instructed to go out and have some fun."

Yuri chose to ignore the sarcasm in my voice.

"Things have changed."

Yuri was serious, more serious than I had ever seen him before.

"Your replacement is gone. She's disappeared," he said.

"The new girl? The one who was supposed to replace me?"

"That's right. Get dressed, Katyusha. You're doing the mission."

The girl had, what, *vanished*? I badly needed a shower. I stumbled into my old bathtub and turned the faucets with a quick twist of the wrists. Cool water flowed over my face and shoulders and somewhat brought me back to life. I dried my hair with a towel and put on a dark blue tracksuit. Yuri had made some coffee while I showered, and I quickly drank two cups and ate two pieces of toast. I also swallowed two Motrins, drank a large glass of water and silently thanked the inventor of ibuprofen. It had been no more than twenty-five minutes since Yuri had shown up, and I was almost ready to go.

I noticed that my partner wore a brand new, midnight blue track suit, one with little inserts of reflective fabric in all the right places. How many did he own? His closet must have been full of them.

"What's with the new suit?" I said.

Yuri chose to ignore the cutting tone of my remarks for a second time. He really had a thing for clothes but couldn't buy as many as he wanted. He had to keep in mind he was a McGill student, and always be careful about the way he dressed.

"You ready?" he said.

"Uh-huh. So, what exactly happened with that girl?"

"Nobody knows. Her and I met on Friday night and everything seemed fine. We trained together yesterday morning and she went home. I told her I would come by her place in the afternoon, then we'd go out for dinner. But when I went to her apartment, no one answered. The door wasn't locked, so I went in. All of her things were there. Her keys, her wallet, her suitcase. Everything except her phone. I tried calling her, but she didn't answer. That's when I knew something was wrong."

"If she's been gone for almost twenty-four hours, she could be anywhere."

"I know. The Service is working around the clock to try to find her. So far no one knows anything."

"And because of that I was reinstated?"

He nodded.

"Central Control has decided to go ahead with the mission regardless of her disappearance. Apparently, the info we're getting from Alford is worth taking the risk of moving forward as planned, even though your replacement vanished into thin air. You should know that not everyone was in favour of bringing you back. Irina was against it. But in the end, it was obvious you were the best candidate to do the job. You've got friends in high places, Katyusha. The order came straight from Moscow."

That could only have been Uncle Ivan. I imagined him sitting behind his massive desk and barking my rehiring orders into his telephone.

Yuri looked at his watch.

"It's almost ten. We have to go," he said. "Someone's waiting for us at the office."

In the jargon of the Service, a field office temporarily set up for a specific assignment was referred to as 'the office'.

We left my apartment and climbed aboard the Jetta, which Yuri had left double-parked with its lights flashing in front of my home. We drove north on Avenue du Parc, cruising along Mount Royal to our left and the grassy field of Parc Jeanne-Mance to our right, then through Outremont, past a mix of stores, cafés and low-rise apartment buildings.

"What did you do last night?" Yuri said.

"I went out with Stacey."

"To a bar?"

"No. To someone's apartment."

A number of blocks further north, we passed under a viaduct that supported a swath of railroad tracks and emerged into a bleaker landscape. There were vacant shops and a half-deserted strip-mall, also a few lonely looking apartment buildings scattered among squat commercial properties. We had arrived in a different part of town, a much poorer one, where fewer people lived.

"So, my replacement, what was she like?"

My partner knew where I was heading. He shot me a glance and ignored my question.

"Alright. So, who are we meeting with?" I said.

"Our mission supervisor. His name is Anton."

I thought about Irina not wanting me back on the mission and wondered if it had anything to do with what I had told her.

"How do you know that Irina didn't want me back on the team?"

"Anton told me," Yuri said.

"Do you know why?"

"No. But, it's obvious it had to do with your episode with the police. I mean, there's no other reason."

"None."

"Exactly. Like I said, Central Control is going full steam ahead on this one, no matter what."

Yuri turned right on a narrow side street that ran between old industrial brick buildings two to three storeys high. We were in that portion of the Mile-Ex neighbourhood people call Marconi, a long-neglected section of Montreal that was being revived by the tech industry. Run-down commercial properties stood next to recently renovated ones, easily identifiable by their brand-new windows and freshly refurbished front lawns. New money was slowly eating away at the derelict and the old.

We made a left turn, followed by a right one. Yuri then slowed down the car and stopped in front of a single storey construction in pockmarked stucco that might have been white originally but was now the colour of dirt. A sad looking place on which a 'for sale' sign had been nailed to the front facade.

"We're here," he said.

Yuri shut the engine and turned towards me as we sat in the car. He looked much fresher than I did with his chin closely shaved and his hair messed up just as it should be. And right at that moment, both him and his newer brand of cologne really bothered me. Where did he think he was going? To a casting call for a *babushka* photo calendar? I was tired and not in the best of mood.

"What?" I said.

He let out a sigh.

"If we meet anyone, you and I are interested in buying this place. Anton is waiting for us inside. If need be, he'll pretend to be an architect we've hired to have a look around," Yuri said.

He got out of the car, and I did too, went around it and took out a large canvas bag from the trunk that seemed to be empty. He folded it under his arm and disappeared around the side of the building and I followed him, all the way to the back where he stopped in front of a beaten door. Yuri took out a key from his pocket and opened it, then let me in first. I entered the building and realized the door had a brand-new lock on the inside and was much sturdier than it seemed.

We stepped into what must have been an office space, where pieces of cardboard and broken office furniture lay on a dirty floor half covered with ripped linoleum. It was a sad place, exhibit one in a case study of corporate abandonment. A mantle of thick, grey dust covered every surface.

I followed Yuri through a doorway into a long rectangular room where most of the windows had been covered with newspaper. The room was empty, except for a table and three chairs at the other end of it. A man with short grey hair was resting against the table with his arms folded over his chest. He wore black jeans and a grey t-shirt and looked to be about fifty years old. Yuri walked up to him and shook his hand.

"How's it going Anton?"

"Not bad. Is that our little prodigy?"

The man looked me up and down. He was strong, with a compact body, but a thickening waist betrayed the dawn of his declining years.

"Sit," he said to me, as he pointed to one of the chairs.

I took one step forward and instantly bent in half with pain.

"Ow!"

The asshole had hit me in stomach with a reverse punch. I had avoided it in part by slightly twisting sideways at the very last second, but his fist had still found its way to my abdomen. *What the hell?* I turned around to face him. The prick was smiling, his beady eyes shining at me with malevolent pleasure. He moved forward and tried to hit me again. I took a step back and responded with a kick to his face, but he lifted his left arm and blocked it. That son of a bitch was testing me. I spun around quickly and kicked him again, faster and with much more force than the time before. My foot squarely met the underside of his chin, shutting his jaw in a snap. He lost his balance and fell backward into the arms of Yuri, who caught him, like a gymnast who had missed his landing at the end of a triple somersault.

My partner helped the asshole back on his feet.

"I told you, Anton. She knows what she's doing."

The spark of pleasure in the man's eyes had been replaced by a mix of respect and resentment. He and I were off to a magnificent start.

The three of us sat at the table, with Yuri and I facing my newest friend. Anton kept looking at me, but I pretended not to notice. My mobile vibrated inside the side pocket of my track pants. I took it out and turned it to silent mode without looking at it, then quickly put it back. Meanwhile, our mission supervisor had reached under the table into a big black bag and dropped two large plastic envelopes in front of us.

"These are your ID documents," he said.

Each envelope contained a series of plastic cards, some with photographs, and a passport.

"Each of you will have two separate identities, a principal one which you will use for the mission and a backup identity to be used only in case of an emergency. Karine Demers and Fabien Racine are your backup identities. These two people actually really exist. They live together in a house fifteen minutes away by car from the hotel and are presently vacationing in South Africa. Their house is situated at walking distance from the outer limit of the green zone. It will be empty and doesn't have an alarm system. If shit hits the fan, you'll be able to use it as a safe house then make your way out of the green zone on foot if necessary. Your principal identities, those you'll be using for the mission, are under the names of Juliette Després and Finn Martens and are completely fictitious. The two of you will be certified coaches in yoga and wellness. Based in Ottawa."

Certified coaches in *wellness*? I thought for a moment this was some kind of joke. The asshole read my mind and looked at me pointedly.

"That's right. Yoga and wellness. The activities you'll be in charge of providing at the G7 to a select group of people that includes the spouses of our world leaders."

Anton grinned a malevolent smile.

"What's the matter? You don't think all these nice people deserve to be taken care of?" he said. "Also, make a note that the two of you are landed immigrants from Belgium to account for your foreign accents."

Anton reached under the table again and placed a USB key in front of me.

"This is your game book, little girl. Operation Riding

Hood. Cute name, isn't it? It's the code name we're using for Alford. Everything that you need to know is on the key. The plan of the hotel, the description of your assignment, your instructions."

He looked at Yuri.

"I meant to give this to Lana," he said.

It seemed that my would-be replacement had been called Lana and was known to our mission supervisor.

"Any news?" Yuri said.

"None."

Anton paused for a second, as if he needed to digest the information he had just given Yuri, then turned his attention back to me.

"The two of you are leaving on Wednesday morning," he said, "in separate cars."

"Why two cars?" I said.

"It's better to have two vehicles in case something happens," Yuri said.

Anton leaned forward and looked at me.

"You have two and a half days to learn everything there is to know about the mission, princess, including the security measures you'll have to get through to access the site. You think you can manage?"

What was the asshole saying? Two and a half days was more than enough to prepare for the mission. The jerk was patronising me.

"What do you think?" I said.

I looked at him steadily and he finally pushed his chair back, crossed his arms over his chest and spoke to us both.

"Alright. Now listen up. I want the two of you to be on high alert. Lana went missing yesterday, which means that she was likely compromised *before* she was told in greater details about the mission. At this point, we don't know if she left willingly or not. And with a bit of luck, we can assume whoever is responsible for her disappearance wanted her for something different."

"But whether or not she was kidnapped or jumped ship, don't you think she won't have a choice but to spit out everything she knows?" I said.

The maniac shot me an angry look. He hesitated for a second and I caught a tiny glimpse of anguish in his eyes, which vanished almost instantaneously.

"Whatever the circumstances, she won't have much to say," he said. "And regardless of what may be happening to Lana, Central Control has decided that we should go ahead with the mission, so that's what we're doing. The assignment is all yours, little girl. Although for some unknown reason, it seems you weren't anyone's first choice."

I shot a sideways glance to Yuri. *Not a word.* This wasn't the time to get into a discussion with Anton about what had happened to me on the street the other night. Yuri looked away, stretched his legs and put his hands in his pockets. Our mission supervisor ignored our little dance and continued with his instructions.

"From now on until Wednesday morning, the two of you will carry a weapon at all times, wherever you are. Including at home."

"What weapon?" I said.

Anton made a show of pretending he was amused by my question by staring at me and raising his eyebrows. He reached into his black bag once again and placed two stubby handguns on the table, each of them no more than fifteen centimeters long, in matte brown colour. A dirty brown the colour of military camouflage that reminded me of those muddy places in the world where people who kill other people die, every day, light years away from happiness.

"These weapons," he said. "You're both getting a Beretta Nano, 9-millimeter. Small but powerful. Specially designed for concealed carry."

He took one in his hand.

"It has a polymer frame and a detachable metal slide. But be careful when you play with it. There's no external safety."

Our mission supervisor smiled at us with what looked like a row of shark teeth, but his eyes stayed cold like those of a mental patient forced to remain on his best behaviour until the visiting crowd had left. *Now, now, Anton. You be a nice boy. No cutting people up in pieces this afternoon.*

"There's some ammo in the bag. You'll be taking the guns with you to Charlevoix on Wednesday," he said, "in separate parts."

The three of us left the building fifteen minutes later. Before leaving, Yuri filled the empty bag he had taken from the trunk of his car with the guns and our identity papers. He and I shook hands with our pseudo-architect on the sidewalk, in full view of anyone who may have been watching us and thanked him for his time. Anton walked away to his car. I noticed his jeans were a size too small and formed a crease under his thick square butt. I couldn't believe the Service had put this psychopath in charge of our mission. He was a mental case. The only possible explanation for his involvement was that he must have been one hell of a field officer. That, at least, was a reassuring thought.

Yuri and I made a show of looking at the sad stucco facade for a couple of minutes before leaving, with all the appropriate hand gestures. Back in the car I let myself fall on the passenger seat and stretched my legs as much as I could. I was thirsty. And hungry, too.

"What do we do now?" I said.

"You need to go home and start reviewing everything that's on the key Anton has given you. And you need to practice taking the gun apart and putting it back together."

"And you don't?"

"I've done it before."

"And tomorrow?"

"Same thing. Plus some training. And the same thing again on Tuesday. We're leaving Wednesday morning at six."

"I'm hungry," I said.

Yuri started the car. I pulled my mobile from the side pocket of my pants. I had three text messages from Stacey and two missed calls. *Theo wants ur number. Call me.* Theo? I felt a flutter inside my chest. I looked outside my window to conceal any changes in my facial expression and placed the phone back into my side pocket. The thought of Theo asking for my number had made me happy, a surprising feeling. And there it was again, this desire to be free. As soon as the Service held me firmly in its grip, I resented my cage and wanted to break loose. I needed to be on my own one more time before the mission, if only for a little while. I crossed my legs and looked at Yuri.

"I'll have to see some of my friends before I leave on Wednesday," I said.

He gave me a blank look.

"Why do you say that?" he said.

"I made some plans when I saw them last night. If I just disappear without an explanation, they might find it strange."

Yuri kept on driving without a word.

"Look, I was told to go out and have a good time," I said. "You were there. You know that's what Irina said I should do."

My partner kept his eyes on the road as he spoke to me.

"I'm not the one who should be telling you what to do, Katyusha. But this job is by far the most important work you've ever been asked to carry out. Something this big may not happen to you again for a very long time."

For someone who thought he shouldn't be telling me what to do Yuri really wasn't faring very well. He was rubbing me the wrong way that morning, with his supposed greater knowledge of the mission and what was at stakes. He seriously got on my nerves.

"I can manage," I said.

The car stopped at a red light and Yuri looked at me. His right hand fell on my thigh and held it. There was concern in his eyes, which took me by surprise. Yuri was tall and strong like a bear, a big brown bear from the Kamchatka peninsula. But at that moment he looked like a little rabbit I could have held in the palm of my hands. My heart softened for my official boyfriend, but it was too late. I had read Stacey's text messages and wanted out of my pen.

CHAPTER 8

"Sorry. We're out of strawberries."

The waitress with pink mermaid hair who stood at our table didn't look a day older than sixteen. A tiny crystal shone on the side of her left nostril.

"Okay, so I guess I'll have mango," I said.

"*Parfait*," she said.

Service was fast in this small eatery in the Mile End where Yuri and I sat, alone. Our hand-made pizzas, two irregular ovals covered with arugula, portobello mushrooms and fresh cheese, landed on our table no more than fifteen minutes later. My mango smoothie also arrived, brought to me in a thick milkshake glass. I took a sip of it and felt a soothing coolness cover the inside of my stomach.

"So, what exactly did you do last night?" Yuri said.

"Not much. I went out. To a party."

"Oh yeah? Whose party was it?"

"Some guy in law school."

Yuri was curious to know more but played it cool. He took a sip of his San Pellegrino, leaned against the back of his chair and crossed his legs. We had chosen a table in the corner furthest away from the cash register, at a distance from any prying ears.

"Have you heard back from the police?" he said.

His change of subject made me smile. A not-so-subtle shift from my activities of the night before.

"You mean about that scuffle I was involved in the other night?"

I was teasing him, pretending to be coy. Yuri rolled his eyes and stared at me, but he wasn't angry.

"No, nothing," I said. "I haven't heard from them at all. I guess they haven't caught the guy yet."

"If they contact you, we'll have to tell Anton about it right away."

"You mean Irina."

"No, Anton. He's our mission supervisor. For the duration of the job he's the one in charge. His authority overrides Irina's. He's the one calling the shots."

For me to volunteer any information to that maniac? Not a chance in hell. If anything happened, he would be the last one to know. I wasn't reporting anything back to this asshole.

"What's his background, Anton?" I said.

Yuri bent forward and spoke in a whisper.

"Syria. He was out there for seven years. Then he got injured. The Service reassigned him and moved him to the States about a year ago. Central Control uses him for high-risk operations. Abductions, extractions, that kind of stuff."

"And before that?"

"The GRU. Special forces."

"And why are they using him for this particular mission?"

"Because it's an important one. And because he's one of the best in the Service to create and implement false identities."

"He seems a bit over-qualified for what we're doing. I mean, we're not going to war."

"That's because you don't know what's on the key, Katyusha."

He pulled back and drank what remained of his mineral water. It was my turn to bend forward.

"What's on the key?"

Yuri put his glass down.

"Some photographs of young girls. Naked. Some of them underaged."

"You mean juvenile pornography?"

"I guess some of it would qualify as such. But mostly people doing things. Together."

"Who?"

Yuri brought his face next to mine and took one of my hands in his. We must have looked like a young couple in love, whispering sweet nothings to one another.

"The president of the United States."

The president of the United States. Mitchell Baker, a man in his early sixties with a full head of the most elegant silvery grey. A self-declared conservative, belatedly adopted by the religious right which he nonetheless convinced of his commitment to promote a socially conservative agenda "for those who wanted it." A candidate concerned with climate change who was able to rally a slice of the liberal electorate. Married, with a telegenic wife always ready to dab her eyes with a tissue in moments of joy or sorrow. A venture capitalist by trade who was known for his level-headed approach to governing and his willingness to reach across the aisle. Elected to the White House after completing two terms in the Senate during which he was known as the wealthiest member of Congress. A man of probity whose prodigious philanthropy had preceded his career in politics. *A pedophile.*

"The *president?*"

Yuri nodded.

"That's insane," I said.

"Nope."

"How young? The girls?"

"Teenagers. On the lower end."

A mix of repulsion and outrage started to rise inside of me. My partner lifted my hand to his lips and kissed it.

"And some young men, too. But not underaged so that's legal and it's not on the key. A lot of people have secrets, Katyusha. Some are just more horrible than others."

Half an hour later Yuri drove me back to our student neighbourhood. He stopped the car in front of my apartment, and I got out without much of a goodbye.

"I'll call you later," he said.

"Sure. But I may be seeing my friends."

There wasn't going to be any exercising in the nude that afternoon. I wasn't in the mood for it, and I also had a fair amount of catching up to do.

Inside my home, I unzipped my tracksuit jacket and pulled out the silencer and the ammo I had stuck under my left arm for the quick climb to the front door of my apartment. I retrieved the Beretta from my lower back, where it held in place with the elastic band of my pants. My phone vibrated in the pocket of my jacket, and I placed all my new toys on a small table in the living room to look at it.

It was Stacey, again. *Where are u????* I wrote to her that I would call her back in an hour and sat on the sofa. I put my left hand into the side pocket of my pants and with the tip of my fingers felt the contour of the USB key Anton had given me. I suddenly felt very tired. I kicked off my running shoes without untying them and fell sideways on the sofa like a dead tree falling in a forest. I could have gone to sleep right at that moment, lying on the soft cushioned seat of the sofa, but I knew I shouldn't. I had to start preparing for the mission. I thought about the director of the orphanage. Seeing me now, she would have no doubt scolded me. *Ekaterina Yegorova, you lazy little sloth. What do you think you're doing? Vacationing on the Black Sea?*

I went to the kitchen and sat at my Ikea table, a rounded thing supposedly large enough for a Scandinavian family of four. I opened my laptop and inserted Anton's flash drive into the USB port. On it I found a multitude of documents, including a timeline of the mission, my specific instructions, and a detailed plan of every floor of the hotel and of its surrounding grounds with the parking lots, the golf course, the pool and the tennis courts. There was also a topographic map that showed the different levels of the terrain as well as the roads and any building within a ten-kilometer radius of the hotel.

The *Manoir du Cap* was located five hundred meters from the main road. It was a large construction with 405 guest rooms, numerous conference facilities and a sprawling land-scaped *terrasse* that overlooked the Saint Lawrence River. The small town of La Malbaie, five kilometers to the north, was home to eight thousand people. On the map and each of the plans, markings in yellow indicated where the security fences had been installed for the duration of the G7. There were two separate security enclaves, one inside the other. The red zone, immediately surrounding the hotel, and the green zone, which extended around it and covered an area of about fifteen square kilometers.

Starting Monday, the owners of the properties located inside the green zone would be subjected to restrictions. Any person wanting to access the green zone, or wanting to leave it, would have to pass through one of the designated check-points set along the road and present a specially issued identity card. These cards had been distributed ten days earlier to the green zone homeowners and the other individuals who needed to travel in and out of the restricted sector. Our fall-back identities, those of Karine Demers and Fabien Racine, the couple who lived in the green zone, came with green zone identity cards.

The red zone was essentially the *Manoir* and its private

land, a sprawling piece of real estate, some of it forested. A three-meter-high metal fence had been put up around it and enclosed it in an irregularly shaped semi-circle that faced the river and included the cliff on which sat the grand terrace of the hotel. Cameras and motion detectors were attached to the fence at regular intervals. Its base was anchored into concrete and buried underneath the ground.

Members of the RCMP, the Royal Canadian Mounted Police, as well as soldiers would be stationed every fifty meters along the fence. Close to three thousand agents, military personnel and police officers, from all over the country, and dozens of trained dogs, were already deployed at the site and would remain so until the G7 was over. Joined by members of the *Sûreté du Québec*, the *Service de police de la ville de Québec* and the local police, that number would swell to five thousand people on the opening day of the summit.

The dignitaries would arrive by plane at the nearby military base of Bagotville and would be flown to the *Manoir* by helicopter. For that reason, the air space in a radius of fifty kilometers around the hotel would be restricted starting Monday as well. As for the waters in front of it, the coast guard already patrolled them around the clock.

Juliette Després and Finn Martens, the individuals we would pretend to be for the duration of our mission, were red zone cardholders. Anton and his team had implanted our false vetting by the Ottawa office of the RCMP in the security system of the G7. Our photographs would appear in the database of the officers manning the checkpoints every time our identity cards were scanned. As permitted to some of the personnel of the hotel, Yuri and I would be allowed to enter the red zone with our vehicles before the start of the summit and leave them in a specifically designated parking area, far from the *Manoir* and the helicopter landing pad. That permission to drive to the hotel given to some of the staff ended at noon on Wednesday. From then on, only the authorized vehicles, the large SUVs operated by the RCMP and the police and the military cars and trucks, would be allowed through the red zone checkpoint.

Yuri and I would be leaving early on Wednesday morning in separate cars and arrive at the *Manoir* at around eleven. The world leaders and their spouses would arrive the following day at lunch time, but that didn't mean the two of us were free to do what we wanted in the meantime. "You've been asked to teach a yoga class for the organizers of the summit on Thursday morning," Anton had said. According to our mission supervisor, this was an initiative of the Prime Minister's wife, a team-building activity for those in the Prime Minister's entourage who had been dispatched to Charlevoix the previous week to handle the preparations. Apparently, yoga classes were all the rage at corporate retreats.

Brett Alford would arrive at the hotel on Monday and Anton and his computer whiz team would make sure that his bedroom would be situated somewhere quiet at the back of the building, with a garden or pool view. Not a bad thing considering the poor guy might have been tempted to throw himself down the cliff if he had been given a room with a view of the river. Life could be tough for those who fell in the clutches of the Service. But as much as I imagined the mental anguish Alford might have been suffering from, I couldn't really feel sorry for him. I couldn't understand how someone raised in privilege could be foolish enough to screw it all up. I had zero to none empathy for spoiled brats.

Thanks to Anton's team of computer hackers, my bedroom would be located on the same floor as Alford's. To give us a wide range of movement, Yuri would be assigned a room in a different wing of the hotel.

My phone rang. It was Stacey. I hesitated for a second before picking it up.

"Yo. Where *are* you?" she said.

"I was at the mountain with Hans."

"Is he still there?"

"No. He went home. He still has a ton of work to do to try to catch up."

"Theo wants your number."

"I know. I read your messages."

"Can I give it to him?"

I hesitated. My mind teleported me back to the party of the night before. Theo, my laid-back beer-pong opponent who didn't seem to care. The guy with a fringe that fell to the side of his face. I had to admit I wanted to see him. I couldn't help myself even though this clearly wasn't the time to even consider developing a crush on someone. I was supposed to know better. I had to prepare for the job. And if I said yes to Stacey, how would I prevent Yuri, or my parents, from finding out about him?

I wasn't supposed to develop an intimate relationship with anyone other than Yuri without the prior knowledge of the Service. At the very least, I was supposed to disclose any such encounters without delay after they happened. That same rule didn't apply to Yuri, which of course was unfair. But to start seeing Theo, three days before the start of our assignment? It was madness. Yet there I was, holding my mobile telephone, incapable of saying no. Just the thought of it seemed to compress my ribcage as if I had no choice but to say yes to Stacey in order to keep on breathing.

"So?" she said.

"Sure. Give it to him."

She giggled.

"Cool. I'll do it right away."

I knew what she was thinking. That I had just joined her rumbustious quest for love. But it really wasn't like that at all. In my case, it was more of a quest for oxygen by someone on the cusp of asphyxiation. I wondered what the people at the Service would say if they discovered I had secretly allowed a private side-life for myself to flourish. A hidden corner in which I hid the few things I could truly call my own. I imagined Uncle Ivan sitting in a big leather chair, distractedly stroking his enormous mustache. "Ekaterina? Such a promising young woman." But I didn't care. All I wanted was to see Theo again.

Fifteen minutes later my telephone vibrated on the kitchen table. *Hi it's Theo do you want to go for a drink tonight?* That one sure didn't waste any time testing the waters. He seemed to be the kind to dive in headfirst, and if he hit the bottom only hurting himself once. Yes, I did want to go and have a drink. Absolutely. At that moment, it was the one thing I wanted the most. Us two, alone for an entire evening without anyone knowing about it. And then I would prepare for the mission.

I wrote that I would meet him at eight at Thomson House, the Golden Square Mile sandstone mansion up on McTavish Street that housed the McGill Graduate Society. Yuri would never go there in a million years. He hated it. "That place is full of scruffy looking people," he said. I, on the other hand, didn't mind going to Thomson House once in a while to have a drink. There was a great bar in what used to be one of the mansion's living rooms. The mood of the place was casual and on a Sunday night it would be almost empty.

CHAPTER 9

At ten minutes past eight I sat at the bar with a margarita when Theo arrived, at once completely at ease with our surroundings. The room we were in was large and elegant, with wood panels, a soaring ceiling and heavy sliding doors made of solid oak. My date walked in as if he owned the place. We were the only two people there.

"Hi," I said.

Theo kissed me on the cheeks and sat on a stool. He smelled nice. Just a subtle hint of a masculine lavender scent. He wore a wrinkled blue shirt that fit perfectly over his shoulders. I hadn't noticed how physically fit he was the night before at the party.

"Good evening," he said.

"What are you drinking?"

"A gin and tonic."

I knew the guy who worked behind the bar that night. His name was Sid, a graduate student in astrophysics. Sid had retreated to a corner when Theo had arrived, and I gestured for him to come over. He took our order, placed a highball glass on the bar and filled it up to the rim with ice cubes and gin and the required amount of tonic.

"There you go," he said. "Want some more ice?"

I ordered another margarita. Sid had decided he was serving us doubles. He didn't care. He also gave us a whole bag of pretzels before retreating to his corner to read his book.

"It's an interesting place, this house," Theo said.

"I love it. It's beautiful."

"It really is. But don't you find it strange that it was built in the nineteen thirties? In those days the majority of people in Montreal barely had enough to eat."

A man with a social conscience. That was another thing I liked about my date. We talked about the usual, at first. He said he had two older sisters. I was an only child. I told him I had lived in Spain. He told me about growing up in Quebec and going to camp every summer, up north in the Mauricie region. His mother spoke French, his father English. We alternated between the two.

"I was eighteen the last time I went. We were gone for a whole month, on the Broadback River. That was a *long* canoe trip. Five hundred kilometers all the way to James Bay. With wolves and flies and no cell phone. And *limited* toilet paper."

Theo was funny, too.

"Sometimes when I was a kid, I would just fall off my chair for no reason. Like, literally fall off it as if someone had pushed me. And then my father would say, "Should we give you lessons on how to sit on a chair?" Or he'd look at me with a serious face and say, "I think we should buy you a helmet to wear at the table.""

We talked about all sorts of things, including my place of birth.

"Where in France?" he said.

"In Lyons."

"Do you still have family there?"

"Only a grandmother. Both my parents are only-children. I don't have any uncles or aunts. I don't have any cousins."

He smiled.

"Really? That is so strange. At that rate you'll be an extinct species pretty soon."

I knew my official life story by heart. I never once hesitated as I told him about myself growing up. Everything was documented. If need be, we had someone in Lyons to play the grandmother. A perfect *mamie* with nice silver hair, a cat and a membership to the local library. Theo and I could have flown there for a visit. She was a charming woman, an agent for the Service for the past fifty years. According to Irina, she had been the mistress of the American ambassador in Vienna in the seventies.

Two drinks later, we were still sitting alone at the bar. It was a quarter to ten and Sid suddenly shut his book and decided he'd had enough of doing nothing.

"I'm leaving," he said. "You guys don't mind, do you? If you want another drink just help yourself and leave the money under the counter. Someone will lock up later, when they close the place."

Sid grabbed his coat and left. As soon as he was gone Theo went to close the sliding doors and turn off the lights. He came back and we kissed, with me sitting on a stool and him standing between my legs. His hands slowly moved under my sweater and mine under his shirt. He pressed his lips against my own and his fingers slid under the straps of my bra which fell off my shoulders.

"Come over here," he said.

He lifted me up and sat me in front of him on the bar. He raised my sweater and started to fondle my breasts while my hands travelled down the side of his chest and wrapped themselves around his waist. We kissed again. His fingers slid inside my pants and mine into his. We were enthralled by each other, unaware of anything else and almost didn't hear a shuffling noise behind the doors. Theo instantly back, and I quickly pulled down my sweater. A second later the panel doors slid open, and the lights came on.

A young guy with a beard immediately took a step backward and lifted his hand to his chest as if he'd suffered a heart attack. He took a deep breath and intentionally looked sideways as I slipped off the counter.

"Sorry guys but the bar closes at ten on Sundays," he said.

"Really? Ah, sorry dude. We didn't know that," Theo said.

I started to laugh. And Theo did too. He'd just said the stupidest thing. As if making love on the bar counter would have been fine before closing time.

Outside, we laughed some more as we walked down McTavish towards the lower part of the McGill campus.

"I can't believe we were caught," Theo said. "What the hell happened?"

"I don't know. What were we thinking?"

"And this guy, oh my God."

McTavish is one of those downtown vertical streets with a thirty-degree inclination at its higher end. Theo placed his arm around my shoulders and held me tight.

"So, what is it that you like to do apart getting caught naked in public places?" he said.

"That is so unfair. You made me do it."

"I did not."

I was having the best of times. The world that existed begun and ended with me and Theo. We crossed Doctor Penfield Avenue and walked down the cement staircase that led to the grounds of the lower campus. Below us, the quad was dark and quiet. At the far end of it, beyond the Roddick Gates, the illuminated skyscrapers of Montreal shone their neon glare into the open sky. We circled past the Arts Building, a stately Greystone neoclassical, and reached the east entrance of the campus at the corner of Milton.

"Where do you live?" Theo said.

"On Durocher. You?"

"On Lorne Crescent."

That was the street on which I had fought my attacker the other night. The coincidence surprised me.

"Where exactly on Lorne Crescent?" I said.

"One house away from the corner of Aylmer."

"In the dead-end?"

"No, on the other side of the street. At the end of the curve."

He placed one hand behind my neck and kissed me again.

"Do you want to come over to my place?" he said.

I wanted to but knew I shouldn't.

"I can't. Not tonight," I said.

He stared at me.

"I have to wake up at five tomorrow morning to finish reviewing an article for my thesis supervisor. We have a meeting at nine. I shouldn't have gone out tonight, but I really wanted to," I said.

His grey eyes looked deeply into mine. He was being cautious now. Like a minesweeper carefully threading onto new ground.

"Yeah. I know what you mean. I also have a ton of work to do. I have an exam tomorrow afternoon and another one on Wednesday. What are you doing Wednesday night?"

I pretended to think really hard about that for a second, to try to make him smile.

"Wednesday? Sure," I said. "That could work."

I already knew I would have to lie to him again and invent a reason for not being able to see him. He smiled and I wished upon a million stars that I too could smile with the blissful happiness of an innocent mind.

"See you Wednesday," he said.

His lips brushed against my own for the last time. I turned around and started to walk away.

"Oh, by the way, I may be going to Charlevoix on Thursday, for the G7," he said.

I stopped as if I had hit a glass wall and turned around.

"The what?" I said.

I was too stunned to say anything clever. His mouth stretched sideways into a large smile.

"The G7. You know, the meeting of the world leaders, in Charlevoix."

"Why?"

"A friend of mine is organising a protest. I haven't decided yet if I'm going or not."

"That's great. Good night."

Minutes later I was on my way home, alone, and wondering if God, if he existed at all, was some kind of joker. Theo at the G7? That was unbelievable. A one in a million coincidence. Of course, it wasn't something I needed to worry about. Protesters would be kept kilometers away from the *Manoir*, herded inside a designated protest area in La Malbaie. If Theo ever went, he and I would never be at the same place at the same time.

I turned left on my street and walked past a long line of parked cars. No one was out at this hour, on a Sunday night. I climbed the stairs to my apartment and saw that the light was out in Markus and Jacques's living room. Their front windows, like mine, were holes of darkness gaping at the outside world.

I closed the door behind me and stopped. Something felt different in my apartment, as if an alien presence still lingered. I noticed the laces of my sneakers which I had left near the entrance were stuck underneath the soles, something I avoided doing to try to keep them clean. Someone had been inside my apartment while I was out, bumped into my sneakers, put them back in their place.

I slowly moved into the living room and slid my hand under a cushion of the sofa where it found the plastic handle of the Beretta. I retrieved it from its hiding place and waited. I listened carefully but couldn't hear a thing. Not the slightest crack, nothing at all. I started to move towards the back of my apartment. I looked into the bedroom, then the bathroom. In the kitchen I turned on the fan light above the oven. My laptop was still on the kitchen table with the lid shut, just as I had left it. But I could have sworn the chair facing it had been moved. I placed the palm of my hand on the seat of the chair. It was neither warm nor cold.

If anyone had been in my apartment it was likely to be Yuri. My partner had a key to my place, and he had been unusually curious about my activities of the past few days.

I decided to call him.

"Hey," he said.

"Hey. Did you come over to my place while I was out?"

"No. Why?"

"Nothing. I just thought someone had been here. But I guess I was wrong."

"Is everything alright?"

"Yeah, yeah. I suppose I must be experiencing a bit of post-traumatic stress or something."

"Because of the other night?"

"Yeah, maybe."

"Do you want me to come over?"

"No, no. I'm fine. I'm going to bed anyway."

In the bedroom I took my clothes off and put on a large t-shirt that fell to the top of my thighs. I wondered if Yuri had told me the truth about not having been in my apartment. Something had changed in my partner lately. A whole new side of him had grown, and I couldn't read his mind as easily as I used to. I turned off all the lights in my apartment and took the gun with me to the living room.

I positioned myself on the right side of the windows to take a look outside. There was no one on the street as far as I could see. I moved to the left side and glanced up the street towards Prince-Arthur. Nothing moved. I was about to go to bed when I caught sight of a silhouette emerging from the shadows along the side of a building and my heart started to beat faster. The stroller was coming towards my apartment, on the other side of the street. He wore a short black coat, a sort of windbreaker, and a dark baseball cap and I knew immediately that he had to be the man Markus had seen a few days before. He slowed down in front of my home, stopped for a second and looked straight at my windows from across the street.

I dropped down on the floor and quickly moved away from the windows on my hands and knees. I stood up again near the entrance, put on my Navy coat and forced my bare feet into my running shoes. I shoved the Beretta into my coat pocket and carefully opened the front door. The man had kept on walking, and I saw him just as he was about to turn right at the corner of Milton. I climbed down the stairs as noiselessly as I could and started to chase after him as he disappeared around the corner entrance of the local *dépanneur*, the neighbourhood's all-hours convenience store. I started to run and almost collided with a couple coming out of the store. The woman lost her balance and dropped her shopping bag and a milk carton and a box of cereals fell out of it on the sidewalk.

"Hey! Watch where you're going!" the man she was with shouted at me.

I ignored him, only to realize that the sidewalk ahead of me was empty. The man I was chasing had disappeared. There was a back alley a few meters ahead to the right and I figured he must have gone there to hide. I jogged to the entrance of the alley, a narrow one-car lane that ran along the back of the houses on the next cross street and stopped. The alley was dark, and I didn't want to fall into a trap for a second time. I took a few steps forward, looking to my left and right, and heard footsteps behind me, on the sidewalk.

"Nina?"

I spun around. It was Aaron, my redheaded beer pong teammate. I stared at him for a second too long.

"It's Aaron. From the party," he said.

"Aaron. Of course. Sorry. Hi."

He looked at my bare legs and at my floppy t-shirt. I closed my coat and crossed my arms over it.

"What are you doing?" he said.

"I was in my living room and I saw this man outside of my apartment who was lurking under my windows. So, I ran out after him."

"You mean like a peeping-tom?"

"Yeah," I said.

"You really shouldn't have done that, running after him. It could be super dangerous. I mean, who knows what these guys are capable of."

"I know. You're absolutely right. I just didn't think about it. I just ran out."

"You must be freezing," he said.

"Yeah, kind of. My apartment is just around the corner."

"I'll walk you back."

"Thanks," I said. "I'm actually really freezing."

We started to walk back to my place. A police car slowly passed us by as it cruised down Milton like a big white shark swimming in shallow water. I didn't dare to look at it. With my kind of luck, I would have probably found Constable Manuel sitting behind the wheel. Inside my coat, my chest felt clammy and cold.

"It's right there," I said. "Thanks for escorting me back."

"No problem. Go make yourself a hot tea or something. And lock your doors."

I quickly climbed up the stairs and went inside. There was a folded piece of paper on the floor, right behind the door. It was a note, scribbled in blue pencil ink. *The blond guy was inside your apt.* I was astounded. The man with the baseball cap had left me a message. He had come back to my apartment while I was talking to Aaron and had slipped it through the mail slot. I stared at it. The 'blond guy' could only have been Yuri. I didn't have any other blond male friends, except my neigh-bour Jacques, with his dyed blond *coiffure*. But he was off to Brussels as of yesterday.

Was it true, what the message on the piece of paper said? And if it was, why had Yuri lied to me? I shivered and felt very cold. I kicked off my shoes, took the gun from my coat pocket and threw my coat on the sofa.

In the bedroom I placed the gun on the floor right next to my bed, just below my pillows where I could easily reach out for it. I wrapped myself in the duvet and tried to fall asleep, but I couldn't. Who was the man in the baseball cap and what did he want? What was his connection to the agents caught in 1995? If my birth mother was Maria Serov, I was certain she had died. But what about my father? Dead also, probably. If not, how had I been placed in an orphanage in Moscow? My mind continued to swirl for a long time but in the end it surrendered, defeated, and sleep got the best of me.

CHAPTER 10

On Wednesday morning I left for Charlevoix at sunrise in a car rented with a throwaway credit card. It was a small four-door model, metallic grey. The most basic of vehicles with pale grey vinyl seats, a USB port and a cheap set of speakers. I followed the directions of my GPS navigation app and drove all the way to the north-eastern tip of the island of Montreal, past the oil refineries of Pointe-aux-Trembles, then onto Highway 40, the concrete ribbon that rolls towards Québec City on the north shore of the Saint Lawrence River.

The road was monotonous from the start. A two-lane bed of asphalt that stretched forward between thick rows of pine trees, most of them planted by the *Ministère des Transports* to prevent whiteouts during the windy days of winter. I tried not to dwell too much on what awaited me in Charlevoix. I lowered my window to get some fresh air. I turned on the radio and found nothing interesting to listen to. My mind eventually switched to auto-play, and I started to think once again about the events of the past few days.

I hadn't told Yuri what had happened on Sunday night after I'd gone out for a drink with Theo. If the message the man had left me was true, Yuri had lied to me about being at my apartment while I was out. I felt uneasy about it and wondered what he'd been looking for. Since Monday morning, he and I been together almost constantly to prepare for the mission. We'd made love once in his apartment, in front of the mirrored sliding doors of his bedroom closet. Things left unsaid prevented us from truly being close to each other. Our intimacy, once so familiar, was now troubled by the lies both of us were responsible for. But Yuri was a model agent, and I couldn't believe he would do anything other than faithfully follow orders he received from the Service. Unless something extraordinary had taken place.

I was now convinced the man who looked at my windows and followed me was the same man who'd left me the newspaper article at the restaurant and also possibly the one who had come to my rescue the other night. I hadn't seen him again since I had chased after him in my coat and t-shirt, but I knew he had been out there for the past two days, close by and probably watching me. I had looked for him at night, sitting on a chair in my darkened living room but he had known better than to take a walk past my apartment. I needed to know who he was and couldn't wait to speak to Irina. As for the man who had attacked me, I wondered if he might have been responsible for Lana's disappearance.

And then there was Theo. He had called me the day before and the few words we had exchanged on the telephone still resonated like a sad song I couldn't get rid of.

"Hey," he had said.

"Hey."

I had asked him about his preparation for his last exam. We had chatted for a while. And then I had told him what I wished I didn't have to say.

"Listen, I'm really sorry but I won't be able to see you tomorrow night."

"Really? Why?"

"I have to go see my mother. She really hasn't been feeling well and I'll probably sleep over at my parents' house tomorrow."

"Wow. I hope it's nothing serious."

"I know. She's lost consciousness recently a couple of times for no reason. Her blood pressure kind of drops unexpectedly. And tomorrow night my dad has a dinner, a fundraiser thing with some of his clients. So, I'll be spending the evening with my mom."

"Right."

At that precise moment uneasiness had set itself at the other end of the line. Uncertainty had taken root in Theo's heart, where I had reluctantly planted it, and there was nothing I could do to prevent it from growing. On my end of things, I felt a giant well of regret grow deeper as the hours passed. I really liked Theo and I wanted to see him again. Once the mission was over, I decided I would, no matter the consequences.

There was a sign on the highway that indicated I was getting closer to the city of Québec. I looked at the digital clock on the car radio. I had been driving for almost three hours. The highway circled around the old city, past its center, and as I left the *Capitale Nationale* behind, it became a boulevard with a series of traffic lights, and the traffic slowed. I continued heading north and it eventually became a two-lane road that veered inland, away from the river and with fewer cars on it.

Road 138, the only throughway to the Charlevoix region, cut through fields and forests that seemed to stretch indefinitely on both sides of it. The scenery made me think of Russia, or at least what I remembered of it. The buildings were different, but the land brought about a similar state of mind. Mostly, a feeling of emptiness.

After another hour of driving the road split in two just before the small town of Baie-Saint-Paul. I veered right on Road 362, back towards the Saint Lawrence River and was finally able to catch a glimpse of it. A blue body of water so large it could have been the sea. The road went up and down a series of bumpy hills. The hotel wasn't much further along the way, an additional forty-five minutes of driving at most.

But twenty minutes later, after a slow climb up a valley that offered a breathtaking view of the river, I came across the first road check. A series of orange plastic cones and a portable stop sign placed in the middle of the road. Four police cars were parked along the curb, with officers standing by in the black pants and the dark olive jacket of the *Sûreté du Québec*, the provincial police force known as the SQ. I counted seven of them.

There it was. The gateway into the green zone. The entry point to a swath of farmland and semi-residential wooden lots converted into a tightly controlled gated community for the duration of the summit. The SQ had a list of everyone who lived or worked in the green zone. But that morning I wasn't one of them. I was a red zone passport holder. A very special guest.

I slowed down and one of the officers gestured for me to bring my car closer. I came to a full stop next to him and lowered my window. He asked me to turn off the engine.

"Vos papiers?" he said.

About thirty years old. A close shave, light brown hair. Nice looking.

"Sure," I said.

I handed him my red zone passport. The officer looked at my ID and shot me a glance to make sure I was the woman on the photograph.

"What's the reason of your presence at the G7?"

"I'm a yoga teacher. I've been hired for the event."

I smiled. He didn't.

"They've organized some activities for some of the guests. I'll be doing yoga classes," I said.

No reaction.

"Can you please step out of your vehicle?" the officer said.

I grabbed my handbag and came out as he pointedly peered inside the car.

"Do you have any firearms with you? Any hunting gear?" he said.

"No."

Another officer came to join the one I was talking to.

"D'you need help Mathieu?" he said.

He moved towards the rear of my vehicle.

"Can you open the trunk?" the first officer said.

I reached inside the car for the release button. I had dismantled the Beretta in separate parts and placed them in three small plastic bags hidden inside the car. The slide and the barrel were in a small pouch in the glove compartment with a tire pressure gauge. The springs and all the smaller parts were in a bag taped under the parking brake pedal. The biggest part, the handle, was taped to the side of the windshield washer reservoir under the hood of the car. The bullets I had placed inside the speaker in the car door on the passenger side.

The first officer opened the rear door of the car on the driver's side and bent down to look under the seats. His hand moved blindly under the front passenger seat while his friend inspected the carpet lining inside the trunk. I took a deep breath and tried to concentrate on the beauty of the landscape.

A loud roar rose from the valley and a group of motorcyclists came to a noisy stop at the SQ roadblock. The first officer pulled out of my car and walked away to meet them. They were about a dozen, each of them riding a Harley Davidson, leather-clad and wearing the distinctive patches of a criminalized biker gang. After a brief exchange of which I understood nothing, the leader of the group put his two-wheeled beast to sleep, and the rest of the gang did the same.

"Where are you going?" the officer said.

"We're going to a friend's birthday party," the leader said.

"You need a special pass to access the green zone during the G7 summit."

"The green *what?*"

"The green zone. During the G7 summit. You need to have a special ID document to be allowed to go through."

"What document? We're just going to our friend's birthday party. In La Malbaie."

"I'm sorry but the road is closed."

"Until when?"

"Next Sunday at noon."

The biker' face suddenly turned a deeper shade of pink.

"Next Sunday? *Comment ça tabarnak?*"

A yellow school bus that had been chugging up the valley screeched to a stop behind the motorcycle squad. A banner tied to its side proudly declared that Imperialism deserved to die in bold capital letters painted red. Chanting burst out of the opened windows.

"*Le G7 faut que ça pète…G7 la même cassette…*"

A school bus full of protesters. I quickly turned around and took out a pair of sunglasses from my handbag. Theo couldn't possibly be on that bus. He had an exam that afternoon. But his beer-pong buddy could. Or anyone else from McGill who could recognize me. Granted, there would be busloads of protesters driving to the site over the next hours but all it took was one person for my cover to be blown.

The first officer was still arguing with the leader of the biker gang.

"You need a special ID card. If you don't have one, you have to go back to the 138 at Baie-Saint-Paul and stay on it all the way to La Malbaie," he said.

"That's gonna take us all day!" the leader of the bikers said.

Two officers went to join their colleague while a third one spoke to the driver of the school bus. The officer who had been looking inside the trunk of my car closed it shut.

"You can go," he said.

I didn't wait for him to change his mind. I drove for another fifteen minutes and turned right on a private access road that led to the hotel and the red zone checkpoint. That road was the only one that remained open. The other lanes, the ones used for maintenance and delivery, had all been temporarily closed off with heavy blocks of concrete.

This time the obligatory stop resembled a port of entry into a country at war, with two rows of metal barriers, German Shepherd dogs and a contingent of RCMP officers in full tactical gear. I slowed down and stopped in front of the first barrier. A heavy-set officer holding an assault rifle opened it and raised his hand and I turned off the engine and lowered my window. Another officer, his identical twin, came up on the other side of the car and looked inside as I reached for my handbag. I handed my ID document to the first one.

"Your name?"

"Juliette Després."

"You work at the hotel?"

"No. I'm a contract employee, a yoga teacher. I've been hired for the activities that will be offered to some of the guests."

"*Merci*. Please wait in the car."

The first officer took my red zone passport and passed it through the opened window of a checkpoint cabin on the left side of the road, a container-like rectangular box dropped into place for the duration of the summit. I knew they would be scanning my ID document inside that mobile shed, spreading it flat on one of those glass-top devices used by customs agents around the world. As I waited, an officer approached my car with a big dog pulling on its leash. Another officer followed with an inspection mirror.

"Can you step out of the vehicle?" the officer with the dog said.

I promptly opened the car door.

"Just step over there please. Are you afraid of dogs?"

"No," I said.

"Good."

He immediately released the large beige and black canine, which started to circle around me, sniffing at my feet and pushing its thick dark snout up against my ass.

"*Prince. Ici!*"

His handler pointed to the car and the dog immediately left me and started sniffing at the car tires, which seemed infinitely less interesting than my rear end.

"Sorry miss. The dog's just doing his job."

"No problem."

The dog circled the car with its long pink tongue hanging out of his mouth while the officer with the inspection mirror moved it slowly along the sides. Once he was finished, he returned to the driver's door and opened it. I swallowed hard and looked at the checkpoint cabin where my ID document was still being examined. I turned around and looked at the car again. The officer with the mirror had opened the rear door of the car on the driver's side and was reaching with his hand under the back seats. I forced myself to look at the sky, seemingly interested in the weather. *Breathe slow.*

"Okay miss, you can go back to your car," the K-9 officer said.

He clipped his furry friend back on its leash while his colleague shut the doors of my rental, then signalled to a couple of men on the other side of the second barrier that I was allowed to go through. A hand appeared at the checkpoint cabin's window with my red zone passport and the officer to whom I had first given it picked it up and gave it back to me.

"After the barrier, you turn right and continue driving all the way to parking F. *Bonne journée.*"

After crossing the checkpoint, I turned right as instructed and continued past a series of ambulances parked on the side of the road with a group of medics who sat on beach chairs in their winter coats and played a game of cards.

The lane took me away from the hotel, past a series of empty flower beds. It hadn't been warm enough yet in Charlevoix for the spring perennials to come out of their winter slumber. Still, one could see the grounds of the *Manoir* were beautifully maintained. The carpet-like grass was neatly trimmed, the secondary buildings all freshly painted.

A dozen SUVs and military vehicles were parked further along the way. As expected, the place was crawling with officers, security agents and military personnel. And in twenty-four hours, there would be even more of them, with the arrival of the heads of state and their security details.

I found *stationnement F* at the end of the lane and parked the car in a deserted corner. As instructed by Anton, I left the Beretta in detached pieces inside the car, to be retrieved only if I absolutely needed it. I took my carry-on out of the trunk and followed a pedestrian walkway that cut through the grounds of the hotel all the way to the grand entrance of the *Manoir du Cap.*

Closer to the building the walkway led to a ramp to the side of a large stone staircase. A handful of valets in red coat-tails with shiny gold buttons stood at the top of it, ready to welcome the more important guests. They resembled a group of circus masters, bored and waiting for a bear or a lion to show up. One of the red-clad attendants saw me and came to meet me down the ramp.

"*Bonjour et bienvenue,*" he said, as he took hold of my suitcase. "Are you part of the Canadian delegation?"

"No, I'm afraid not. I'm just a yoga teacher."

"*Ah bon,*" he said over his shoulder. "For the activities?"

"Exactly."

I followed him up to the massive front doors of the hotel where the other valets warily eyed the driveway for incoming cars.

"Well, if there's any room left in your class let me know," he said, with a wink.

"Sure. I'll take it from here. Thanks a lot."

The lobby of the hotel reminded me of a grand hunting lodge. Heavy beams of dark brown wood criss-crossed an elevated ceiling where medieval-looking iron chandeliers hanged overhead at regular intervals. Whoever had designed this hotel, about a hundred years earlier, had obviously been a fan of the Neo-Gothic architectural craze.

The reception desk was straight ahead from the entrance at the end of the room, but I couldn't get to it directly. Ten meters away from the doors, a yellow ribbon stretched across the room funnelled all newly arrived guests towards a security check identical to those found at international airports. I lifted my carry-on onto the nearest conveyor belt and emptied my pockets into a rectangular plastic bin.

"This way, please."

I reclaimed my suitcase after being scanned and blasted with short puffs of air in a plexiglass cabin and walked to the reception desk. Security personnel with dark jackets and not-so-discreet earpieces stood inconspicuously in different corners of the lobby. I counted five of them. I handed my red zone passport to a woman behind the desk who greeted me with the unwavering amiability required of those working in the hospitality business.

"Miss Després?" she said.

"That's right."

She looked at her computer, typed something on her keyboard and gave me a cardkey.

"Your room is on the second floor of the Saguenay wing," she said. "Through the lobby, to your right."

I took the elevator to my floor and rolled my suitcase down a long corridor, all the way to room 214, the one nearest the emergency exit. Inside, I threw open the curtains. Below my window were the green carpets of the hotel's estate and the grey rectangles of the tennis courts.

I placed my suitcase on the luggage rack, sat at the foot of the bed and closed my eyes for a moment. There I was, at the *Manoir du Cap*. I had successfully made it through. All these years of training with Irina and Dmitry, finally put to use. The day it all fell into place.

The décor of the room was traditional in style, with heavy floor-length draperies, a large mahogany desk, a chair and a king size bed. Pleasant overall, with walls painted a creamy white and brand-new carpeting. The usual updates included a large flat-screen television, a minibar, a Nespresso machine and decent air conditioning. One of the least expensive rooms in a five-star hotel. I suddenly felt tired. I removed the quilted bed cover and dumped it in the closet next to the entrance, then lay on the bed.

I closed my eyes for a moment. If everything went as smoothly as my arrival at the hotel, the mission would likely move forward without a hitch. "A walk in the park" as Yuri had said. But it was too early to know with any certainty what kind of park it would be. I needed to stay on my toes. The *Manoir* was buzzing with security personnel. Anything could happen.

I got up, took a long, hot shower and lay on the bed again. I turned on the TV and watched some old episodes of Friends. At four thirty, I started to get dressed and at five o'clock sharp headed downstairs to the hotel bar. A drink at the bar was my first visual *rendez-vous* with Alford, who had been told I would wear a yellow sweater and would order an

Aperol Spritz, a bright orange cocktail even a legally blind person would have no problem spotting on a bar table.

"*Bonsoir.*"

A waiter welcomed me as I walked in. The in-house drinking hole was located on the ground floor of the building on the river side and was almost empty. The place was dark and solemn, in the same style as the lobby, with a long wood-panelled counter and plush upholstered chairs. I looked around and saw that Alford hadn't arrived yet. There was a small table stuck in a corner with a view of the entire room and I took a seat there and waited.

Panoramic windows at the back of the room offered a spectacular view of the outdoors. A set of French doors led directly from the bar room to a *terrasse* where clipped potted shrubs and Adirondack chairs waited for the warmer weather. Immediately behind it, a short flight of stairs led to the prom-enade where the hotel guests could enjoy scenic views of the river.

Alford and I weren't supposed to make contact that night. My presence at the bar was meant to let him know that we had arrived safely, and that the operation was going ahead as planned. His instructions were for him to give me the USB key the following morning, as we would both exit our bedrooms at the same time. I opened my laptop, a brand-new machine with nothing on it, and started surfing the news sites on the Internet.

"Good evening. Would you like something to drink?"

A waiter stood next to me. I lifted my eyes and saw Alford entering the bar.

"Yes, please. I'd like an Aperol Spritz," I said.

Alford walked to the counter and sat on a stool. He spoke to the barman and clumsily looked over his shoulder. I noticed his cheeks were flushed. Our D.C. mole seemed to have had a drink already, which was highly possible given his known penchant for alcohol and the pressure he must have been under. Having to deliver a USB key with such highly compromising content to his Russian tormentors had almost certainly turned him into a nervous wreck. And a good stiff drink was likely to be his preferred medication.

The waiter came back to my table with my *apéritif*.

"There you go miss. Enjoy."

Alford twisted sideways and looked across the room, his eyes jumping from one table to the next until he saw me. I purposefully looked down at my screen and typed on my keyboard. When I looked up again, he was drinking what appeared to be a double whisky on ice.

I took a sip of my fluorescent drink. More people arrived at the bar. A whole crowd of gophers, aides and assistants. Members of various delegations sent more than a week in advance to the *Manoir*, before the truly important people showed up. A heavy-set man walked up to Alford, slapped his back and sat next to him at the counter. Alford turned slightly towards him and while doing so looked in my direction again. The idiot wasn't being very subtle. I continued typing on my laptop and glanced at him from the corner of my eyes. He raised his glass and finished his drink in one gulp and he and his friend gestured to the barman to come over. Another double whisky on ice landed in front of Alford, who clinked it lightly against his drinking buddy's pint glass filled to the top with beer.

Alford's friend was as loud as a French horn. The sort who doesn't understand that a roomful of people minding their own business might not be interested in what he had to say. I was mercifully too far away from the bar to follow his every word but once in awhile his booming laughter would project across the room and find its way inside my ears, like bad breath into someone's nostrils.

I took another sip of my Aperol and pretended to look outside through the panoramic windows. Alford's friend rose from his seat and ambled towards the bathrooms and as he did Alford picked up his glass and looked at me again. He must have been drunk by then, and I realized I had better leave the bar before he did something stupid. I shut the lid of my laptop and quickly scribbled my room number on the bill the waiter had placed next to me on a small silver plate. I made my way towards the antique-looking patio doors while Alford kept looking at me as I left the room.

Outside, I sat on a bench at the far end of the promenade and sent Yuri a text message. Finn Martens and Juliette Després worked as a team but were not a couple. For the duration of our mission, Yuri and I were co-workers who lived in Ottawa, nothing more. I admired the view of the river as I waited for him to show up. In front of the *Manoir*, it was more than forty-kilometer wide and smelled like the sea. A cool breeze blew from behind the hotel, but the building acted as a shield and I sat there, quite comfortable and protected from the cold. Yuri appeared on a gravel path that came from the hotel grounds. He sat next to me and crossed his legs.

"Did you have a good drive?" he said.

"Forget about the drive. I just saw Alford at the bar. He already had a drink before he showed up and kept on drinking like a fish all the time I was there."

Yuri nodded.

"We already knew he was drinker."

"I know, but he looks like a complete alcoholic. He's still sitting at the bar as we speak, getting plastered. I don't know if we can trust him. And I don't trust his judgement. He kept looking in my direction when I was there. For a moment I even thought he was going to walk up to me to say something," I said.

"He wouldn't do that. He's too afraid."

"I'm not so sure about that. There was something reckless about his demeanour. As if he didn't care about his own safety anymore."

"He'll be alright. He's just having a hard time processing it all."

In the middle of the river a freighter slowly sailed north, on its way to the Gulf of Saint Lawrence and the Atlantic Ocean.

"I'm hungry," Yuri said. "Let's go inside and have something to eat."

My partner was right. It was time for us to go and find some dinner. We rose from our seat and walked inside the hotel to one of the restaurants. We dined at the least fancy one, a bistro-type dining room unimaginatively named *Le Café du Fleuve*, then headed to our rooms after we had finished.

"Everything will be fine," Yuri said, before we parted.

I nodded and he disappeared across the lobby. I took the elevator to my floor and inside my room lay on the bed for a few minutes. It was early still, not even past eight, and I decided to go out for a walk. I put on a pair of jeans and a dark blue windbreaker and returned to the promenade, carefully avoiding the glare of the large windows as the light from the inside illuminated the smooth plane of the hotel *terrasse*. I sat on a chair at a safe distance outside the bar and looked inside the room for Alford.

The bar was still packed but I couldn't see him. That, at least, was an encouraging sign. Riding Hood had probably had enough to drink, and I assumed he must have retreated to his room for a sweaty night of remorse and soul-wrenching nightmares. Satisfied, I continued my walk along the promenade all the way to the other end, then took a path that circled around the hotel. Back inside my room I watched Rachel and Ross try to make sense of their feelings for another twenty minutes, then turned off my bed lamp and fell into a deep sleep.

· · ·

"And this is your room." Irina opened a door. Behind it was a small bedroom painted a pale shade of blue. A single bed placed against the wall took up half the space. I had never had a bedroom to myself before and happiness swelled inside me like a giant wave. There was a pillow on the bed, and on the pillowcase the image of a red-orangey fish, a Disney character with big friendly eyes. A loud knock resonated against the bedroom wall and it startled me. Then another. The knocking intensified, and a crack appeared in the plaster. I started to breathe more rapidly. Someone was trying to break a hole into the wall of my bedroom. I looked for Irina, but she was gone.

I opened my eyes and sat upright with a start. Someone was banging on the door of my hotel room. I looked at my phone. It was twenty-five minutes past eleven. I threw aside the covers, rushed to the door and carefully looked through the peep hole. Brett Alford stood in the corridor outside my room, barely able to hold himself up.

"What the fuck."

I opened the door and quickly pulled him in. How did he know my room number? And then all of a sudden I knew. I had scribbled it on the bill before leaving the bar. Alford had seen me do it and the waiter might have momentarily left it somewhere close to him, perhaps even on the bar counter. While his friend was in the bathroom, he'd obviously taken a look at it.

"What the hell do you think you're doing?" I said.

I threw my words at him in a violent whisper. He looked at me with unfocused eyes and I pushed him against the wall so that he could lean against it.

"Don't move," I said.

I turned around and grabbed a pair of sweatpants from my carry-on. As I pulled them up Alford swayed forward, tried to put his foot down and tripped sideways, then hit a corner of the desk. We were most definitely in trouble. He tried to regain his balance, then found the desk chair and slowly sat on it. He planted his elbows on the desk and held his head in his hands.

"I don't wanna do this anymore," he said.

"Keep your voice down."

"I've had enough of this shit. I'm done."

The idiot couldn't have managed a more efficient way to risk alerting the entire floor. I bent over him and twisted one of his arms upward behind his back. He was too inebriated to offer much resistance.

"Ouch. You're hurting me."

Alford tried to wriggle out of my hold, but his heart wasn't into it. I twisted his arm tighter, and he let out a cry. I leaned over his shoulder and brought my mouth closer to his ear.

"Lower your voice or I swear I'll pop your shoulder."

Riding Hood started to whimper.

"You can all go fuck yourselves, you fucking Russians," he said.

"Listen to me very carefully," I said, in his ear. "Number one, you keep your voice down. Number two, a deal is a deal. Tomorrow, you're going to give me the flash drive with all the information on it, as you said you would, or we'll make sure you go to prison for betraying your country."

"I'm going to prison anyway."

"Not if you do what I say."

Alford was dead drunk and I couldn't reason with him. But I could make certain that his next stop would be his bedroom, and more specifically his bed. I let go of his arm. He didn't move and stayed seated on the chair like a sulking child. I quickly slipped my feet into my sneakers and put on a sweater over my camisole. I came back to him and grabbed his arm.

"Brett, listen to me. You've had too much to drink. What we're going to do now is go to your room so that you can lie down and get some rest."

I slowly pulled him upward. He resisted at first.

"Get up," I said.

He mumbled something as he struggled to lift himself up while keeping his balance.

"What did you say?" I said.

"I said it's too late."

"Too late for what?"

"For the flash drive. I don't have it anymore. I gave it away."

My stomach immediately tied itself into a knot and I forgot to breathe for a couple of seconds.

"What do you mean? What did you do with it?"

Now the asshole had decided to stay quiet.

"Brett, what flash drive? The one you were supposed to give me?"

He nodded.

"I gave it to the CIA," he said.

I felt my legs grow weak. If the CIA had taken hold of the key, and if they were even remotely aware of what Alford had agreed to do with it, it could be a matter of minutes before a team of officers burst into my room to arrest me. I pushed him against the wall and placed one hand on his chest and the other one around his neck, immediately below his windpipe. I wanted to kill him.

"What do you mean?" I said. "Where is it?"

"At the front desk. I put it in an envelope."

"When?"

He seemed to lose himself for a moment, and I squeezed my fingers around his throat.

"Tonight," he said, barely able to speak. "And then I... to the bar."

"What kind of envelope? One with a name on it?"

He nodded.

"What name? Who did you address it to?"

"To Martin... Ber," he said.

I let go of his neck.

"Martin who?"

"Bergensen," he said.

"Martin Bergensen? The director of the CIA?"

He nodded yes.

I couldn't believe what the moron had done. While still functionally drunk, he'd managed to lumber his way to the front desk and leave the USB key in an envelope addressed to the director of the Central Intelligence Agency. Someone who wouldn't even be at the G7. There was no time to waste. The envelope could still be at the front desk and I had to try to get it back immediately.

"Alright. Listen up. We're going to go to your room now. And you and I are going to talk about this tomorrow morning," I said.

I searched his pockets for his magnetic cardkey. Thankfully, he hadn't lost it.

"Let's go."

I opened the door and we stepped into the corridor. Alford's room number was 208. There were five doors between my room and his. We started to amble slowly as I held Alford firmly under one arm. He was taller and heavier than I was, and because of it I kept him close to the wall so that he could rest against it if he lost his balance. We walked for no more than five meters before he started to keel starboard and rubbed his right side against the wallpaper. I held on to his arm and pulled him upright.

"Keep going," I said, in a whisper.

He and I made it to another portion of the wall before he stumbled again. This time, he put his hand against it and closed his eyes, as if he needed to rest. At such a pace, it would take us a good ten minutes before we reached the relative safety of his room.

"Listen," I said. "I'm going to count to three and then you

and I are going to walk in one shot all the way to your door, understand?"

He nodded.

"Alright. One, two, three."

Alford took off, throwing his weight onward and carrying me with him as he miraculously put one foot in front of the other at an accelerated pace. I jerked forward and was reminded in a flash of a teenage girl I used to see walking her dog in Spain, where I had stayed with Irina and Dmitry. Every morning an enormous Mastiff dragged her down the winding streets of the village as the girl flew behind it and tried not to let go

I released Alford's arm, unable to hold on, and saw him heave dangerously left and right as he kept moving forward down the corridor. He started to lose his balance again and crashed against the nearest door, which thankfully happened to be his. I inserted his magnetic card into the lock and as it clicked and flashed a green light, I heard the elevator doors on our floor open.

The elevator shaft was around the corner from Alford's room and mine, less that thirty meters away. I pushed Alford's door open, jumped over his crumpled body and pulled him inside as hard and as fast as I possibly could. His feet cleared the threshold and the heavy door started to slowly close on its own. It clicked shut, locking us into safety, just as the shuffling of feet passed us by on the carpet of the corridor.

Riding Hood had decided to sleep. He lay motionless on the bedroom floor, his arms spread peacefully to his sides with his palms up, as in communion with God. I removed his shoes, then pulled his pants down his legs. If Alford was to wake up before morning, I didn't want him to rush out of his room. I hid the shoes and the pants in the mini-fridge and grabbed the door hanger from the doorknob. I looked in the hallway. There was no one there. I stepped out of the room, closed the door and hung the do not disturb sign on the doorknob, then quickly walked to the elevators.

A couple of floors down, the lobby was busier than I had anticipated. Some of the chiefs of staff of the G7 leaders as well as their entourage and various officials had arrived late in the evening. Their planes had landed at the nearby base, a quiet air strip now probably busier than a beehive. All these people were tired and wanted a room. Behind the front desk, four employees were busy distributing cardkeys and wishing the newly arrived guests a nice and pleasant stay. I placed myself in line and waited until one of the employees, a petite blonde woman in her mid-forties her gold name plate identified as Brigitte, was free to see me.

"*Bonsoir...*"

A booming voice rudely interrupted our conversation.

"Miss! I said I needed *two* room keys. Not just one. There's only one in the envelope."

A man with a German accent ungraciously bawled at Brigitte. I looked over my shoulder at the culprit who stood right behind me and stared angrily down at her. He was a tall man with brown hair and an obnoxious expression pasted to his rosy face. Some people are naturally unpleasant, and this man seemed to be one of them as he stood there like a hot serving of sauerkraut no one had asked for.

"Sir, it's behind the first one. In the cardholder," Brigitte said.

The boor turned around and disappeared without the slightest thank you. I shot a sympathetic glance at Brigitte and raised my eyebrows. She rolled her eyes ever so lightly, only for me to see. A secret was exchanged. She and I were friends. On the dark wood counter to her left a telephone buzzed, almost imperceptibly, and next to it I caught sight of a white envelope.

"Hi. *Je viens chercher une enveloppe pour* mister Bergensen," I said.

I had chosen to speak to her in French with an English accent on purpose. A gut decision that proved to be the right one. To the exhausted Brigitte, an English-speaking woman who made the effort to speak to her in her native French was worthy of an immediate reward.

"Here it is," she said, with a tired smile.

She took the envelope and placed it on the counter. Brigitte didn't seem to know who Martin Bergensen was, and that was a good thing.

"Can I have your name?" she said.

I needed to give her a room number and a name other than mine that matched it.

"Brett Alford. Room 208. *Je suis l'assistante de* Mr. Bergensen."

She punched her keyboard and looked at a screen below the counter.

"Brett Alford. There you are."

She lifted her eyes at me.

"I didn't know Brett was a woman's name," she said.

I gave her a big smile.

"It is. It's not very common but it's also used for girls. My parents were Hemingway fans."

Brigitte didn't know Hemingway, but she still handed me the envelope.

"There you go," she said.

I left the front desk and went straight to my room like a wolf hungrily taking a prey back to its den. Alford's USB key was inside the envelope, without any message or note. I threw myself on the bed and sent a text message to Yuri. The plan had fallen apart, but the mission was saved. I had the key, the USB key the Service wanted. And that was all that mattered.

CHAPTER 11

My phone started to ring, and I picked it up from the night table next to me.

"*Allo, Juliette? C'est Maryse Jetté.*"

Maryse Jetté was the communications director for the wife of the Prime Minister. She and I had exchanged email messages a couple of days ago, using an address connected to a false yoga studio website. The site was the exact replica of an existing one and had been created by Anton and his team three months earlier to respond to a tender notice posted on a Canadian government website for yoga teaching services to be provided at the G7.

"Sorry for calling you so early," she said.

It was six forty-five in the morning.

"No problem."

"Do you have a minute? I wanted to touch base with you before the start of the day."

"Sure."

"Alright. So, the yoga session will begin at eight, no changes there, but we want you to do it outside, on the *terrasse*. Right in front of the gazebo, you know? The one facing the river. It's a bit cold this morning but the sun is out, and since the press will be there we want the shots to look great, with the big blue sky in the background."

The press? I'd have to make sure I wasn't in any of the photographs.

"You don't have to worry about anything. The hotel is taking care of the mats and the towels."

"Thanks. That's great. At what time do you want us to be there?" I said.

"Five minutes before eight will be fine. Oh, and if you could please wear some light-coloured clothing? We'd like everyone to have a fresh morning look. No black spandex, if possible."

"Sure," I said. "I'll send a message to Finn."

"Don't bother. I'll do it myself. See you at five minutes before eight."

I got off the bed and popped a capsule in the espresso machine. Fit and good-looking were the attributes required to participate in our morning session of yoga, now set to take place *al fresco*. The communications director had compiled the list of participants herself. In politics, nothing was ever left to chance. I took a sip of coffee and looked at my mobile telephone. It was five minutes before seven. I couldn't believe I was still there, in my hotel room at the *Manoir du Cap*, and not sitting in my car on my way back to Montreal.

After retrieving Alford's envelope the night before at the front desk, I had written to Yuri and waited half an hour for his reply. When he had finally written me back, his words had seemed at first to be some sort of joke. *Good work. We proceed as planned. No changes.* I couldn't believe it. With Alford falling drunk at my door a couple of hours earlier and the near miss we just had with the flash drive? His response didn't make any sense. I had written him back immediately. *Why? And what do we do about Riding Hood?* This time his answer had bounced back to me like a fast ball in a tennis match. *I'll handle it.* To say that I was upset was an understatement. Yuri and I were now clearly at risk. Our safety was being jeopardized by Alford's unpredictable behaviour and for us to be required to stay at the hotel was inexplicable.

I took a quick shower and put on a pair of loose-fitting yoga pants and a thick, white cotton hoodie over a long-sleeved t-shirt. I found my identity card, a large piece of plastic attached to a neon green lanyard and hung it around my neck. Alford's USB key was safely tucked under my left arm in a tiny pocket sewn inside my bra. The instructions with respect to the key had always been clear. Once obtained, I would keep it in my underwear at all time until I safely delivered it to Anton. I looked at my phone. It was twenty minutes past seven. Time to get some breakfast.

In the corridor, I slowed down in front of Alford's room. The do not disturb sign still hung on the door handle. I listened for any signs of life but couldn't hear a thing. I wondered what he was doing, alone in his bedroom. Sleeping? Writing a confession then slicing open his wrists? If Alford believed the envelope he had left at the front desk had somehow been forwarded to the CIA and its content discovered, he was likely having a well-deserved moment of panic, afraid as much of his own people as of his Russian friends. One way or another, the man was a ticking time bomb.

I took the elevator to the ground floor and counted four agents scattered across the lobby. I passed by a piano lounge and further down a hallway found the only restaurant of the hotel open for breakfast. Located in a vast solarium on the east side of the building, it had crisp white tablecloths and a view of the garden and of the blue waters of the river. I sat at the back of the room next to a window and ordered a bowl of yogurt with fresh fruits and a cup of coffee. Yuri appeared at the entrance of the restaurant two minutes later and saw me the moment he entered the room. He didn't look at me directly until he had made his way past the other tables and stood in front of me.

"I know what you're thinking," he said.

He pulled out a chair and sat.

"We need to leave," I said.

A fresh-faced waitress came to our table and smiled at Yuri as she wrote down his order on her paper pad. I crossed my legs and looked outside at the trimmed lawn and bushes. I wasn't in the mood for any lighthearted chit-chat and waited with my mouth shut until she had left.

"We need to leave this place," I said.

"You're over-reacting. I spoke to Anton last night. Everything's under control. I've taken care of it," Yuri said.

"Taken care of what exactly?"

"The situation. I've taken care of Alford."

"What do you mean?"

"I spoke to him."

"When?" I said.

"Twenty minutes ago. I called him. We had a nice chat."

"What did you tell him?"

"We talked about his family. I told him I knew where his sister lived and how cute her kids were. He got it. He's not going to do anything," he said.

"Isn't that what you said yesterday?"

The waitress brought Yuri his coffee. He rewarded her with a smile and took a sip of it. Yuri was very relaxed. Way too relaxed for the situation we were in.

"We should leave," I said.

"That's not what Anton said."

"Fuck Anton. I *have* the flash drive. This is what we came here for. We should leave right after the yoga class."

"Absolutely not. We're staying. We're not supposed to leave until tomorrow at noon and that is exactly what we're going to do."

A waiter brought us our food. Yuri had ordered two eggs with sausage and toasts. He started to eat the eggs, holding his fork in one hand and a piece of bread in the other. Two men came and sat at a table to our right. They spoke Italian and one of them translated the breakfast menu to his friend. I finished my yogurt in less than two minutes.

"It's time to go," I said. "They want us to do the yoga outside, on the *terrasse*. By the way, didn't Maryse Jetté call you to tell you to wear white?"

Yuri's steely blue eyes met mine for a fraction of a second.

"Shit. I forgot. I'll see you there in a few minutes," he said.

I got up from my chair and dropped my napkin on the table. Yuri took a sip of coffee and looked outside the window. The hell with him.

I left the restaurant through a set of French doors that led to an outdoor seating area and a gravel path. The path circled around the hotel in a sinuous loop and offered the guests the possibility of a pleasant stroll. It connected to the promenade, on the river side, and to other pathways at the front of the hotel that led to the tennis courts, the outdoor pool and the parking lots. A separate trail, almost a kilometer long, led to the golf course and the club house. I started to walk towards the promenade, past clipped hedges and empty benches, and said good morning to a couple of RCMP officers making their rounds.

The presidents and the prime ministers of the G7 were arriving at lunch time and security had increased tenfold since the day before. At a short distance, I could see groups of armed personnel stationed behind the barren flower beds. I couldn't understand how Yuri could be so oblivious to the danger we were in. Was it some kind of bravado on his part to impress our mission supervisor? His thinking was wrong. I also felt that he wasn't being completely honest with me about what Anton had said. *The blond guy was inside your apt.* I thought about the message the man in the baseball cap had left at my apartment and decided to plan for an exit on my own, in case it had to happen quickly. If Yuri didn't want to prepare for the possibility of a run-for-your-life situation, so be it. But I wouldn't be the one getting caught.

I followed the pathway around the corner of the *Manoir* and cut through the manicured green grass of the hotel lawn for a quicker access to the stone-paved promenade. The sun was out but pockets of cold air still lingered. It was a beautiful day and the Saint Lawrence shimmered in a light breeze like a million silvery flags. I walked to the balustrade and rested my elbows against a black metal guardrail. At the bottom of the cliff two zodiacs cruised upstream in shallow water along a narrow beach. Nothing was being left to chance. I couldn't wait to go back to my room to pack my things.

I heard chatter behind me and turned towards the hotel and its five storeys of medieval imposture. A group of approximately thirty people had gathered on the promenade. Mostly men, of various ages. All wearing a bright orange lanyard with an identity card dandling around their neck. About half of them carried some equipment, in large bags and boxy metallic cases, while the others were smartly dressed in casual business attire with a laptop bag slung over their shoulders. It seemed the press had arrived for the day, freshly disembarked from their minibus. Right on time for my opening *namaste*.

I looked at my mobile telephone. It was seven minutes before eight and I started to walk towards the opposite end of the promenade, where our yoga session was scheduled to take place. From a distance, I could see Maryse Jetté hard at work. She was talking and gesturing at a couple of hotel employees as they placed blue yoga mats on the lawn.

"No, no, no. Closer together. Then another row right behind it."

She saw me and I waved to her.

"Hi, Juliette," she said. "I recognize you from your website photo."

We shook hands.

"Can you believe no one took care of this earlier? That's

the one thing I hate the most about my job. I can never, ever take anything for granted. Where's your partner, Finn?" she said.

"He should be here any minute. He had to go back to his room to change."

"Really? What for? I spoke to him right after we hung up to tell him about the clothes."

It hit me that Yuri probably hadn't really forgotten about wearing light-coloured clothing. What was he playing at?

I looked at the hotel again. A couple of very agitated people had come out of a set of doors and were having a word with the journalists. A woman in a pale grey pant suit left them and quickly headed in our direction.

"Maryse, can I talk to you?" the woman said.

She was part of the Canadian delegation, as I could see from the red and gold maple leaf pin she wore on her lapel, identical to the one worn by Maryse. She took the communications director's arm and led her away as she spoke in a low voice. Maryse looked startled and she and the woman exchanged a series of quick words before the woman walked back to the hotel.

"We're postponing the yoga session," Maryse said. "The participants won't be available until later. Something came up. Can you call me on my cell in an hour?"

"Sure," I said.

I cursed under my breath. I wanted to pack my things and be ready to leave. Being on standby for Maryse meant having to report back to her at any time. And where the hell was Yuri?

"Please tell Finn," Maryse said.

"I will."

She turned to the hotel staff and told them to haul the yoga mats away. I started to leave but stopped. The news people who lingered leisurely on the promenade a few moments earlier had morphed into frenzied ants, briefly interacting with each other then stepping aside in different directions, mobile in hand. Some were sending messages, others talked loudly on the phone. Something newsworthy was obviously happening.

"The president of the United States has canceled his visit to the G7."

I looked to my right. A short man with a wild bush of grey hair and a windbreaker worn unzipped over a wrinkled shirt had wandered next to me. His chino pants were also quite wrinkled and in need of a good ironing, as was his face, which seemed to have only recently left the armrest of his seat on the press minibus.

"What did you say?" I said.

"Mitchell Baker. The American president. He's not coming."

The man was a journalist, which was obvious from the giant press card he wore around his neck. His name, printed on it in letters big enough for me to read, was Peter Frankel. He threw his right hand at me and I shook it.

"Pete," he said.

"Juliette."

He had a strong hand, dry and pleasant.

"Kind of chilly this morning," he said.

Pete zipped his windbreaker and put his hands in the pockets of his pants. Someone came out of a door on the right side of the hotel and held it opened as two hotel employees carried a large rectangular box through it made of black-painted plywood. The box was about two meters long and the two men carried it all the way to the edge of the paved area on the hotel *terrasse*. As they put it down, I realized it was a portable podium. Apparently, someone was about to give an impromptu press conference. Pete turned to me and winked.

"Showtime," he said.

We moved closer to what was by the second becoming the hottest ticket in town. His colleagues had beaten us to the front of the pack, standing room only, and we stationed ourselves casually at the back of a fast-expanding crowd that included many of the hundreds of assistants and staff members who'd flown to Charlevoix in the last twenty-four hours, in advance of their respective masters. As we waited for the presentation to begin, Pete and I started to talk.

"Who do you work for?" I said.

"The Associated Press," Pete said. "I work out of their Washington bureau."

"And you wanted to cover this live from Charlevoix?"

"God no. There was a younger guy who was supposed to do it, but his wife gave birth prematurely. So, they asked me to do it, the old sucker. It was a last-minute thing."

"So, what exactly happened with the president?" I said.

"The first lady had some kind of health scare. No one knows exactly what happened."

"And that's it? He's not coming?"

"As far as we know. But there's also a rumour."

"What rumour?"

"Well, according to some of my sources at the White House the president was told by some of his aides that a couple of senior people on the French and the German delegations were overheard making stupid jokes about him."

"What kind of jokes?"

"Silly stuff but also kind of condescending. Something about having a special menu for him for the state dinner. Everybody knows the president is particular about his food. Nothing too spicy or too exotic. Everything well cooked. Beef and ketchup. Anyway, someone was heard making a joke about ordering him a McDonalds' Happy Meal. You know, with the toy?"

"And what, just because of that he's going to miss the summit? You must be joking."

"Absolutely not. I swear this is true."

"You're pulling my leg."

He grinned.

"I'm not. Now, of course, that doesn't mean the president is *really* upset. I'm sure everybody on the French and German sides is biting their nails over the blunder. And knowing Baker, he's probably using this to his advantage. One of the red-hot topics of the summit is the continued presence of American troops in Europe. The French and the Germans are opposed to any reduction in number but at the same time they don't want to pay for any of it. So, my guess is Baker is making them sweat a little over the possibility that he may not show up. We'll see what the US delegation has to say about it."

The sun was getting warmer. Standing there and listening to Pete under a blue sky, I nearly forgot how badly I wanted to leave. There was something about the crumpled journalist I liked. Something about his company that was easy and natural. There was still no sign of Yuri but for a moment, everything was back to normal, and I almost felt comfortable about the flash drive hidden inside my bra. Until a group of three people came out of the hotel, two men in dark blue jackets and a woman in a bright fuchsia dress, and I saw Alford rush out to join them from the pathway on the side of the hotel.

"Well, well. Isn't that Madam press secretary in person. I didn't even know she was here," said Pete.

The men in the blue jackets moved to the front of the podium.

"Can you all please take a few steps back," one of the men said.

They were the Secret Service, doing their job. I supposed no one was allowed to get an upward shot of the press secretary's nostrils. The cameramen who had planted their equipment too close to the portable stage were forced to pick up their tripods and move back with the rest of the crowd. Microphones were quickly reattached to longer boom poles. Once a safe distance of about twenty meters had been cleared between the crowd and the podium, the woman climbed on it and offered a perfunctory smile to the dense group of watchers.

"Good morning," she said.

She was a tall woman with black hair, impeccably coiffed. A strange mix of the physically strong and the conventionally feminine, or more accurately of a physically imposing woman trying to camouflage her strength under the customary attributes of femininity. The heels, the lipstick, the nail polish. All of it looking like a fresh coat of paint over rough cement.

"As some of you may have heard, the president of the United States was held up in Washington this morning and as a result will be arriving in Charlevoix later this afternoon."

There was a rumble in the audience. Pete snorted.

"When that one retires, she should buy a home in Las Vegas. She'd have one hell of a second career as a professional poker player," he said.

Alford had retreated slightly behind the podium. He looked faint and sweaty, with his face as white as a sheet and his arms tightly crossed over his chest. There was something awkward in the way he stood. Oddly, his clothes didn't seem to fit. His buttoned jacket stretched tightly over his chest and looked one size too small, as if he'd borrowed it from someone slimmer. His shoulders moved slightly every time he breathed while his eyes remained low. Meanwhile the White House envoy carried on, straight on message.

"The president is anxious to sit down with his friends at the G7 and is very much looking forward to having productive meetings with his counterparts on the issue..."

"Pete, I'll be back in a minute," I said.

I wanted to get a better look at Alford and needed to move closer to the podium. The crowd was tightly packed in front of us, making it impossible for me to cut through. I decided to squeeze out of the lump sideways and to circle around it in order to get nearer to the side of the podium, where I would see him in profile. I positioned myself a few meters away to the right, as close as I was allowed to by the Secret Service. Alford didn't look well at all as he stood there and breathed heavily. There seemed to be something pressed against his chest under his jacket. But with his arms crossed over it, I couldn't see what it was. He turned his head sideways and saw me, and an expression of pure hatred flashed across his face.

I was startled and took a step back, then decided to move away to the promenade where a couple of benches faced the flowing river. Where the hell was Yuri? Something was wrong. As I walked away from the podium, I placed a hand over my brows to shield my eyes from the diagonal rays of the sun and tried to look for him.

"Nina!"

I froze. Someone had shouted my student name, which no one at the G7 was supposed to know. That voice. I could have sworn it was Theo's. I heard another voice behind me. Some noise. I started to turn around and a gigantic mass violently hit me from behind with the blunt force of a train engine. Something enormous pushed me forward onto the gravel path and I hit the ground like a raggedy doll. My eardrums were gone. I couldn't hear a thing. I didn't even know if my head was still in one piece. I felt dizzy and could barely lift it off the ground. I moved an arm, then another. My entire body ached. One of my legs felt warm. I looked down and saw that my yoga pants were ripped and that my right knee and the area around it was badly scraped and was bleeding against the dirt of the pathway. The blast of an explosion had sent me flying forward. I bent my other knee and slowly managed to lift my head and my torso off the ground. There was ringing now, in my ears. I looked in the direction of the hotel and discovered a true scene of horror.

The podium was gone. As was the press secretary and her fuchsia dress. Also gone was the group of people standing, replaced by a few lying bodies which rested on the ground in grotesque poses, many covered in blood. Cries rose through the air as my hearing slowly returned. Moans of pain and shrieks of panic. A contingent of officers erupted from the hotel with their weapons drawn. Throngs of soldiers came running from the hotel grounds, as did some medics.

"Get down! Get down!"

Whoever hadn't run away and still miraculously stood upright was ordered to lay face down on the ground by the screaming officers. Mayhem broke out as some of the uninjured and the hotel personnel tried to rush back inside. A woman, crying and yelling, fought madly against an employee who held her in his arms. A waiter vomited. As did a soldier. And a medic. The officers yanked every uninjured person they could get their hands on into a kneeling or lying position. A fire alarm started to ring. From behind the hotel, the high-pitched wails of sirens soared above the bloody mess of the dead and the mutilated.

I lied down on the ground again. I couldn't hold myself up and felt nauseous as my mind spun into a drain.

"Miss, are you okay?"

An enormous head stood above me, dark against the bright blue sky. My senses started to run amok, freed from any logical constraint. I felt every drop of blood that oozed out of my battered leg, heard every scratch of my rescuer's shoes against the gravel path. A heavy smell of sweat, deodorant and chewing gum assailed my nostrils. The sun disappeared and everything turned to black.

CHAPTER 12

I thought for a moment that I was back in my dormitory at the orphanage, when a sick girl would cry herself to sleep. But the whimpers to my right weren't those of a child. And when I opened my eyes, I saw wooden beams that criss-crossed a white ceiling and formed identical squares of plaster like some giant gameboard, upside down.

I lifted my head and realized I was lying on my back in one of the hotel's reception rooms. There were about ten of us resting on yoga mats and bed sheets stretched across the floor or sitting against the wall. A medic was busy tending over the ankle of an injured man. To my right a woman cried silently, not so much in physical pain but from nervous shock. She panted more than she breathed, as if an enormous hand violently squeezed her rib cage every five seconds and made her gasp involuntarily. I looked down at my injured knee and saw that the right leg of my yoga pants had been cut with scis-sors at mid-thigh and that my knee was bandaged with white gauze held in place with an elastic wrap.

I moved one arm, slowly. Then the other. Then my legs. My limbs were as stiff as those of a mummy waking up after a thousand years, but luckily everything seemed able to func-tion. I lifted my torso and looked more attentively at my battered neighbours. The medic, his shirt sleeves rolled up, was now listening to the heartbeat of a man sitting on a mat, who also bled from his forehead and the side of his lips. All of us looked haggard and more or less beaten up, but no one in the room seemed in need of urgent medical care. The more severe cases had obviously been sent someplace else.

The double doors of the reception room had been left wide open and outside in the corridor a couple of people briskly walked by. I wondered if Yuri was injured and lying in another room somewhere in the hotel. I knew I shouldn't try to look for him. If all hell broke lose, our instructions were to try to get away separately as fast as possible.

The medic saw me move.

"I'm coming to see you. Stay where you are," he said.

"Juliette."

I twisted sideways to look behind my shoulder. Pete the journalist sat with his back against the wall, his shirt stained with dried blood. He shot me an exhausted smile. His right arm was wrapped in a cardboard splint kept suspended over his chest by a piece of cloth knotted around his neck. I carefully pulled myself in a sitting position and turned to him.

"Pete, are you okay?"

"Sure. I'm not as bad as I look. The blood's not mine."

"What happened?" I said.

"There was an explosion. A bomb. There was a commotion at the front of the podium with the Secret Service and then the thing exploded."

A bomb. I thought about Alford, holding his arms tightly crossed over his chest. About his jacket one size too small. Christ. Had Alford been wearing a *suicide vest?* That didn't make any sense. For a start, how could he possibly have had access to explosives? Alford had arrived by plane and it would have been impossible for him to smuggle them in. The only plausible way explosives could have been brought inside the red zone would have been by car, then left outside the hotel to avoid detection. But with the police dogs at the red zone checkpoint, it seemed highly unlikely. Unless the explosives used were the undetectable kind.

Dmitry had taught me all there was to know about plastic explosives. When I was eighteen years old, he had given me lessons in their compositions, their uses, their drawbacks and their advantages. Some were white, others yellow or a deep orange hue, all had the appearance of bars of plasticine. A few were more powerful than others, and every different kind was manufactured only in a very small number of countries and possessed its own particularities. C4 was mostly made in the U.S., Serbia and the United Kingdom. Plastex in Switzerland. Semtex in the Czech Republic and in Israel. Semtex was Dmitry's favourite because it was waterproof and resisted much lower and higher temperatures and because it was made from PETN, which people called PENT, an explosive compound almost completely undetectable. "PENT is the perfect bomb-making material," Dmitry had said. "You can even make some on your own."

PENT was sold on the black market as a crystalline white powder. It was insoluble in water, stable, gave virtually no vapor and was extremely difficult to detect if sealed in a container or in a plastic bag. It could be made at home with pentaerythritol, an alcohol, and nitric acid. The only downside of using it in a bomb was that it was hard to ignite and required the use of another explosive, as a fuse, to trigger its explosive properties. An electrical detonator could do the trick. And acetone, commonly found in nail polish solvent, could also be used to dissolve PENT and trigger its explosive reaction.

"Juliette, are you okay?"

"Sorry Pete. You were saying there was a commotion with the Secret Service?" I said.

I remembered hearing voices behind me, a second before the explosion.

"Yeah. There was a disturbance at the front. A guy who stood behind the press secretary suddenly came to the front of the podium and shoved aside one of the Secret Service agents, then started to walk away towards the promenade, like he was on a mission or something. I could see you over there and the guy seemed to be going straight towards you. The other Secret Service guy lunged at him and grabbed him by the jacket, I guess because no one understood what the hell he was doing, and that's when it happened. The explosion."

"Are there many people dead?"

"I think four, as far as I know, including the press secretary. It seems the bomb didn't have any nails or pieces of metal in it. It was the blast that killed those people. We were lucky the Secret Service had cleared everyone away from the podium."

No metal in it? The bomb had likely been made entirely of plastic, with a small detonator which could have easily been carried inside the hotel, even aboard a plane, in an electric razor or toothbrush.

"All the top people were evacuated. They're not allowing anyone else to leave. Unless you're injured, of course," Pete said.

"Why? Are they looking for suspects inside the hotel?"

"I don't know. But where else could they be?"

I nodded and slipped my hand inside the pocket of my shredded yoga pants. My mobile telephone was still there, miraculously. But no messages from anyone. I slid my fingers under my left arm and inside the fabric of my bra and found the little rectangle of plastic still in place.

"You were lucky to be far enough from the explosion," Pete said. "A moment before you could have been right where it happened."

I nodded.

My name. Someone had shouted my student name just before the explosion. I thought about Alford's look of fury when he'd seen me a moment before. If Pete's recollection was accurate, Riding Hood had abruptly left the podium and decided to come after me as I was walking away towards the promenade to blow us both to pieces. Someone had understood what was happening and yelled after me to warn me. That person could only have been Yuri. And he'd shouted my student name to get my immediate attention, before it was too late.

"Pete, did anyone come looking for me when I was out?" I said.

"No. Why? Are you here with someone?"

"Yes. A colleague from Ottawa. Finn Martens. A tall blond guy, my age."

"No. I haven't seen anyone who fits that description."

The medic came over and lowered himself next to me on one knee. He took out a small penlight from his breast pocket and pointed it at my right eye.

"Can you look straight into the light?" he said.

He blinded me for a few seconds in one eye, then the other.

"Any headache?"

"No."

That wasn't entirely true.

"Do you feel nauseous?"

"No."

"Alright. How are you feeling now, generally speaking? Any dizziness? You were semi-conscious when they brought you in."

"Really?"

I didn't remember a thing about being carried inside the hotel.

"Yes. And if you don't remember any of it then it's obvious to me that you've suffered a concussion. Which means no strenuous physical activity for at least a week. No reading, no TV and no computer. Unless you suddenly start to feel worse, you should see a doctor in about a week for a follow-up."

"Okay. Thank you."

He stood up and put his pen light back inside the front pocket of his shirt.

"By the way, you were mumbling quite a lot when they brought you in," he said.

"I was? What was I saying?"

"I have no idea. It sounded like you were speaking in a foreign language."

Great.

"That's weird. By the way, is there a washroom I can use?" I said.

"It's right outside, to your left. At the end of the hall," the medic said.

I slowly rose to my feet. Pain shot up my right leg as I bent my knee.

"Juliette, I don't think we're allowed to leave the room," Pete said.

"I have to use the washroom. The medic said it was alright."

"I know but before you do there's an RCMP guy you're supposed to talk to. He was here five minutes ago."

"I'll find him."

I needed to leave this room immediately and get some of my things. Soon the rounding up of everyone inside the *Manoir* would begin and I had to be gone before that happened. I shot a glance at Pete and gave him a smile in lieu of a proper goodbye.

"I'll be right back," I said.

I took a few tentative steps towards the entrance of the conference room as a light headache pulsated above my brow. On the brighter side, the pain in my right leg seemed to ease every time I put a foot forward, as if my body had agreed to get on with it and stop complaining.

Outside the hallway was empty. To the left, past the wash-rooms, it led to a dead end and an emergency exit. To the right, it stretched towards the lobby of the hotel, where I could see a small group of men talking. Two of them wore police uniforms, the others casual clothing. A man in a blue shirt and a holster strapped across his chest appeared from the left and joined them. He was of medium height, with strong shoulders and a fit, compact body, oddly familiar. He moved his hands energetically as he talked, as if asking for some information and giving out orders.

The man turned his head slightly towards me as he kept on talking and I let out a gasp. All at once I saw the short beard and the patch that covered his right eye. My heart started to pound my ribcage. My attacker of the week before was right there, in the lobby, no more than a few meters away. What the hell was he doing at the hotel? Was he a policeman? An RCMP officer? *Was he looking for me?*

I turned around quickly and hobbled down the hallway towards the emergency exit. I pushed open the heavy door and climbed the stairs to the second floor, then stumbled down the corridor to my room. I needed my car key and my backup identity documents, including the green card issued to Karine Demers. I also needed my house keys, my wallet and a charger for my mobile telephone.

I took off my ripped yoga pants, changed into a pair of jeans and put on my navy-blue windbreaker over my hoodie. I swallowed a couple of Motrins and prayed I wouldn't die of a brain hemorrhage. I thought of calling Yuri but decided against it in case he'd already been caught. I left the hotel room with the rest of my things in it and went back to the emergency exit. I climbed down the emergency stairs all the way to the basement this time, careful not make any noise as I passed by the door of the *rez-de-chaussée*. Pain travelled up my right leg every time I lowered it on a metal step, but I was getting used to it. Or perhaps it was the adrenaline that numbed my injuries.

At the basement level the staircase ended in front of a heavy metal door. Behind it a concrete corridor painted a sad bluish grey lay straight ahead for about twelve meters then turned right. I knew the plan of the hotel by heart. The hotel kitchen was in the basement as well as the laundry room, the employees' changing rooms and a side exit onto a pathway that led directly to the staff parking lot.

I quickly walked down the corridor all the way to the turn, flattened myself against the wall and looked around the corner into a large rectangular room. It was a sort of central room, located directly below the lobby. On the left side of it, large laundry carts were lined up against a wall and a set of opened doors led to the laundry room. On the right side, opened doors and long wood benches marked the entrance to the employees' locker rooms. Straight ahead, at the end of the room to the right of the service elevators, a red exit sign glowed over a service door.

"*Arrêtez!*"

A woman's voice stopped me dead in my tracks, less than fifteen meters away from my emergency hatch. Whoever was behind me hadn't politely asked me to stop moving. She had given me an order and I stood still and silently cursed my haste. The woman must have been in the laundry room or one of the locker rooms. I hadn't seen her as I had hurried past but she, in turn, had definitely caught sight of me.

"Raise your hands," she said.

I did, slowly. The woman spoke with a strong *Québécois* accent, the kind you hear mostly in the *régions* outside of Montreal. I slowly turned around to face her. She was a policewoman in black pants and a black shirt who pointed her gun at me. She held it with both hands, aimed straight at my chest. Her legs were slightly bent at the knees, her feet set apart just right. She had a long blond ponytail and a healthy tan. The attractive police-woman everyone at the station must have had a crush on. A girl, my age, who today had decided that she was going to be a hero.

"You have your identity card?" she said.

"Yes."

I slowly lowered my right hand inside the front of my jacket to pull out the ID card I still wore around my neck.

"Take it off and throw it to me," she said.

She was using the familiar '*tu*' in French when she spoke to me, to assert her authority. I removed the lanyard, rolled it around the card and weakly threw the small bundle in her direction on purpose. It landed a mere two meters in front of me.

"*Excusez*," I said, pretending I was sorry for my lousy performance.

I wanted her to believe that I was a clumsy girl who didn't know how to throw things properly. The archetype of the awkward girl at school she must have surely known as a kid, who was bad at sports and kept to herself at recess. The one she had probably laughed at with her little friends. That girl who existed in every school around the world. I took a couple of steps forward, lowered myself to pick up my ID card and pretended to lose my balance. She lowered her left arm and took a step forward. A mistake only a rookie would make.

I jumped at her from below and hit her right wrist with my forearm as hard as I could. Her gun flew in the air and landed against the wall. I hit her under the chin with the palm of my left hand. She tried to grab her baton, but I seized her right arm and twisted her over my shoulder. She fell and hit the floor. I quickly picked up her gun and pointed it at her. Pain travelled up my back and through my right leg. I was lucky to have been caught by a police princess and not by one of her heavier male colleagues.

"Not a word," I said. "Keep your mouth shut."

My new BFF didn't appreciate being on the losing side of

things. I could see anger in her eyes. I pointed towards the laundry room with the tip of the gun.

"This way. Slowly," I said.

I needed something to tie her up and the laundry room seemed to be the right place to find it. I followed her through the opened doors and saw a rack of terry cloth bathrobes to my left, each with a long tie belt.

"Stop right there," I said.

Her shoulders stiffened as she understood what I was about to do.

"Lie down on the floor. Face down. And put your hands behind your back."

The princess pretended to do as I said then started to sprint forward towards the washing machines. What a complete waste of time that was. Just by looking at her I knew I was quicker. I started chasing after her, grabbed her shirt with my left hand and knocked her hard on the back of the head with the butt of her handgun. She fell to her knees and I almost tripped and landed on top of her. A sharp pain shot through my lower ribs. I wasn't enjoying any of this. I pressed her gun to the side of her head.

"Enough with the fucking hero shit," I said. "If you do this again, I swear I'll shoot you. Stay down and put your hands behind your back."

She obeyed without any resistance this time. I grabbed a couple of bathrobes' belts and tied her up, then stuck a face cloth into her mouth. A used one I found in a laundry cart.

I left the laundry room and limped towards the exit. There was a water fountain near the service door, also a metal sink and a large mirror bolted against the wall. I took a sip of water and dared to look at myself in the mirror. No doubt about it, I was a scary sight. My right cheek was bruised at the cheekbone. My lower lip was puffed and my forehead dirty and full of scratches, as if I had been pushed face down on a gravel path. Which in fact I had been, due to the force of the explosion. I took a paper towel and tried to wash my face with water. It didn't improve matters much.

I came closer to the door and looked outside through its wired glass window. A pathway across the lawn led directly to a wooded area, and to what I knew were the parking lots immediately behind it. But there were some people on the lawn. Lots of people. Some officers, some soldiers. All fully armed and on the lookout for those responsible for the carnage that had taken place. A girl with a beaten face in a dirty white hoodie and a windbreaker wouldn't go unnoticed. I was bound to be stopped.

But staying put was not an option. I needed to leave the *Manoir* as fast as possible. I took a step back. The princess and I were about the same size. With her police uniform, I would be able to pass by these guys and reach the parking lots. It was my only way out.

CHAPTER 13

I shut the basement service door behind me and followed the gravel pathway to the end of the lawn. By walking slowly and at a regular pace, I was able to do so without much of a limp. Straight ahead, two men in jackets and sunglasses were coming towards me. I pulled a tissue out of my pocket and lifted it to my face.

"Hi," one of them said.

He was a tall guy with short brown hair, good-looking. The confident type. I responded by sneezing into the tissue pressed against my nose and a little wave of the hand.

"Bless you," he said.

The princess' sunglasses only covered part of the damage to my face but her uniform fitted me beautifully. I was dressed head to toe as a policewoman of the SPVQ, the *Service de police de la ville de Québec*. The shoes, the pants, the jacket. Everything a near perfect fit, except that the princess' hips were slightly larger than mine and the seat of her pants was loose. But who was I to complain? I had a handgun, a baton, a radio attached to my shoulder and, in a stroke of unimaginable good luck, the car key to a police cruiser.

I had to insist, forcefully, before the princess finally agreed to tell me where her car was parked. She and I had not become friends. But in the end, she had accepted defeat. After I had pressed my foot, clad in her very own police shoe, on her pink-manicured toes, she had reluctantly nodded her surrender. I had taken the face cloth out of her mouth and she had spat the location of her car like a mouthful of foul milk. The police cruiser was parked right outside the lot nearest the grand entrance of the hotel.

If the car was truly parked where my new police friend had said it would be, the quickest way to get to it was to cut through the lawn in front of the hotel, but that was too risky. Some of the princess' colleagues would be milling about. The *Service de police de la Ville de Québec* was too small an organization for a never seen before policewoman not to raise suspicions. There was also the possibility that my attacker with the eye patch would be strolling around. I had no choice but to play it safe and follow the pathway to the remotest parking lots then turn back and walk towards the hotel using the lanes that connected them. With a bit of chance, I would also be able to retrieve the Beretta from my rental car in parking F. I didn't mind the Walther that came with the policewoman uniform, but the Beretta was too nice and handy a weapon to leave behind.

I had stuffed the few personal things I had taken with me in the pockets of the police uniform and as I kept on walking, I took my phone out. There was still no sign of life from Yuri or anyone else connected to the mission. No text messages. No emails. Operation Riding Hood had gone completely silent. Not a surprise in our present circumstances.

My rental car waited for me in a corner of the last parking lot, one of approximately thirty parked vehicles. I started to walk across the lot when two SQ officers entered it from the opposite side. They had a dog with them, a big brown Labrador. I immediately stopped next to the nearest car and took out my telephone. I pretended to take photographs of the car and its license plate, then moved on to the next. The SQ guys were coming towards me. The two of them similar in size and gait, neither of them very tall, with broad shoulders and wrap-around sunglasses.

"*Y'a-tu quequ' chose qui s'passe avec les chars?*" the one with the dog said.

A gem of pure *Québec* lingo which meant, roughly, 'is there somethin' happ'nin' with the cars?' I feigned not to be interested in a friendly chat and tried to hide the bruises on my face by looking intently inside one of the cars.

"No," I said, in my very best *Québécois* accent. "We need a list of the vehicles. To check the plates."

"Right," the one with the dog said. "While you do that, we'll have the dog take a sniff at the cars."

"*C'est beau,*" I said, which meant that I was fine with it.

I moved on to another car. It was a good thing there were many different police corps on the ground conducting parallel operations. My presence was not a surprise to the SQ guys. To them, I was a novice Québec City policewoman, an obvious newbie, who had been given the very uncool task of making a list of the parked vehicles.

The two look-alikes walked their dog to a minivan at the end of a row. I kept on moving from one vehicle to the next and taking pictures. I could kiss goodbye to the Beretta but at least I'd be able to slip away to the next parking lot in a minute or two. Soon the officers moved on to a red Audi, two cars away from my rental while I moved on to a blue Ford Focus parked at the edge of the lot. The plate number on the Ford started with an F, which meant that it was a leased vehicle. I wondered f that was the car Yuri had rented.

The officers finished with the Audi and with a white Honda next to it and moved on to my car and as soon as the dog was close enough to it, it stopped and lay down in front of it. The officers reacted immediately. One of them grabbed his phone and started talking while the other walked the dog away from my rental.

"What's going on? Has the dog found something?" I said.

"Explosives," the one with the Lab shouted back. "Stay where you are."

Explosives? *In my car?* A cold sweat broke at the base of my neck. How was that possible? I retreated to the furthest corner of the parking lot and took a few additional photographs of the cars closest to me. The K-9 officer quickly walked his dog past the remaining cars to finish his round while a SQ box truck emerged from the service lane and roared into the parking lot. It screeched to a halt and five men in olive green coveralls jumped out. The bomb squad had arrived. I pretended to be taking a call on my telephone and slowly moved away with my mobile stuck to my ear.

Explosives? I had picked up my rental the previous morning at an Avis location in downtown Montreal and driven straight to Charlevoix. No one could have placed explosives in it until I had left it in the parking lot of the hotel twenty-four hours earlier. Which meant that since my arrival, someone had deliberately used it to hide explosives. Or even worse. Someone was trying to frame me. But who? *Yuri?* The thought chilled me to the bone. And yet, his earlier disappearance and his incomprehensible willingness to stay at the *Manoir* until the following day all pointed to a possible betrayal. But why?

I followed the lane through the series of parking lots and reached the one closest to the hotel. A white police car was parked just outside of it on the right side of the lane, exactly as the princess had said. I pulled the key ring from my pocket to look at it. Car number 3234 was the one for which I had a key. The number painted on the side of the car was 7567. The policewoman had lied to me. I slowed down my walk to try to have a look around. Her car had to be parked some place else. I just had to find it.

Assuming my new police friend had rushed to the scene, she would have driven her car as close as possible to the hotel and left it in a place where it didn't block access to the entrance or the car port. So, where was it? There was a reserved parking lot to the left of the grand entrance where a number of emergency vehicles were parked, including some police cars. But there was a regular flow of people in that parking lot, coming and going, with police officers being part of the mix. I took a deep breath and started to head towards it when someone shouted after me.

"*Excusez! Madame l'agent!*"

I stopped and felt my shoulders stiffen. *Breathe slow.* I turned around and saw one of the red-clad valets rushing up the lane to meet me. The same one who had helped me with my suitcase the day before and given me a wink. He came up to me and panted heavily as he tried to catch his breath.

"Can I help you?" I said.

His fancy red coat was opened, showing an old t-shirt, and his hair dishevelled. So much for the polished appearance of the previous day.

"Excuse me. Do you know when the hotel staff will be allowed to go home?" he said.

He coughed loudly. Fear and a high dose of stress had turned my luggage hauler into a nervous wreck.

"There's nothing official yet, but it should be later this afternoon or early this evening," I said.

The man looked at me attentively. I could see the confusion hatching in his eyes as he remembered seeing me the day before as a guest but couldn't understand why I was now wearing a police uniform. He hesitated. In his panicked state of mind, he didn't trust himself.

"If I were you, I would immediately go to the hotel lobby and give my name to the people there. They've set up a table. The sooner you get on the list, the quicker you'll be going home," I said.

Nothing is more convincing to the desperate than a piece of good news. The valet instantly lost interest in having seen me the day before.

"They're doing this now?" he said.

"They just started. First come, first served."

"Thank you."

I took a deep breath as he walked away briskly towards the hotel. I was being lucky. How long could I keep this up? Only a couple of medics remained in the reserved parking lot and I quickly made my way to the first police car. And there it was. Car number 3234. I unlocked the driver's door and sat behind the wheel. I pressed the ignition and the engine started. I took another deep breath and exhaled slowly as I shifted into drive. To be sitting in that car, ready to leave the hotel, was nothing short of a miracle.

Police cars are generally equipped with GPS tracking devices and this one was probably no exception. As soon as the princess was found the SPVQ would start looking for its missing cruiser, if not earlier. Which meant that I could only use the car for a short period of time. I slowly drove onto the access road towards the checkpoint and saw an ambulance coming behind me with its red lights flashing. I slowed down and allowed it to pass me. There was a control panel mounted under the secured laptop bolted to the right side of the dashboard, with a red and blue rectangular button on it. I pushed it and in the rear windows of the ambulance saw the reflection of the cruiser's red and blue roof lights as they started to flash.

I followed the ambulance to the red zone entry gate, which now resembled Checkpoint Charlie at the height of the Cold War. The armed personnel manning the area had quadrupled in number and included a platoon of soldiers deployed on both sides of it. The ambulance stopped at the first portable fence and an officer quickly opened its rear doors to take a look inside. He closed them almost immediately and, having assumed I was escorting the ambulance, gave us the all-clear. One of the men signaled to the others to let our convoy go through and they immediately opened the metal barriers to let us pass. I thanked the officer nearest to my left with a slight wave of the hand. As I drove across the fences, soldiers positioned right outside the checkpoint gestured for us to keep going without making a stop.

I looked in my rear-view mirror and watched the fences and the soldiers grow smaller. I lowered my window and took a breath of fresh air. I waited until I was out of sight, then turned off the police cruiser's lights and allowed the ambulance to speed ahead and lose me.

The forest was quiet by the side of the road. I stopped the car and pulled Karine Demers' green zone identity card from the inside pocket of my jacket. Number 1050 on Route 362, the *Route du Fleuve*. Now was the time to make use of our fallback plan. Go to the safe house, ditch the car then get away from the green zone on foot. I knew I needed to get there as soon as possible, find a change of clothes and leave. But what if Yuri was already at the house? I couldn't trust him anymore. Not until I knew what had really happened at the *Manoir du Cap*.

CHAPTER 14

Anton had planned our operation well. Karine Demers' home was a peaceful retreat located at the bottom of a gentle slope. A white clapboard house at the end of a winding dirt lane, hidden from the road by a forest of thick spruce. There was a large, screened porch attached to it with views of the river and an annex used as a two-car garage. I stopped the car at a fair distance from it and carefully approached it on foot.

Only one vehicle was parked in the garage, an older SUV. I looked inside the house through one of the windows and caught sight of a large rustic kitchen that opened into a dining room. The house appeared to be empty but with Yuri, that meant very little. If he wanted to, my partner could make himself invisible.

I pulled the Walther from its holster and slowly moved around the house to have a look inside the other rooms. There were no signs of life inside the property nor was there any indication of a forced entry. I entered the screened porch. There was a small window behind an old rattan couch to the left of the main door through which I could see the landing of the central staircase. I broke its lower pane of glass with the foot of a chair, unlocked it and lifted myself inside.

It took me about five minutes to clear both floors of the house and make sure I was the only one there. I then went back to the police cruiser and parked it inside the garage next to the SUV. Hiding it wouldn't buy me more time, but it was the prudent thing to do nonetheless, to prevent any wandering neighbour or walker from seeing it.

I returned inside the house and went looking for a glass in the kitchen cupboards. I was dying of thirst. As I filled it with water, I noticed the key for the SUV was in a large marble ashtray on the counter, full of small change and bits and pieces of junk. Leaving the green zone would perhaps be easier than I had anticipated.

I knew I shouldn't linger and hurried back upstairs. In the bathroom, I washed my face again, this time more carefully, and brushed my hair. I discovered a tube of concealer in the drawer of a cabinet below the sink and used it to cover the bruises on my cheek. I took off the police uniform and quickly examined my injuries in the bathroom mirror. A dozen purple hematomas had appeared on my body in various places, mostly on my legs and arms. I washed the dried blood below my wounded knee but decided not to undo the bandage. That would be for later, if I ever made it to a later time.

Karine Demers was a nurse. That much was evident when I opened her bedroom closet to look for a change of clothes. I picked up a set of pale pink scrubs, a buttonless short-sleeve cotton shirt and matching cotton pants with an elastic waist-band. I also found a pair of white mushy shoes, the kind worn by health care workers in clinics and hospitals. The pants were too short, and I pulled them lower over my hips. The shoes were half a size too small and squeezed the tip of my big toes. In a cupboard, I found a pair of sweatpants and a heavy wool sweater which I packed in a canvas bag with the police-woman's shoes, her gun holster with the Walther in it and the few things I had taken with me when I had left my room at the hotel.

I returned downstairs and opened the fridge, which was almost empty. In a cupboard I found a box of crackers and put it in the bag. It was high time to leave. I stepped outside and quickly examined my surroundings. At the end of the lawn a meadow gently rolled downhill from the house, all the way to the blue waters of the Saint Lawrence. A pack of seagulls squawked loudly in the distance. After the violence of the past hours, the scenery was almost surreal.

Halfway to the garage my phone vibrated inside the pocket of my elastic waist pants. It was a text message from Stacey. *So whats up with u and Theo?* Then a second one. A fire emoji and a laughing face. A message from another spacetime dimension wouldn't have felt any different. Somewhere, a couple of galaxies away, a normal world existed.

I took the old SUV and drove to the same green zone check point I had gone through on my way to the hotel, where the number of SQ officers had increased to about twenty. All of them were wary and heavily armed. Two officers, a man and a woman, came towards my car. I lowered my window to speak to the man while his colleague looked inside my vehicle. He was nervous.

"*Bonjour.* Where are you going?" the officer said.

"I'm going to work. In Baie-Saint-Paul."

He looked at my face and at the photograph on my ID document.

"What kind of work do you do?" he said.

"I'm a nurse. I work at the *Résidence des Saules*, it's a seniors' home."

"You know about what happened at the *Manoir* this morning?"

"Of course, I do. *C'est épouvantable.*"

"If you notice anything unusual, anything at all, around your house or elsewhere in the area, it's important that you call 911 immediately. It could be some people you've never seen before or an abandoned car. Anything that seems strange to you, for any reason. Just call immediately."

I looked at the officer with the eagerness of a hardworking nurse.

"Absolutely."

"*Merci*. You can go."

I drove for almost an hour, then exited onto an access road south of Baie-Saint-Paul that led to a tourist information center. The center was closed during the week at this time of year and a handful of drivers used the parking lot and the picnic tables next to it to stop for a short rest or snack. I could park the car there and stay for a while without running the risk of looking suspicious.

I took off the pink nurse uniform and put on the sweat-pants and the sweater I had brought in the canvas bag. I threw the white cushioned loafers on the backseat of the car and put on the heavy police shoes of the SPVQ princess. I ate some of the crackers and thought about the big brown dog in the parking lot at the *Manoir*, and the way it had lain in front of my grey rental. *Explosives. In my car.*

The thought of Yuri betraying me made me sick to my stomach, but I couldn't rule it out. Something had shifted in him recently. And he could have easily smuggled the explosives inside the red zone. Had he forced Alford to blow himself up by making threats against his sister and her kids? I knew he was capable of it. But why throw me under the bus, not to mention almost having me ripped to pieces by the explosion?

It didn't make any sense. None of it did. I had the flash drive with me. Having me arrested, or killed, even by accident, would have rendered our operation useless. Unless something completely unexpected had happened. Something gone terribly wrong. I thought of Yuri at our breakfast table and the way he had mentioned speaking to Anton. Had Yuri been following some orders I wasn't privy to?

'Silo instructions' was something the Service was known to use for certain assignments, Irina had once explained to me, years before, as she had sat one evening at the foot of my bed. There was this mission once, she had said, so secret the Service had decided it should be divided into separate compartments, with the agents never knowing about each other and the entirety of what they were doing. Separate cells, each with their own sets of instructions. Smaller missions within a larger one, like a series of diminishing matryoshka dolls, one fitting into the other. Was that how Riding Hood had been set to unfold at the G7? If so, retrieving the flash drive was only one piece of a larger operation, one that Yuri obviously knew about, and I didn't. I imagined Anton and Yuri discussing it on their own and felt a growing sense of unease. Was it even possible there were other agents at the *Manoir* I didn't know about? But why have Alford blow himself up?

If the explosion was part of a master plan, such plan had clearly put me at risk of dying. It had also made our escape from the *Manoir* almost impossible. And again, that didn't make any sense unless the timing of it had gone wrong. But why use my car to store the explosives and possibly assemble the bomb? *The blond guy was inside your apt.* I thought about that note and wondered what else Yuri had not been telling me.

I started my drive back to Montreal shortly before three in the afternoon. I drove slowly, very slowly, on my way back to town, hoping that some instructions would be sent to me by the Service before I arrived. I took a few back roads to slow my return home even more. Dirt lanes that reconnected to the 138 after taking me past strange, isolated houses where I wouldn't have wanted to stop to ask for directions.

Further south I made a detour around Cap Tourmente, a bucolic national park along the river, and stopped there for a while to watch the seabirds. Later, as the sky turned pink, I stopped at a self-serve station north of Quebec City to buy some gas and looked at the news on my mobile telephone. I stopped two more times along the way, after the night had fallen. Once in a deserted rest area and a second time at a convenience store off one of the exits, to buy a coffee and a pack of cigarettes, even though I don't smoke. I sat on the hood of the car and lit one up, smoked half of it then threw it and the entire pack into the nearest garbage can. And each time I stopped I checked the news again on my mobile telephone.

The explosion in Charlevoix, which had officially been branded an act of terrorism, was being reported by all the news outlets around the world. But so far there was no mention of precisely how it had happened and no mention either of a possible female suspect on the run. The emphasis was on the bloodshed and on the people who had died or been injured. The blood and the killings. I felt ill as I remembered the bodies I had seen lying on the ground like raggedy dolls.

Traffic was sparse when I later reached the edge of the metropolitan sprawl. It was thirty-five minutes past eleven. One hour before the last run of the trains of the Montreal Metro, from one end of the lines to the other. I drove into the city a few moments later, flying along rooftops on the elevated portion of Highway 40 until the exit for Boulevard Pie-IX. I turned left as I got off the ramp, drove under the highway and stopped at a red light. I was so tired my hands were shaking. I was completely burnt out. And still no instructions from the Service.

I drove south on Pie-IX, past an endless collection of almost identical duplexes and triplexes, two to three storeys-high. Things were eerily quiet in this unassuming part of the city, ten kilometers from downtown. Straight ahead, the illuminated concrete mast of the Olympic Stadium rose like the bow of an interstellar ship above the flatness of the Maison-neuve borough. Two street corners north of the *Parc Olympique*, I turned left on a side street and parked the SUV next to a lonely tree. I took the gun holster out of the canvas bag and strapped it over my shoulder and across my chest under the thick fabric of the wool sweater.

It had been a little more than twelve hours since I had left the policewoman tied up under a pile of laundry and I figured that she must have been found and rescued by then. There were video cameras inside the hotel, including in the base-ment, and I had undoubtedly been filmed leaving through the service door in her police uniform. Images of me were almost certainly being analysed and shared and my description circu-lated among the various law enforcement agencies working around the clock to find the criminals responsible for the killings. My rental car had likely been identified and searched and my room examined by a forensics team. With a bit of luck, my cover would hold for perhaps another couple of hours before Juliette Després crumbled and disintegrated into thin air. And then I would become the woman whose identity was a mystery. A possible terrorist. I searched the Internet on my phone one more time for news of a possible suspect but couldn't find any. There was still no mention of anyone having fled the site of the summit. No mention of a female fugitive.

I decided to go back to my apartment to spend the night. I figured I could stay there for a short while, no more than a few hours, and get some rest. Hopefully, I would hear from the Service before having to move to another hiding place. Central Control was surely working on a plan to get me out and it wouldn't be long before they got a hold of me. I took the canvas bag with my personal things in it, closed the door of the SUV and walked south again on Boulevard Pie-IX. On my way to the metro station two blocks down.

A few cars passed me by as I walked alongside the impene-trable darkness of the Botanical Gardens, immense and eerily quiet. I crossed a street and continued past the gigantic circular structure of the Olympic Stadium. At the end of a long city block I finally reached the low concrete bunker of the Pie-IX metro station, a masterpiece of Brutalist architecture comrade Brezhnev would have approved of.

I disappeared below ground into the bowels of the station and rode the escalators down to the platform as the warm breath of the metro blew into my face. There are many cameras in the tunnels of the Montreal metro, and I kept my head down, never once raising it as I made my way to a yellow plastic bench. I sat down and waited, as did a few other people, for the *dernier métro*.

In Montreal, the last train of the evening is a popular one, and that night was no exception. There are always more people in the very last metro than in the one just before. It is the train of the last ride home for those who would rather not sleep on someone else's couch, pay for a taxi or wait on a deserted sidewalk for an all-night bus.

I climbed aboard the train and sat opposite a tired looking youth in a leather jacket who stared blearily at his mobile telephone. There are eight stations on the green line between Pie-IX and McGill, the station nearest my apartment, and I looked at my reflection in the window next to me as the train carried me from the darkness of the tunnel to the next brightly lit platform, and then through darkness again. *What had happened to the Riding Hood mission? And what was I supposed to do now?*

The train slowed down and stopped at the McGill station. I followed a pedestrian tunnel to the exit nearest the university, one street corner south of the McGill campus, and emerged from the metro on a sidewalk in front of a high-rise building. Downtown was asleep and the streets were deserted. I crossed Sherbrooke street and hurried on my way home through the dim, tree-lined avenues of my student neighbourhood.

I climbed the stairs to my front door two by two and

quickly opened it, then closed it shut behind me and stood still. My apartment was completely silent. I pulled the Walther from under my sweater and carefully ventured in. I inspected every room and opened every closet. I checked the windows to see if they were locked. I finished my round and sat on the sofa in the living room, exhausted. The tension in my shoulders and my neck slowly eased away. I shivered. A gigantic wave of tiredness washed over my entire body. I was completely wiped-out. I couldn't walk anymore, I couldn't think. I looked at my phone. It was twenty past one. I closed my eyes and fell into a deep sleep.

I was jolted awake by the roar of a garbage truck outside my windows. The first lights of dawn had chased away the darkness. I looked at my phone. It was almost six in the morning. I rose from the sofa and took a few steps. My entire body hurt, with different parts of it suffering from various kinds of pain. In the kitchen, I made myself a piece of toast and a cup of coffee, sat at the table and opened my laptop.

On almost all the news websites live coverage was dedicated to what was referred to by Radio-Canada as *l'attentat*, the attack, at the G7 summit. On CNN live broadcasting from the *Manoir* was interrupted at regular intervals by replays of some earlier and more dramatic footage. I visited the Cyber-Presse website, a local Montreal newscaster. Then the Washington Post and The New York Times. All of them dedicated a major portion of their reporting to the G7 bombing. But again, I couldn't find a single mention of a possible female suspect. Someone, somewhere, had decided to keep my existence secret. And still no instructions from the Service.

I took a steamy shower with my phone placed within reach on the bathroom sink and tried to clear my mind, but I couldn't. Every time I closed my eyes I was back at the site of the explosion, a gruesome slideshow I couldn't get rid off. I saw the maimed bodies again and felt nauseous as I remembered the rancid scent of blood. I thought about Yuri and the explosives inside my car. I thought about the man in the baseball cap and wondered what he knew and why he had tried to warn me about him.

In my bedroom, I fastened my bra around my chest, with the USB key still tucked inside the underarm fabric. I put on a clean pair of jeans and a t-shirt over which I strapped the nylon holster of the SPVQ princess, then slipped on a large McGill hoodie. Something Stacey had borrowed indefinitely from a long-forgotten date, then lent me one chilly afternoon at the university. I went back to the kitchen, made myself another cup of coffee and ate a bowl of cereals.

The more I thought about the bloodshed, the more sickly I felt. Collateral damage was not a concept I was particularly fond of, especially when the explosion seemed to serve no purpose and had come close to killing me. I still couldn't make any sense of it. The Service badly wanted Alford's flash drive. It was the reason I had been sent to Charlevoix in the first place. For our plan to go haywire in such a spectacular way, something I didn't know had most definitely taken place at the G7.

I reached for the tiny rectangle under my armpit. What if the USB key was a decoy? What if there was nothing on it? The entire mission to retrieve it a farce, a distraction from something else. Something I had been used for, unwittingly, that led to my possible slaughter like Riding Hood with the big bad wolf. Was *I* Riding Hood? I pulled the flash drive from inside my bra. I wasn't supposed to look at its content. Those were the rules. Deliver the device without reviewing any of the information on it. But there were no rules anymore. Not after what had happened. I inserted the key into the USB port of my laptop and clicked on the menu bar. The key wasn't empty. It contained a folder.

I clicked on it and found a series of JPEG photographs.

The first one was of a group of men, sitting in what seemed to be a private lounge in a large sports stadium. Among them the Commander in Chief, about thirty years younger, if not more, smiled for the camera. His smile wasn't so much an expression of joy as an affirmation of power, a clenching of the jaw while showing a row of white teeth. Next to him with an arm around his shoulders was Bart Wallace, an infamous billionaire financier recently condemned to fifteen years of prison for sex trafficking. Someone whose notoriety had exploded over the past six months as reports of his salacious activities had surfaced in the press following his arrest. The president of the United States and Bart Wallace, together at a football game. I swallowed and felt my throat tighten.

I looked at the next photograph, which had been taken elsewhere, probably inside a luxury hotel room from what I could tell from the décor and the furniture. The president was sitting on a sofa, with a young girl on his knees. The girl seemed to have been fourteen or fifteen years old, with black hair and skinny limbs. She wore a miniskirt and a bra, and a pair of high heels. She smiled for the camera, but her gaze was unfocused, as if she had been drunk or high. The president looked inebriated too. His cheeks were flushed, and his facial expression lacked the composure of the previous shot.

The following photograph was a clear indication of what would come next. The current tenant of the White House was sitting on a large bed with the girl standing between his knees, his pants unzipped and his shirt unbuttoned. The girl was naked now, except for the high heels and a black string that rose up her crotch. The president's hands cupped her small breasts as she stared blankly off camera. I scrolled quickly through the three following shots. I didn't have to look at any of them for long to understand what had happened. A fat motherfucker abusing a young girl. The darling of the Evangelical right having sex with a minor, a teenager with the eyes of a dead woman.

I shut the lid of my laptop and rested my shoulders against the back of my chair. The USB key was real. The photographs were top-notch *kompromat* material. There was no way anyone at the Service would have wanted to see them destroyed. I wondered how Alford could have had them in his possession in the first place. Surely, such sensitive material would have been rounded up and obliterated from the face of the earth the minute Mitchell Baker would have considered a life in politics. Granted, his arrival on the political stage was relatively recent but a man of his financial means would have easily bought, bribed or threatened anyone holding any unsavoury memento from his civilian past.

I opened my laptop again and looked at the first photograph taken in the private lounge of the sports stadium. I didn't recognize any of the men apart from Wallace and Baker but something about the football field in the background caught my attention. There was a big logo in its center. Two letters, one over the other. An A overlapping a U, which I Googled immediately.

The men had attended a football game at Auburn University, Brent Alford's alma mater. Also, possibly the alma mater of his father. I searched the Internet for a photograph of the older Alford, using a combination of the words 'Alford', 'republican' and 'Alabama' and quickly found what I was looking for. Douglas Alford, the chairperson of the Republican Party for the state of Alabama. A political operative who had been rubbing shoulders with the rich and the powerful for the past four decades. I went back to the photograph of the men in the stadium and spotted him immediately, sitting to the right of the sex-trafficking billionaire with a tall glass in his hand. The likely local organizer of the little *soirée* and of the entertainment that came with it.

There was a time when photographs could be taken and forever forgotten. A bygone era when no one could have imagined what the Internet would do years later with a candid shot taken in a private setting. The photographs had likely been kept by Douglas Alford. And by the look of them, it seemed possible the president of the United States may not even have remembered they were ever taken. That was probably why they still existed. Because no one knew about them. Until his son, somehow, had stumbled upon the jackpot.

These photographs were worth an absolute fortune. Perhaps the younger Alford, strapped for cash, had tried to sell them. Maybe that was how our agent in Washington D.C. had first heard about them and about their owner. Regardless of the circumstances, someone at the Service had caught a goose and the phenomenal golden egg that came with it.

I pulled the key from my laptop and replaced it inside my bra. What if the purpose of the explosion *was* to kill me and Alford, and to destroy the flash drive? If that was the case, there was little doubt about who benefitted the most from preventing the Service from getting its hands on the *kompromat*. Whoever was behind the bombing was protecting the president. And if that person was Yuri, then he was a traitor, a double agent working for the United States. *The blond guy was inside your apt.*

I felt cold and suddenly very tired. I also felt vaguely nauseous thinking that my partner had possibly bought me a one-way ticket to the afterlife. A VIP voucher to a never-ending sit-down with Saint Boris while my human shell slowly rotted away in a damp casket buried in the corner of a cemetery. I picked up my telephone and went back to my bed and my set of pillows. What was I supposed to do now, with the key? It was seven in the morning. I lay down with the Walther next to me and pulled the duvet over my battered limbs. I closed my eyes and fell into a slumber almost immediately, rescued by Morpheus from a growing pool of loneliness.

CHAPTER 15

I opened my eyes for no apparent reason and stared at the ceiling. I had slept on my back, with my shoes on, in the same position I had been when I had lost consciousness, with my right hand resting on the Walther. I found my phone next to me. It was five minutes before nine, still early in the day. Again, no messages from anyone. And still nothing on the news about a possible female suspect. I wondered if I should wait in the apartment a little while longer. Wait with the key with the *kompromat* on it. The key the Service wanted. It wouldn't be long now before someone would come and get me. I was about to be extracted. Taken away somewhere, never to come back.

I stared at the ceiling again and wished I could disappear in a similar sea of white. Perhaps after being away for a few years I would be forgotten and could come back to Montreal and live a normal life. Start over. I closed my eyes as my mind slowly drifted. The doorbell rang and startled me.

I sat up and grabbed the Walther, then carefully walked down the hallway towards the front of my apartment. The old-fashioned bell unleashed its fury a second time as I slipped into the living room and lowered myself under the windows. I took a peek outside and immediately recognized the dyed-blond hair of my neighbour Jacques, who stood at the top of my staircase under an umbrella. I shoved the Walther in its holster and breathed a sigh of relief.

Jacques seemed especially glad to see me as I opened the door.

"Nina. Thank God you're here."

His eyes immediately travelled to my cheek and to my lower lip.

"Jesus. What happened to you?" he said.

I realized I had momentarily forgotten about the bruises on my face and what my lower lip looked like.

"Oh, that? Don't worry about it," I said. "I fell."

Jacques looked at me for a second too long.

"I was jogging down the stairs on Mount Royal, you know, the ones that lead to the belvedere, and I tripped and tumbled down. I almost broke my arm."

"*Mon dieu,*" he said, then seemed to remember why he was there.

"Markus has something for you."

"For me? What is it?"

"An envelope. Two days ago, when he was at the grocery store, a man came up to him and gave it to him."

"A man?"

"Yes. It was very bizarre. Can you come over to our place? Markus will tell you all about it. We've taken turns ringing your doorbell for the past two days."

"Alright. I'll be there in a minute. I just need to grab my keys."

I closed the door of my apartment. A man with an envelope? That was the man with the baseball cap again, no doubt. After the newspaper article and the scribbled message about Yuri, he had given Markus a third message for me after not seeing me for a couple of days. Perhaps he knew what had really happened at the G7. Perhaps he was the key to understanding the madness.

I went to the bathroom and dabbed some concealer over my cheekbone to try to cover a bluish spot the size of a silver dollar. For my lower lip, there was nothing I could do but luckily its puffiness had noticeably diminished since the night before. I took my phone, my keys and my wallet and put on a short black coat over my hoodie, one of those water-resistant North Face jackets. I left my apartment and crossed over to Markus and Jacques' place. I rang the doorbell and Markus quickly opened the door.

"Come in," he said. "I'm really happy you're finally home."

I followed him to the back of his house, through the entry with its large wooden staircase and into a smaller room with ancient cupboards that reached all the way to the ceiling. We were in a walk-in pantry, connected to the kitchen and the dining room by heavy swing doors. A small staircase in a corner led to the basement below. Markus opened one of the cupboards and pulled out a white envelope.

"Let's have a seat in the kitchen," he said. "I know Jacques already told you how it happened."

I followed him to a kitchen twice as large as mine with shiny aluminum appliances and marble counters. Jacques was already there, seated at a long rectangular table and drinking coffee. Markus sat next to him, and I took a seat on the opposite side. Dickens strolled into the kitchen and ignored us, as cats usually do.

Jacques put his arm around Markus' shoulders as he handed me the envelope across the table.

"This is it. The envelope the man at the grocery store gave me," Markus said.

I took it and held it in my hands as they rested on the table in front of me.

"Thank you."

"These past few days have been slightly nerve-racking to

say the least," Markus said. "With that horrible terrorist attack at the G7 and everything else."

"I know," I said.

"Markus and I have been worried sick about you," Jacques said.

"We didn't see you for three days and you were never home. We thought the man I caught looking at your windows had done something to you," Markus said.

"We even thought about calling the police."

"I'm so sorry. I… how can I say this? The past few days have been a bit difficult," I said.

"Well, aren't you going to open it?" Jacques said.

My eyes fell on the envelope. By the look of it, it contained no more than a piece of paper, a delivery similar to the two previous ones. Was there a reason for not wanting to open it in front of my friends and neighbours? My life as Nina was over. I would likely be gone by the end of the day. Whatever was in the envelope, I could explain to my friends as insignificant or as a stupid joke. And even if my explanation rang hollow, I wouldn't have to live with it for very long as I was likely seeing Markus and Jacques for the very last time that morning.

"You can go into the living room if you want some privacy," Markus said.

"No, it's alright," I said.

"You know, Markus is right. Why don't you turn around to open it? Then you can decide if you want to show us what's in it or not," Jacques said.

I twisted sideways on my chair and ripped the envelope open. There was a single folded page of paper inside. A copy of a birth certificate for a child named Sofia Nicola Jankowski, born on September 7, 1994, at the John Hopkins Hospital in Bethesda, Maryland. Was she the baby mentioned in the article of The New York Times? It is customary in Russia to give newborns a middle name that is a derivative of their father's first name. Giving the baby Nicola for a middle name was probably an Americanized attempt at naming her after her father, Nikolaï Belinski, one of the Russian agents mentioned in the article. The certificate appeared to be genuine. It was signed by a doctor, presumably the obstetrician, with his name typed underneath his signature. I felt a shiver travel down my spine.

I placed the copy of the certificate on the table in front of me and lifted my eyes at Markus and Jacques. They both stared at me intently.

"What is it?" Markus said.

"It's a copy of a birth certificate," I said.

"A birth certificate? For who?" Jacques said.

"I don't know. Some baby born in the US."

"May I?" Markus said.

He lifted the photocopy off the table.

"Oh, look. There's something written on the back of it," Jacques said.

Markus turned the piece of paper over for us to look at it. A message had been scribbled in blue ink. 'I will see you soon,' it said.

"Why are you getting this?" Markus said.

"I have no idea."

"This guy sounds like he's obsessed with you," Jacques said.

"Nina, Jacques and I are your friends. If you need to talk to someone about anything at all, you know you can trust us," Markus said.

He waited. I looked at them both, so earnest and filled with genuine concern and I wished at that moment that I could tell them everything and choose their world over mine. Toss my life over and jump forever into theirs. My friends. The few of them I could rightfully call my own.

"What is it?" Markus said.

"Nothing. I mean, I really don't know."

"You know, I think this man is the same one Markus

caught looking at your windows. Look, Nina, you can tell us what's going on. We're here to help you and protect you. I mean, what about those bruises on your face? Nice work with the concealer by the way," Jacques said.

"Oh, no. No, Jacques, you're getting this whole thing completely wrong," I said. "I've been having a couple of rough days, which is probably why I almost killed myself on those steps while I was out jogging. My mom hasn't been feeling well and I went over to my parents' house to see her. I'm sorry you guys thought something bad had happened to me. And I honestly have no idea who this man is. What did he look like, physically?"

"About fifty years old. Clean looking, with nice clothes. There was nothing weird or creepy about him. He looked normal. He came up to me and apologized then gave me the envelope and said it was very important that I give it to you in person. I was stunned at first because he obviously knew I was your friend. But he was very polite, very articulate. I don't know how he did it, but he put me at ease," Markus said.

I immediately thought of Dmitry, with his irresistible good manners and engaging smile, and felt a weight being lifted off my shoulders.

"Did he have salt and pepper hair? And dressed kind of nicely, like a Frenchman would?"

"The hair, sort of, yes. Although I would say it was more like salt and brown sugar, not pepper. About the clothes, I wouldn't say he dressed like a Frenchman. More like an American, you know? Kind of a Brooks Brothers look. And he seemed fit. In good physical shape. A little less than six feet tall. He also had very blue eyes. Just like yours," Markus said.

My newfound sense of relief dissipated instantaneously. Dmitry's eyes were light brown, like a pair of polished chestnuts.

"Does that ring any bells?" Jacques said.

"I thought so for a moment, but no. None whatsoever," I said.

That, at least, was the truth. Jacques took the photocopy to look at it.

"That baby was born in Bethesda in 1994," he said. "Today, she'd be about your age."

My neighbour had stated the very obvious. But more to the point, Sofia Jankowski wasn't just a girl who would have been the same age as me. She was possibly me and this birth certificate was possibly mine. I had known this the moment I had looked at the name and the date of her birth.

But even though the document seemed genuine, it could still be a forgery. There is no greater bait for a child of unknown parents than the tantalizing possibility of finding out who he or she really is. Anyone who knew I was an orphan could have used that against me. And what better way to have me fall into a trap and get hold of the USB key hidden inside my bra than to lure me with the fairy tale possibility of a family reunion? On the other hand, whoever would have thought of that plan would have had to know about my real identity and about the Riding Hood mission.

My telephone vibrated inside the front pocket of my hoodie. It was Theo. *Hi are u back from your parents house?* I felt my face getting warm.

"Some good news?" Jacques said.

"Actually, yes. My mom. She got some test results from the hospital."

Markus looked at me with a little smile.

"Funny how that made your cheeks flush," he said.

"No, really, both of you. That's where I was for the past two days. In Saint-Lambert with my mother."

"Well, if you plan on staying over at your parents' house again could you please let us know?" Jacques said. "With all these weird things happening Markus and I would really appreciate knowing about it. Especially if Markus ends up being used as your special delivery person again."

"Of course," I said.

My phone vibrated a second time. A repeat of the previous message. I looked up at Markus and Jacques who both stared at me, but I was no longer with them.

"I have to go," I said. "I'm meeting my parents at the hospital."

I folded the copy of the birth certificate and slipped it in the back pocket of my jeans.

"But what about this birth certificate? And that man stalking you?" Jacques said.

"I don't know what to say. I guess I'll have to deal with all of it later. I'm really sorry you guys were worried about me. I'll let you know what happens," I said.

Markus walked me to the door.

"514-998-2317," he said.

"What's that?"

"My number. Just in case."

"Of course."

I took out my phone as he repeated it and typed it in.

"It's funny that we never called each other before," he said. "And you know, about that man, you really should be careful. If we see him again and you're not there we'll probably call the police."

I looked up at Markus with his black-rimmed eyeglasses and felt a lump inside my chest. This was our last goodbye.

"Markus, thank you for being my friend. I really mean it," I said.

"Don't be silly. Of course, I'm your friend. And so is Jacques. We love you. I guess we'll figure out what that birth certificate is about over the next few days. Why don't you give us a call later this afternoon when you're back at your apartment? If you want, you could come over for dinner tonight."

"Sure. I'll do that."

He rolled his eyes as if he didn't believe me.

"Alright darling. Just be careful. And whoever that person is who's sending you those text messages, he better be gorgeous and super nice to you."

We air kissed on both cheeks before he let me out.

I walked down the staircase and texted Theo. *Yes I'm back.* His reply came almost immediately. *Wanna come over now for some coffee?* I hesitated. Was it safe to visit Theo's apartment? Probably no less than staying at my own place. I texted back. *Sure.* If the Service contacted me while I was at Theo's, I would have to leave, that was all. And I really wanted to see him one last time. Before my life changed forever and my face started being shown on the nightly news. My phone vibrated again. *3644 B Lorne Crescent.*

The rain had stopped but it made no difference to me. I was giddy. A strange sensation after the horror and misery of the past twenty-four hours. I looked behind my back to make sure I wasn't being followed and started to walk up the street, on my way to something that was entirely mine and which I knew would be over before the end of the day. A brief moment of happiness, inconsequential, before Central Control got a hold of me and the flash drive inside my bra.

CHAPTER 16

3644 Lorne Crescent was a narrow, semi-detached house of red bricks. Victorian in style and likely built at the turn of the past century. I climbed a short flight of stairs to a black-painted porch and pressed the doorbell for apartment B. Footsteps clambered down an interior staircase. The door opened and Theo was there, in a t-shirt and a pair of jeans.

"Hi," he said.

He locked his arms around my waist and pulled me close. Our lips met and any and all logical thoughts left my head at once. The Service was gone. I didn't care about the key or who I really was. My body took over from my brain, which excused itself and said it would be back later. Desire washed over me, but I suddenly remembered the Walther strapped to my left side under the hoodie and quickly pulled away. Thankfully, it rested higher up on my ribcage than the lock of Theo's arms, but not by much.

"You okay?" he said.

"Yeah. I just..."

He took my hand.

"Come," he said.

I followed him up the stairs. The door to his apartment was open. It was a nice place, with framed posters hanging on white painted walls, a long brown leather couch and a couple of armchairs. An open plan layout with a kitchen connected to a dining area that flowed into the living room. More than a notch above the average student home.

"Do you live here alone?" I said.

He seemed slightly embarrassed, or at least pretended to be.

"Yeah. My parents bought this place when I started at McGill. They thought it made more sense that having to pay rent for four years."

I smiled. Theo, the cool one who didn't seem to care much about anything because, on his end of things, there really was nothing to worry about. Theo the casual holder of a silver spoon that stuck out of his back pocket. I didn't give a damn. It didn't matter to me. And I certainly wasn't in any position to fault him for being discreet about certain aspects of his private life.

I took off my windbreaker and dropped it on the couch.

"Can I use your bathroom?" I said.

"Sure. It's down the hall. First door to your right."

I locked the bathroom door and removed my hoodie. The nylon holster was heavy with the weight of the police handgun and I slipped it off my shoulder and pushed it under Theo's bathtub, as far underneath it as it could go. It was an antique cast iron tub, almost identical to mine. A heavy tank set on short stubby legs. I put my hoodie back on. Flushed the toilet and washed my hands.

I found Theo in the kitchen.

"How's your mom?" he said.

"Better. But she's having some tests done. To make sure there's nothing sinister going on."

"It's a good thing she's feeling better."

He pointed to an espresso machine at the end of the counter.

"Would you like a short, a latte or an *allongé*?"

I leaned against the counter.

"Actually, I'm fine. Thanks."

Theo came closer and gently pinned me against it.

"No coffee? I thought that was why you came over. What would you like instead? A glass of juice?" he said.

"No thanks."

He kissed me lightly on the neck.

"A glass of water?"

"No."

He kissed me again.

"Is there anything I can offer you that would make you happy?" he said.

"I don't know. I'll have to think about it."

He kissed me on the lips, softly. His hands slipped under my hoodie and under my t-shirt. I slid my right hand around his chest and ran my left hand down the front of his jeans. I wanted him. And at this point, did it matter? His bedroom was next to the bathroom, at the opposite end of his apartment, and on our way to it, we stopped and kissed in the living room, moved a few meters more and stopped and kissed again, in the hallway, and again, against the door frame of the bedroom, until we finally made it to our intended destination.

His t-shirt flew on top of his desk, our pants dropped to the floor almost simultaneously. He unhooked my bra and kissed my breasts. Our underwear vanished. We climbed into his bed. I never felt more at ease than right at that moment, naked under sheets that smelled of laundry detergent and of this man I was with, the sexiest law student I had ever met. He pressed himself against me and I wrapped my legs around his hips. We made love, twice. And after the second time, we lingered in bed.

"What's with the bandage around your knee?" he said.

"I fell down the stairs at my parents' house. I was trying to take my bicycle out of the basement to use it to go to the pharmacy."

"And what, you tripped?"

"Yeah. I caught my feet in the pedals. And my knee landed right on the chain ring."

"Ouch. I also noticed you got all these bruises."

"I know. I banged myself pretty badly. And I also bruise *super* easily," I said.

"I didn't want to say anything when you took your clothes off. But I was, like, this is a bit weird."

He kissed me.

"Do you remember when I told you I was thinking of going to the G7 for a protest?" Theo said.

"Yeah. I do. What happened?"

"Well, that was supposed to be yesterday. Can you imagine being there? With everything that's happened? I'm actually really happy I didn't go."

"For sure."

"It's fucking crazy, what happened," he said.

"I know. I can't stop thinking about it. These poor people, dead."

Images of the carnage were coming back to me.

"Hey, are you okay? Forget about what I just said. Let's talk about something else," Theo said.

"Alright."

I gave him a smile to show that I was fine.

"I have to use the washroom. I'll be right back," I said.

I put on Theo's t-shirt and left the room. When I came back, he was sitting on the side of the bed, putting one foot, then the other through the leg holes of his boxer briefs. His jeans and all my clothes were folded in a pile next to him.

"Do you want a glass of juice? Or should I say, *now*, do you want a glass of juice?"

He smiled.

"Sure. That would be nice," I said.

"I'll be right back."

I sat on the bed where Theo had been a second before and put on my panties and my bra with the little rectangle of hard plastic still in it. I liked his bedroom. It was orderly, with documents and books neatly stacked on his desk. There was an armchair in a corner, with some clothes on it, and next to it a half-opened closet. A window into a normal life. Theo came back with two glasses of orange juice and sat next to me on the bed.

I took a sip from the glass he had given me and heard my phone vibrate under the pile of clothes. I retrieved it and looked at it casually. It was Yuri. *Meeting at 1 at your parents.* I locked my phone and put it face down next to me.

"Everything okay?" Theo said.

"Yeah. My dad just wrote me to say that he got my mom an appointment to see a doctor today at the hospital. I think I should go and meet them."

"At which hospital?

"At the CHUM, downtown".

"At what time?"

"In less than an hour. I guess I should be going."

"Like, now?"

Theo gave me a sad face.

"I'll call you after," I said.

"How about watching a movie later tonight? The new Guy Ritchie just came out on Netflix."

I felt my heart fracture into bits and pieces. I wanted to be that girl who would curl up on a sofa next to him.

"Yeah. Absolutely."

I put on my pants and my t-shirt. My hoodie, my socks and my running shoes. On my way out I stopped in the bathroom again and retrieved the holster with the handgun in it. I strapped it tight against my chest under the hoodie, as high as

I could under my arm. In the living room I put on my jacket as Theo sat on the couch in his briefs with his legs wide apart. I leaned over and kissed him. He took my hand and held on to me.

"I have to go," I said.

"Just, wait a second."

He brought my face back down to his and kissed me a second time.

"I really have to go."

"Call me after," he said.

I walked down Lorne Crescent under a pale grey sky. There was never going to be an after. This was the end of Nina Palester and of her law school boyfriend. I pulled the hood of my jacket over my head and tried to remind myself that getting away was my number one priority. As I moved along the sidewalk, a strange mix of relief at seeing Irina and Dmitry again and of sadness at leaving Theo started to fill my heart. As for Yuri, I didn't know what to think. Except that he seemed to be working for the Service after all. At least officially.

I stopped by my apartment and threw my laptop, a charger and a clean t-shirt into a sports bag. I also took a light down feather vest from my closet and folded it with the rest of my things. I didn't know what else to take. It was my entire life I was leaving behind. My books, my clothes, my personal things. If I couldn't take all of it with me, then perhaps it was better to take nothing at all. I looked at my telephone. It was five minutes before noon. I sent a text message to Yuri. *On my way will be in SL at 1.* Before opening the front door, I pressed my forehead against the wall in the hallway, to say goodbye. I left my apartment without a look back and walked down Durocher towards the bustle of the city center.

I made my way down McGill College Avenue among the downtown midday crowd, a mix of office people, students and shoppers, then walked all the way to *le 1000 de La Gauchetière*, the city's tallest skyscraper. I took the escalator to the bus terminal at the basement level, bought a ticket and climbed aboard bus 55, a safer way to cross over to the south shore than the metro with its many close-circuit cameras. I sat at the back of the bus, which was almost empty, and waited for the bus driver to turn on the engine. We crossed the Champlain Bridge a few moments later and I watched the waters of the Saint Lawrence churn north under the bridge structure towards that hotel in Charlevoix that I now wished I had never visited.

I got off the bus on Victoria Street, the commercial heart of my suburban hometown. I was looking forward to being reunited with Irina and Dmitry, even if that was only for a short while. The bus stop was a ten-minute walk to my parents' house, and I cut through the *parc du soldat*, as we called it, with its life-size statue of a First World War infantryman and continued along tree-lined sidewalks to my parents' cottage. Dmitry's car, a dark blue Volvo, was the only one in the driveway.

I rang the doorbell and waited. No one answered. I rang a second time and listened carefully for any noise coming from inside the house. I tried to open the door, but it was locked, unsurprisingly. I climbed down the front porch and walked around the house on a flagstone pathway that led to my parents' yard, past a side basement door. The garden at the back of the house was a rectangular patch of grass with a bed of crocus set around the base of a magnolia tree, in full bloom at this time of year. A hedge of cedar trees Dmitry had planted many years before enclosed it in a thick, evergreen wall.

I climbed the stairs to the deck at the back the house and looked inside the kitchen through a set of French doors. Everything looked normal except for a wide-open cupboard, something which immediately set off my alarm bells. Irina was meticulous. She never left anything out of place. Neither did Dmitry. A cupboard door left open meant that my parents weren't home, and also that they may not have been the last persons inside the house. I peered into the dining room but couldn't see anything else that wasn't in its place.

I went back to the flagstone pathway on the side of the house and slipped my hand behind the pipe of a downspout that ran along the wall from the edge of the roof. There it was. The key that had saved me so many times from freezing outside in winter or having to wake up my parents after a late night out. Dangling on a rusty nail. I inserted the key into the lock of the side door and opened it, slowly. The door led directly onto a landing halfway down the basement staircase, a mid-level stop between the kitchen and the downstairs TV room.

I stepped inside the house, stopped for a moment and listened but couldn't hear a thing. Was there anyone home? I went upstairs to the kitchen and saw that a drawer had also been left open, something I didn't like. In the living room, a lightbulb burnt inside the giant shade of a mid-century table lamp, one of Dmitry's favourite finds. I dropped my sports bag on a sofa and quickly climbed upstairs.

I reached the first-floor landing and stood there for a moment, too shaken to move. From the top of the stairs I could see inside my parents' bedroom, where cupboards had been left open and closet doors ajar. I took a step inside their room and saw piles of clothes scattered on the bed and an empty suitcase on the floor next to it. Irina and Dmitry had left. They were gone. I tried to swallow but I couldn't. A hard ball had suddenly grown at the back of my throat.

I raced down the stairs all the way to the basement. The secret room behind the water heater no longer existed. The walls had been taken down. The space had been turned into a storage area, with shelves and a couple of lawn rakes set against the walls. I went back to the TV room and sat on the floor next to the sofa, too numb to think.

Irina and Dmitry weren't my real parents. They were my superiors. My handlers. That fact had always been acknowledged, it wasn't a secret. But they were also the individuals who had cared for me and raised me. The two people who had stood by my side all these years, as I had navigated the milestones that mark the passage of time, from youth to adulthood. The first days of school, the birthday parties. They had taught me and made me who I was. The three of us had laughed and argued and kept secrets just like real families do. Regardless of who I was to them, and what they were to me, I loved them. And they had left me. My eyes started to burn and heavy tears rolled down the side of my cheeks.

I heard footsteps above me, in the kitchen.

"Katyusha?"

It was Yuri. I stood up and wiped my tears with the front of my hoodie. I didn't want him to see me cry. I no longer trusted him.

"Downstairs," I said.

My partner came down, looking even taller than usual in the confine of the basement TV room.

"Hey," he said.

He immediately noticed my eyes, which must have been redder than usual, and purposely looked away.

"Irina and Dmitry have gone back to Russia. The orders came down yesterday from Central Control," he said.

His voice was flat, without the slightest hint of emotion. His text message had been silent about my parents' departure on purpose. A surer way to get me to come to Saint-Lambert for a meeting.

"Okay," I said.

Yuri was calm, almost aloof. He was clean-shaven, freshly dressed in clothes I had never seen him wear before. A new pair of jeans and a suede jacket that must have cost a fortune. I caught a glimpse of a heavy metal watch on his wrist that was new to me as well. While I looked at him and tried to decipher his thoughts he went over to the old sofa and sat.

"I spoke to Anton. Your photograph is being circulated to all the law enforcement agencies in North America," he said. "The airports are being watched."

I couldn't think of anything to say. He looked at me in a funny way, then smiled.

"I heard you got into a fight with a policewoman at the hotel."

"I didn't have a choice," I said.

He chuckled.

"That probably wasn't the most discreet thing to do," he said.

"Like I said, I didn't have a choice. I was trapped inside the hotel, like everyone else. And by the way, where were you?"

"On my way here," he said.

"How?"

"I got lucky. After you and I had breakfast, I decided to go for a jog around the golf course. I was on my way back to the hotel when the blast happened. I heard the explosion and I saw all the emergency vehicles converge to the back of it. I thought about trying to find you, but you know as well as I do that's not what we're supposed to do when something happens. So, I went straight to my car instead to get the Beretta. Then I cut across the woods all the way to that place where they have the hiking trails. The two guys who were stationed at the fence never saw me coming. They never thought someone would come at them from inside the fence."

"Why the hell did you go for a jog? You were supposed to meet me on the promenade right after breakfast to do the yoga class."

"I heard the class was cancelled. So I decided to go running."

I nodded but I knew he was lying. Maryse hadn't called Yuri to let him know. She had asked me to call him about the cancellation.

"And then what?" I said.

"After a while I flagged down a passing car. The driver didn't know what had happened at the hotel. I got rid of him and stole the car."

"What did you do with him?"

"He's in the woods. Probably still there."

It was the first time I was seeing Yuri confirm he had killed some people, and he wasn't batting an eyelid.

"How did you manage to leave the green zone in the stolen car?" I said.

"I had my ID cards with me."

"That was lucky."

Yuri raised his eyebrows.

"Not really. I took the whole kit with me when I went out running. It's standard protocol never to leave that stuff inside our room. You know that," he said.

No, it wasn't. Yuri didn't have to take his ID documents with him to go for a jog. My partner was lying. I was certain of it.

"And what about the explosion? Did you have anything to do with it?"

Yuri looked at me quietly.

"No, of course I didn't," he said.

I started to feel angry.

"Really? Are you sure about that? Because you know I almost fucking died because of it. And explosives were detected by a sniffer dog *inside my car*. So, if you had nothing at all to do about it, then who did?"

"I don't know. Maybe Anton will know."

Yuri looked away. Why had he not mentioned calling my name a moment before the explosion? It was obvious he and I no longer shared a playbook. But I couldn't confront him any further alone in the basement of my parents' house. I was at a disadvantage, hidden from view in a subterranean TV room. Even though I wanted to punch him in the face for lying to me so blatantly there was no other choice for now than to play along. I came closer and sat at the opposite end of the couch.

"So, what do we do now?" I said.

"You have the flash drive with you, right?" Yuri said.

"Yes."

There was no point in denying it. Regardless of who he was working for, I had a feeling Yuri would have thrown me on the floor and found out for himself if I had tried to say no.

"Alright. Anton is waiting for us at the office. So far there's been no mention of you in the media, which is a lucky break, but we don't know how long that will last. You and I need to meet with Anton asap, to give him the key. Then we need to get you to a safe place."

"Like where?" I said.

"I don't know. Anton will tell us. I'm guessing they're going to fly us both out."

I tried not to flinch.

"Fly us out to where? *Russia?*"

"Maybe."

"Yuri, why did we have to stay at the *Manoir* after I told you I had the key? Was it Anton's decision?"

"I don't know. He must have been following orders from Central Control."

"I almost got killed because of that."

Yuri looked at me for a second.

"I know," he said.

A mission within a mission, directed by Anton, or someone else at Central Control, that somehow had gone haywire. And Yuri was working for the Service after all. But I couldn't be entirely certain of it, and I still didn't trust him.

"We should go," he said.

I wasn't looking forward to a visit with Anton, but there seemed to be no alternative. If I wanted to be taken care of by the Service, I had no choice but to meet with our mission supervisor. Unless Yuri and Anton were *both* traitors and working for somebody else, it was the better option.

"Alright," I said. "But what do we do about this house?"

"The Service will take care of it."

"How?"

"It's going to be put up for sale," Yuri said.

"Remotely?"

"Sure. Why not?"

"And what about Irina and Dmitry? Are they supposed to have vanished into thin air?"

"The official story will be that they had to fly back to France for a family emergency, and never came back. They'll video-conference with anyone down here if necessary. They'll be reachable, for a while."

"And Dmitry's car?" I said.

"Same as the house. As your apartment."

So that was it. The end of the Palester family. The taking down of a background décor I had almost come to believe was real. I was shocked, which was strange considering I had often wished for my dual existence to end. I had often dreamed of not having to live a double life, and now that it had finally happened, the reality of it brought me nothing but a profound sense of loss. But there was no choice to be had in the matter. I was Ekaterina Yegorova, an orphan raised by the Russian state. An agent working for the Service. A member of the Illegals Program.

"You know, a lot of people are looking for the flash drive," Yuri said.

"You don't say."

"Don't be such a smartass. I don't mean the people at Central Control, or the Americans. That's pretty obvious. I mean the Chinese, for example. And some very rich people in the Middle East. Some of them have already reached out to some free agents, right here, in Montreal, to try to find the person who has it. They all want the key. The sooner we give it to Anton, the better."

"How do they know the flash drive even exists?"

"News travel fast, I guess."

My partner stood up.

"Let's go," he said.

I followed him upstairs. In the living room I picked up my sports bag with the laptop and my other things in it. Yuri waited for me by the front door. As I walked past the mirror in the vestibule, I saw the key for the Volvo on the console table underneath it and took it. Outside the house Yuri walked across the street to his car.

"I'll take the Volvo," I said.

He turned around and shot me an angry look.

"I don't think that's a good idea," he said.

There was nothing he could do about it, out in the open, and I was no longer in the mood to be pushed around. In the past twenty-four hours, I had lost a great deal that was dear to me. Someone I really liked, maybe to the point of falling in love with. An apartment and a neighbourhood I had called my own. A semi-normal life as a student, some friendly neighbours and a best friend. I had also lost the two people I had grown up with for the past fourteen years, the only family I had ever known. And if that wasn't enough, I had also almost been killed. I didn't give a shit who Yuri thought he was or why he believed he could tell me what to do. I no longer trusted him. And I wanted my own car.

"Why? You think I'm not a good enough driver?" I said.

I walked to the Volvo and unlocked it. Yuri didn't move. I sat behind the wheel, shut the door and started the engine and only then did he realize that I was really going to leave with it. He jumped in his car, but he was too late. I pulled out of the parking with the tires screeching and quickly drove away in the direction opposite the one his old Jetta was facing. Yuri and I had been a team once, but we weren't anymore. That too had been lost.

CHAPTER 17

We arrived at the office almost at the same time, Yuri and I. He'd caught up with the Volvo before I got on the Victoria Bridge and managed to stay close behind it despite all I did to try to lose him. Yuri was pretty good at tailing drivers, but I'd given him a run for his money. I'd stomped on the gas pedal at a yellow light, made unexpected last-minute turns on a number of side streets. I had added a couple of detours. As he parked his Jetta bumper to bumper behind Dmitry's car, I looked at his face in my rear-view mirror. It was a mixture of red and white, like one of those big strawberries grown in California. The ones that taste of nothing. He was really pissed off.

"You think you're funny?" he said.

I closed the door of the Volvo without saying a word.

"You go first," he said, "I'll follow."

I wasn't looking forward to seeing Anton, but as things stood, he was the only one who could ensure my ticket to safety. We walked around the old stucco building, with Yuri keeping guard two steps behind.

"What's with the big fancy watch?" I said, over my shoulder. "I guess you're not a student anymore."

Yuri didn't say a thing. We stopped in front of the door at

the back of the property, and I turned around to look at him. He was solemn with his face a mask of flesh-coloured stone. Inside, the long room with the table and the chairs was as gloomy as the time before. The same pieces of broken furniture laid scattered on the floor, dust still covered all things and surfaces. Anton was sitting at the table at the far end of the room, waiting for us while working on a laptop with a thick metal casing. I had seen one of these portable computers before. It was a super secure model issued by the Service to its field agents. The man on the run who had sought shelter at our house in 2010 had left one of those behind, before being whisked out of the country by my parents.

We got closer to Anton and stood, waiting, while he stared intently at the brightly lit screen. I noticed for the first time how old he was, or seemed to be, with his deep wrinkles around his mouth and at the corner of his eyes. A Beretta was strapped to his chest in a holster he wore over a tight black t-shirt. He glanced at us, reclined in his chair, and crossed his arms.

"You took your time," he said.

"Traffic was slow," Yuri said.

That was my partner sticking it to me. Anton nodded and looked at us both, his eyes scanning us from head to toe.

"Sit," he said.

I reluctantly took a seat next to Yuri, across the table from our superior. I hadn't forgotten his little Kung Fu trick from our previous meeting. This guy was at best a casualty of war and at worst a raving lunatic.

"For your information, we're still trying to understand what exactly happened at the G7," Anton said. "We still don't know who provided Alford with the explosives."

What the hell was he saying?

He looked at us pointedly.

"The two of you will have to undergo a complete debriefing later tonight," he said.

I stiffened on my chair. Did Anton really not know what had happened at the *Manoir*? If there was a mission within a mission, one I had assumed he had put Yuri in charge of carrying, he seemed not to have been aware of it. Was Yuri bypassing Anton and taking his instructions directly from Central Control? The other possibility was that Yuri was working for somebody else. That he was a traitor after all. Possibly a double agent working for the Americans. Or perhaps the two of them were working together, with Anton only pretending that he didn't know what had happened to confuse me. Maybe this was a sick little show they were putting on for my benefit, some kind of skit designed to fool me. The ultimate blindside before sending little Katyusha back to Russia, or some other part of the world.

"At this point, the Service is contemplating every possible scenario, including the possibility that someone on the inside has betrayed us, perhaps unwittingly," Anton said.

He stared at us intently as he said these words, his reptilian eyes watching our slightest moves. *Someone on the inside?* If that was true, the principal suspect was sitting next to me with his legs stretched out and his hands shoved into the pockets of his chic suede jacket. Did Anton suspect Yuri was a traitor? I was suddenly grateful for the Walther strapped under my arm.

"Have you thought of Lana? She could have sold us out," Yuri said.

A flash of anger shone in Anton's eyes.

"I don't believe she would have done that. But we're looking into it. The timing of her disappearance is an obvious red flag. The one thing we do know for certain at this point is that a third party interfered with your assignment and that as a result the Riding Hood mission was almost derailed."

"I almost died over there. And if I had, the key would have been lost," I said.

"But you didn't, did you?"

I felt a cold sweat form at the base of my neck. Was I a

suspect as well? Whoever had used my car to store the explosives had obviously tried to implicate me in the bombing. Did Anton know about that? Was Yuri trying to frame me?

"Anton, are you saying that some other people were after Alford's flash drive at the same time as we were?" Yuri said.

"It kind of looks like it, doesn't it?" Anton said.

He was being evasive on purpose. My mind started to spin. A mission within a mission but perhaps not for the benefit of the Service? Yuri using us, using *me*, to carry out somebody else's plan and, ultimately, to take the fall. But whose plan was it? And what purpose did it serve?

Anton reached across the table and presented me with his opened hand, a thick paddle attached to a sinuous arm.

"The key," he said.

I stuck my hand under my hoodie and under my shirt, pulled out the USB key from its little pocket inside my bra and placed it on his leathery palm. He plugged it into his laptop and started to type. His face, lit up by the fluorescent glow, rested impassively at first. Then he started to blink, a few times, then again more rapidly, as his eyes darted from one corner of the screen to another. A deep crease started to form between his brows. He kept on typing but with each second that passed, his face betrayed a rising anger that grew more powerful. He stopped and closed his laptop, then stared at me intensely, his pupils two small beads of barely contained fury.

"What the fuck is this?" he said.

He stood up as quick as lightning, lunged forward and grabbed the front of my coat. His chair toppled behind him as he lifted me up and pulled me across the table.

"Where's the key?" he said, as he brought my face to his.

Yuri stood up as well.

"Anton, take it easy. What do you mean, where's the key?" he said.

"There's nothing on the drive the little *shlyukha* brought us. It's full of empty folders. Completely blank."

He shook me as he said these words, tightening his grip on the front of my hoodie.

I suddenly felt sick. Not so much from being shaken down like an apple tree but more so from what Anton's words meant.

"You're going to tell us what you did every single minute of the past forty-eight hours," Anton said. "Where you were and who you were with."

His eyes were two narrow pits of madness. Black and cold like the bottom of a lake in mid-January.

"Let her go."

I turned my head just enough to see Yuri's Beretta pointed at my assailant's temple. Anton released me from his grip, and I slid back to my side of the table. The Beretta Yuri had supposedly retrieved *in extremis* from his car at the G7. He still had it, tucked in the back of his jeans.

My partner took a step back while keeping the gun pointed at Anton's head with both hands.

"Put your hands behind your head," he said.

Our mission supervisor reluctantly obeyed.

"Katyusha, put Anton's chair back on its feet so he can sit on it," Yuri said. "Then take his gun and give it to me."

His voice was calm and monotonous. Just as it had been in my parents' basement. None of what was happening seemed to upset him. In stark contrast with Anton who was seething with rage. The flash drive empty? A knot had formed at the bottom of my stomach when Anton had spat these words onto my face and the only possible explanation for it made me downright seasick. I had worn my bra continuously since I had left the *Manoir du Cap*, except on two occasions. Once in my apartment, when I had taken a shower, and a second time, in Theo's apartment. *Theo.*

"You're making a big mistake, *mudak*," Anton said.

I gave Anton's gun to Yuri who shoved it in the back of his pants.

"Keep your mouth shut Anton. Katyusha, where did you get the key?" Yuri said.

"I got it from an envelope Alford left at the reception of the hotel. It was addressed to Martin Bergensen. As I wrote to you that night, I went down to the lobby and retrieved it."

"And *then* what happened?" Anton said.

His words oozed from his mouth like dribbling venom. Yuri ignored him.

"Did you look to see what was on the key after you got it?" he said.

"No."

Anton watched me intently as I spoke. I could tell that he knew I had just lied.

"She's lying. Aren't you? You little whore," he said. "The key Alford left at the reception isn't the same as the one you had in your bra, am I right?"

A glint appeared in his eyes as he turned to Yuri.

"You know what has to be done, don't you?" Anton said. "You need to let me have a go at our little princess, to find out what happened. If we don't have the key, you and I don't get paid."

A look of hunger had spread to his face, of growing excitement. It seemed our mission supervisor was also a sadist, and the thought of inflicting me pain had suddenly aroused him. I took a step back. His depravity was repulsive. Yuri saw it too and also stepped back.

"No," he said.

An expression of shock took form across Anton's face. As Yuri's answer sunk in, he realized he was truly on his own.

"Katyusha has nothing to do with this and she's coming with me," Yuri said. "She and I have something very important to do."

"Yuri, what are you talking about?" I said.

"I'll tell you as soon as we leave here," Yuri said.

I slowly slipped my right hand under my hoodie and grabbed the handle of the Walther.

"You're going to pay for this, Yuri Fedorov," Anton said. "And I'll be the one making sure you're sent to a nice work camp where you'll be praying for a quick death every day of the week."

"Shut the fuck up, you fat, fucking loser," Yuri said. "You don't know anything."

Anton suddenly rose from his chair and lunged towards the table. He grabbed his laptop, held it up in front of him like a shield and sprung towards Yuri. My partner shot at him twice, but the bullets ricocheted against the metal casing of the laptop. *The case was bullet proof.* Yuri realized it and shot at him again, this time in the lower part of the belly, just as Anton hit him in the face with the laptop. Anton growled in pain as the bullet buried itself in his gut but kept hitting Yuri with the laptop. Blood started to pour from Anton's wound. Yuri fired a fourth bullet that hit the ceiling as he tried to push Anton away from him, but Anton kneed him in the groin. Yuri bent forward in pain and lost his balance as Anton dropped the laptop on the floor and reached for the Beretta stuck in Yuri's pants. I shot him a first time, in the back. He turned around and pointed his gun at me and I shot him again, in the chest this time. And a third time. Until his knees buckled, and Yuri hit him with the butt of his gun on the side of the head. Our mission supervisor fell to the ground and lay face down on the floor, moaning.

"Let go of your gun'" I said.

Anton uncurled his fingers from the handle of his Beretta. I took a step forward and kicked it. Yuri looked at the blood on his hands and on the front of his jacket. He was truly upset. His chic suede coat was ruined, smeared by our mission supervisor who wriggled in pain at our feet. There was blood everywhere. On the floor. On the laptop. On Yuri's face.

Anton, for his part, was almost entirely covered in it. I was the only one unspoilt. Yuri walked around our common enemy.

"*Suka blyad*!"

His foot hit Anton in the ribs. He barely reacted and rolled on his side like a heap of wet clothes.

"You… will pay," Anton said in a whisper.

Yuri moved to the side to face him.

"What's that you're saying?" Yuri said.

He pushed Anton with his foot to roll him on his back. Anton wheezed a couple of times then took a deeper breath.

"… will… find you," Anton said.

"Is that what you think? You forget who I work for."

Anton opened his eyes and tried to focus on Yuri. He moved his lips, but no sound came out of his mouth. Death was near. It waited for him in the wings, ready to pick him up as soon as the final scene was over. Yuri moved to Anton's feet and stood there.

"I'm going to tell you a secret, Anton," he said. "I know what happened to your girlfriend, little Lana. She didn't betray us. She's dead."

Anton started to breathe heavily. His face contracted in anger. He moved his right hand across the floor, hoping to find his handgun.

"Ttt…," he said, shaking.

"Can you repeat that? I don't think I heard what you said," Yuri said.

"Traitor," Anton said.

The first bullet hit him in the chest. Then another. Each time his body twitched as if it had been hit with an electrical jolt. Yuri lowered his gun and turned to face me. I held the Walther pointed at his head with both hands.

"Who do you work for, Yuri?" I said.

He looked at his gun to see if any blood had splattered on it then slid it inside the top of his jeans behind his back.

"I asked you a question," I said.

Yuri bent down to pick up the laptop on the floor. He grabbed it with the tip of his fingers, placed it on the table and pulled out the USB key. He looked at it and put it in his pocket, then looked at me.

"Where's the flash drive?" he said.

I took a couple of steps back towards the door.

"I don't have it. Why did you kill Anton?"

"Anton was going to hurt you to make you talk. I saved you. And besides, Anton was a pain in the ass. He wasn't told what we're really doing. To him, this was all about the flash drive. He didn't know why your presence was essential. He didn't know what the real plan was. He knew very little. Only what he needed to know. And because of his stubbornness we had to make Lana disappear in order for you to be brought back on the team. Look at it this way. Anton was expendable. He was going to die anyway, sooner or later. Not to mention that he was a tad unpredictable."

I wasn't sure what my partner was trying to say except perhaps that he and I were on the same side after all. That he and I were friends.

I took two more steps backward.

"Who is *we*? Who do you work for? The Americans?" I said.

Yuri stood up straight and faced me.

"I need you to come with me, Katyusha. You and I have to find the key. You know where it is, don't you?"

I did know where it was. I knew it with absolute certainty. And the more I thought about it, the angrier it made me. It was a personal matter. Something I wanted to take care of on my own. Also, the USB key was pretty much my last card. My ticket to freedom. If I could get to it before Yuri, or anyone else, someone somewhere would want it badly enough to come to my rescue. I took a few more backward steps towards the door.

"I'm going alone," I said.

"You can't do that Katyusha. You and I must stay together."

"I know it was you who gave the explosives to Alford."

Yuri thought about this for a second.

"You're right. It was me. But he wasn't supposed to blow himself up until later in the day. It was never part of the plan to put you in danger in any way whatsoever."

"To put me in danger or to risk losing the key?"

He smiled but didn't say anything.

"Your story doesn't add up, Yuri. If Alford had waited until later, the president of the United States could have been killed. And then the key would have been worthless."

"The president was never going to show up at the G7. He was late on purpose. He already knew we had the flash drive, Katyusha. And he did what we told him to do."

"You're saying that the president stayed away because of the *kompromat*? What, you just called up the White House and instructed him to stay home?"

"Much easier than that. When you told me you had the key in your possession, I relayed the information and then someone asked a friend of the president to call him on his cell phone. The President has many friends, Katyusha. People on the outside who hover around him like flies around a piece of steak. People he speaks to on the phone all the time. And one of these friends actually works for us."

Yuri's story was outlandish, but not impossible. Still, it didn't mean it was true. And quite frankly, it didn't change anything about the situation I was in. Regardless of what he had told me, I still needed to find Alford's flash drive before he did, more so now that ever before. And once I had found it, I would reach out to Uncle Ivan, the one person I could trust, and he would arrange to get me out of Montreal. That was my safest way out. But one thing about Yuri's story bothered me.

"If you wanted to get the key so badly, why bother with an

explosion? That was likely to make our escape from the hotel much more complicated," I said.

"Not *our* escape, Katyusha. But yours, yes, certainly. Especially after the explosives were detected inside your car. I was supposed to get you out. To help you get away. But that was impossible to do once that idiot detonated himself earlier than he was supposed to. That's why you need to stay with me now. So that I can protect you."

"You're saying that's why you put the explosives in my car? So that I'd be the one everyone was looking for? Who do you work for, Yuri?"

"I can't tell you that right now. But you're going to find out very soon."

"I'm leaving," I said.

"Don't do it."

I took a few more steps back. I could see Yuri calculate the distance between me and the door. Twenty meters at most. A three second sprint for him, no more. I kept on walking backward while holding the gun pointed at him.

"Stay. What you're doing is useless. You're only slowing things down," he said.

I reached the door and placed my left hand on the doorknob. It turned. I opened the door and rushed outside as fast as I could. I ran on the side of the building, towards the street where the Volvo was parked. I could hear Yuri's footsteps behind me. He was fast, much faster than I was, and I could tell he was getting closer. I reached the sidewalk and pulled the car key from my pocket. Dmitry's car was further to the right. I aimed the key fob at it and pressed the unlock button. The lights of the Volvo flashed. I opened the car door, threw myself in and locked it behind me. Yuri flung himself against the door and grabbed the handle. He was furious.

"Open up," he said.

He took a step back and pulled out his gun, then he and I saw the same thing at the same time. Three men walked out of a building across the street. Two of them immediately ran back inside while the third one grabbed his cell phone and held it up, ready for his moment of Internet glory. Yuri put his handgun back in his jeans. I pushed the ignition button and pressed the gas pedal. In my side mirror, I saw Yuri disappear into the alley at the side of the old stucco building. There was no doubt the police were already on their way. Yuri needed to retrieve Anton's laptop before getting the hell out.

I drove the Volvo through the old industrial neighbourhood and headed south, towards downtown, the McGill Ghetto and an apartment I never thought I would visit again.

CHAPTER 18

I parked Dmitry's car a block and a half away from Theo's apartment. On Aylmer Street, almost at the corner of Prince Arthur. I pulled the hood of my jacket over my head and walked up Lorne Crescent to his home. I saw the porch, painted black, and the window of his bedroom.

I climbed the four stairs to his door and rang the doorbell. I heard the clambering down of feet once again and waited, this time in anticipation of an entirely different kind. How very strange that things looked exactly as they had a few hours earlier but were now so completely different. The door opened and there he was, Theo. In a shirt and a pair of jeans with his hair all messed up. He smiled.

"Hey. You're back," he said.

He leaned over and kissed me. I wished I could believe that moment was real. And I did. I allowed myself to believe it was for a few fleeting seconds. His lips against mine. It made me feel good, the illusion. He closed the door behind me. We went upstairs to his apartment and started to pretend.

"How was it?" he said. "With your mom?"

He knew without a doubt that my mother wasn't sick. Better even, he must have known I didn't have a mother.

"Fine. I mean, they did a CT scan. And some blood tests," I said.

He took me in his arms and kissed me again.

"I'm glad you came back," he said.

These words. They broke something in me. As if a giant mirror had fallen down and smashed into a thousand pieces. And behind it was this guy whose real name I didn't even know. The way he looked me in the eyes as he spoke to me. I peered into his grey blue pupils and saw what he saw. That I hadn't changed my clothes since I'd been to his apartment earlier in the day. That it was possible I didn't even know Alford's USB key was no longer hidden inside my bra. That I may not have realized he had replaced it with an empty one.

I took a step back, pretended I wanted to take off my jacket and threw my fist straight into his solar plexus. I couldn't help it. And I did it just like Yuri had showed me, which is when you hit someone, you imagine your fist passing *through* that person instead of hitting their body. Did I take him by surprise? I absolutely did. But when I hit him, he gasped for air but didn't crumble. He withstood the blow better than I had anticipated. Because he was, of course, in excellent physical shape. But I knew that already. I'd had the pleasure of spending part of the morning in bed with him. The mere thought of it made me see red. As in blood fucking red.

He took a few steps back and brought his arms in front of him, ready for a fight, with his knees slightly bent. His fringe fell over his forehead, half covering those eyes I had fantasized about. Anger exploded inside of me. It rushed to the surface through every cell of my body and erupted like boiling water shooting through the hole of a giant geyser. He had me, this son of a bitch. Like a bait dangled in front of my nose. And I had jumped at him like a naïve little twat. A little *idiotka*. I kicked his fancy torchiere lamp and it fell on the floor of the living room and broke in a resounding crash.

"Easy Nina," he said. "If you make too much noise the neighbours downstairs will call the police."

I pivoted sideways and kicked him in the groin. He blocked me and tried to take a hold of my foot, but I moved back quickly. We faced each other again like two fighters in a ring.

"So, what do you do for a living, Theo? Apart stealing stuff from women you sleep with?"

He attacked me, took two steps forward and tried to hit me. His right fist flew at my face, then his left, then his right again towards the top of my body. I blocked him, twice, and the third time twisted myself just enough to partially absorb the blow. This guy obviously knew how to fight. He knew martial arts. I grabbed a paperweight from the coffee table to my right, a heavy decorative glob of multicolored glass, and threw it at his face. It grazed the left side of his head and flew across the dining room. He reached for a small frame hanging on the wall, a glass plated Ikea clip-on, and threw it at me like a frisbee. I moved out of the way and it exploded against the wall behind me.

"What about the downstairs neighbours, huh? You don't seem too worried about them anymore," I said.

I took two steps forward and threw my right foot under his chin. He moved back. His calves hit the seat of the sofa and he lost his balance for a moment. A tiny fraction of a second, just enough to allow me to move in for the kill. I twisted sideways and drove my elbow into his belly, just below the ribs. He lost his breath and heaved then grabbed my arm and twisted it backward. The pain cut me in half, and I fell to my knees, with Theo pushing his body over mine. I extended my left arm and seized a small table lamp that had fallen on the floor. I hit him in the head with it three times, with the ceramic foot of the lamp pounding the side of his face. He finally let go of me after the third blow. I threw my foot backward and pushed him away then quickly crawled across the room. I turned around, pulled out my handgun and unlocked the safety just as he was about to lunge after me. He stopped and looked at me. There was blood on his lips. He slowly moved backward on his hands and knees to a sitting position and rested his back against the side of the sofa.

"You could have pulled out your gun sooner," he said. "We wouldn't have had to smash this place up."

"Sorry. I needed to get something off my chest."

He dabbed the lower half of his face with the sleeve of his shirt and looked at it.

"Where's the key?" I said.

Theo, or whoever he was, ran his hand through his hair and stared at me. I lowered the butt of the Walther towards his legs. His lifted his right hand in a gesture of appeasement.

"Alright. Calm down. If you shoot me the police will be here in five minutes max. There's no one downstairs but there are some people next door," he said.

"Where is the key?"

"I don't have it anymore. I gave it away."

"To who?" I said.

"To the people I work for. The CIA."

"You're American?"

"Yes."

"I don't believe you. Your French is way too good for that."

"My mother's French Canadian. From Montreal. I spent all my summers up here when I was a kid. My grand-parents had a house on Lake Memphremagog."

"And you just what, happen to be in Montreal?"

"I've been here for a year."

He crossed his arms and bent one of his legs.

"Look. This may come as a surprise to you but there never was any intention on our part to hurt you in any way," he said.

"That's funny. Because someone else said the exact same thing to me an hour ago."

"I don't think that person was telling you the truth. It was me who called your name just before the explosion. I was there. I saved your life."

That voice. I had recognized it. It really had been Theo calling after me. Yuri hadn't come to my rescue after all. That, at least, he hadn't lied about.

"Why are you telling me this?" I said.

"Because I want you to understand that we're not bad people. And that we can look after you."

"In return for what?" I said.

"Everything you know. Look, we've known about Brett Alford for a while. He's been on our watch list for quite some time. When we learnt that he would be attending the G7 summit, we figured he would use that opportunity to pass along some information to someone on the other side. We didn't know what that information was. But we figured it would be passed on to someone who was already here, in Montreal. And our plan was to intervene at the time of the exchange and take you into custody, then offer you a deal. But that plan went belly up when Alford got drunk the night you showed up and decided he wanted to get rid of the key."

"How did you know about me?"

"Your handlers, Irina and Dmitry, are known ex-officers of the SVR. We also know they're not your real parents."

"Ex-officers? You're wrong about that."

"No. We're not. At the very least we can confirm they're not on active duty. We know the three of you came to Montreal as part of the Illegals Program. But the Program was terminated a few years after the arrests of 2010. Why you and your handlers were left in Montreal after the Program was shut down was a complete mystery."

"You don't know what you're talking about."

"I think I do. But that's besides the point. A year ago, we noticed an increase in Russian-based criminal activity in the U.S. Lots of hacking attempts. Lots of unusual chatter. There was a suspicion someone at the State Department was compromised. Alford got onto our radar and with the G7 coming up, we assumed something was in the works. So, we started to pay attention to your little group, in Montreal."

"If you knew so much about what was going on why didn't you intervene to stop the explosion?"

"We didn't know anything about it until the last seconds before the bomb exploded. As soon as we realized you'd managed to get Alford's key back from the front desk, we started to scramble. There were conflicting opinions up our chain of command as to when we should go and grab you. Some people thought we should keep our distance for another twenty-four hours, to see if there were any other people working with you at the G7 we didn't know about. Others thought we shouldn't be wasting any time and just get you out of there, with the flash drive. We started monitoring every email, phone conversation and text message going in and out of the hotel. We also watched what your boyfriend was doing, of course. Dan, the guy you almost turned blind in one eye, kept close to Yuri. And I kept my eyes on you."

"Yuri's not my boyfriend," I said.

"Whatever he is to you is irrelevant. Anyway, the morning of the explosion, Dan saw Yuri leave the hotel in his running gear. So, he followed him to one of the parking lots where he saw him take out a small backpack from your rental car and leave it there, right next to it. Your partner then waited nearby, while pretending to do some stretching exercises. That's when Alford showed up and walked straight to the backpack and picked it up. Dan witnessed the whole thing and called me right away. But then Yuri took off towards the golf course and Dan followed him. I was on the promenade at the time, watching you getting friendly with that journalist. The thing with the president not coming to the summit had just happened a few moments before and all these people were running around and scrambling. But then Alford showed up for the press conference *without* the backpack and I called Dan to tell him to forget about Yuri and to go look for it. We thought that Alford had dropped it off somewhere between the parking lots and the promenade. We didn't know what was in it, but we thought it might have been money."

"And then what?"

"Alford joined the press conference. And you were there, and you moved closer to him, and he saw you. And that's when I understood what you had been looking at, that he seemed to be keeping something under his jacket. But it took me thirty seconds too long. After he looked at you, you moved away almost immediately, and I took out my phone to trigger an alert but right at that moment Alford lost it. He bolted from the podium and tried to go after you. He took off and pushed one of the Secret Service guys who tried to grab him. You had your back turned to the press conference at that point and you didn't see any of it. I shouted your name. And then it was too late."

"Why didn't you come and arrest me when I was unconscious?"

"The blast knocked me out as well. Dan assumed I had you in custody and went after Yuri who he thought was still somewhere inside the red zone. But of course, he wasn't. He killed two men and crossed over the fence. And when I came out of it, you were gone."

"I had nothing to do with the explosion."

"I know. You wouldn't have acted the way you did if you had known about it. No one on our side anticipated anything of the sort either. We didn't expect it because it didn't make any practical sense. And it still doesn't, by the way. That part of the story we're still piecing together. But Yuri definitely has something to do with."

"How did you know it would be me who would be going to the G7?"

"We had some intel that the Russians would be using

someone off the grid, so to speak. A fresh new face. Unknown to any biometrics database. The Agency put a specific tail on you and a couple of others. I was assigned to you six months ago. Could have been worse."

"Spare me."

"Don't be angry. You understand this is part of the job, don't you? This is the work I do."

"Sure. All of it to protect your piece of shit president."

He let out a short, silent laugh.

"Yours isn't much better if I may say so. And if you want to compare notes on corruption and abuse of power, I don't think your side of the fence has any lessons to teach any freely elected government. This isn't about this one person who presently happens to be president of the United States. This is about protecting my country. It's about preventing some corrupt, Russian oligarch from getting his hands on something that would allow him and his friends at the Kremlin to meddle in our internal affairs more effectively than ever before."

"There's no corrupt Russian oligarch. I'm working for the SVR."

"No, you're not. You're working for Ivan Iegorovitch."

I was surprised he knew about Uncle Ivan.

"Ivan Iegorovitch works for the Service," I said.

"Sometimes he does, and sometimes he doesn't. That's the thing about your country. Private interests blend into governmental powers and vice versa. The money scratches the back of the state, and the state does the same to the money."

"Ivan Iegorovitch is not a corrupt oligarch."

"Oh really? How long has it been since you last saw him? Don't you know about the private jet? And about the big house in London and the private island in the Caribbean?" he said.

Uncle Ivan, a wealthy man? Irina and Dmitry had never mentioned it. The image I had kept of him was of a patriot, a loyalist devoted to his country. I was rattled by these revelations of unbridled affluence. He was good, this CIA guy. He knew what to say to get under my skin. In a matter of minutes, he had managed to sow doubt in my mind about some of the things I thought I was so certain of. But Uncle Ivan? I saw him again, sitting behind the director's desk at the orphanage, with his military uniform and his big black mustache that spread sideways as he smiled over a row of white teeth.

"What? You're going to tell me that you didn't know anything about it? That they didn't tell you *anything*? What *did* they tell you, Nina? That you're a full-fledged SVR agent working for the glory of the Russian motherland?"

"Don't call me Nina."

He chuckled.

"We figured at the Agency that they'd kept you in the dark about certain things, but we never knew by how much. You've been told lies about who you are and what you do for a living. All your life. You're not an SVR agent. You never were."

"You're lying," I said.

"No, I'm not. Think about it. How many people at the Service have you ever interacted with? Two? Three at most? The Program was shut down years ago."

"What you're saying doesn't make any sense. Why would Ivan Iegorovitch personally want the USB key?"

"To sell it. There are many people in Russia and elsewhere willing to pay top dollars for that key, including certain people at the Kremlin. So, Ivan Iegorovitch made a deal with the Service. In exchange for some backup and logistical support, he would finance the operation at the G7 summit with his own money and put together his own team to handle it. Then he would share the content of the key with the Service. It was a no brainer. A definite win-win. All that was required was a green light from Central Control and some operational backup."

I looked at him without saying a word. He really was a

pro, this Theo guy. A top-notch manipulator. I admired that about him. He was a damn good agent, one presently subjecting me to the oldest trick in the book. That is, destabilizing me by questioning some of my most profound beliefs. By tearing apart the foundations of some of my innermost convictions. I'd had enough of it.

"Your partner, Dan. Why did he attack me the other night?" I said.

"He didn't. That night he saw you almost at my doorstep and followed you. It was you who attacked him. He was only trying to defend himself."

It was true I had been the one who'd thrown the first punch. Something completely unrelated suddenly crossed my mind.

"How old are you?" I said.

He smiled a sheepish smile.

"Twenty-nine."

What's a girl to do when she's been tricked from A to Z? I had somehow imagined Theo was a year younger than me. And there he was, four years older than I was. It was time to move on and cut my losses. If all good things came to an end on their own, bad things had to be forcibly made to stop. I needed to find the flash drive. That was all that mattered.

"Alright. That's enough. Where's the key?" I said.

"I told you. I don't have it anymore. You can look around all you want," he said.

It was my turn to let out a brief silent laugh. The thought had just crossed my mind that this guy was as good as I was at lying and that I had to do something about it.

"Okay. Slowly, very slowly, I want you to lie face down on the floor and put your hands behind your back," I said.

The object of my short-lived romance did as he was told. I grabbed the cord of the table lamp I had used to hit him in the face and proceeded to tie his wrists together behind his back. I couldn't afford not to tie his feet as well and once I was finished with his upper limbs, I looked around to try and find a rope or a cord of some sort. There weren't any lying about but I noticed a wool scarf hanging on a metal peg next to the entrance.

"Don't move," I said.

I stood up and grabbed it quickly, then came back to finish the job. The scarf was too short for a good solid knot, but I figured it would be enough for what I had in mind.

"So, Theo," I said. "Or whatever your name is. It's not that I don't trust you but sometimes, people get confused about certain things. For example, they think they gave something to someone, but they really haven't. And I just want to make sure that you clearly remember everything about this one thing that is really important to me."

I walked to the kitchen and started to look around. I opened the drawers and the cupboards. I looked under the sink.

"You're wasting your time," he said, from the living room. "I don't have it. And even if you found the flash drive, what would you do with it? Give it to one of those people who lied to you all these years? And then what? Your life here is finished, Nina. They're going to fly you to some sad frozen place from which you'll never be able to leave. I'm offering you a new life. Anywhere in North America. Or even elsewhere if that's what you want. Under a new name."

"Stop talking."

"Why do you think none of the news networks know you even exist? Because we didn't tell them about you. No one did. We wanted to give you a second chance. To cut a deal and to disappear. To live free, for the rest of your life. If you tell me you've never dreamed about this, I won't believe you."

I tried not to listen. So far, I had found a couple of good pointy knives, some Clorox and a box of matches. I put all these things on the kitchen counter and walked back to my prisoner with a chair I picked up in the dining room.

"Don't move," I said.

"By the way, did you know your boyfriend was in the United States when he disappeared for two months in March? I bet they didn't tell you about that. And the fact that he travelled around. Moved from one city to another, stayed for a few days. We know he visited some Russian defectors, but we don't know why he did it. Did you know anything about that?"

"Shut up."

"One of the people he visited is Oleg Kozlov. One of the crazy ones who insist on living openly under their Russian names. Him and your boyfriend had dinner at a fancy restaurant. I wonder what they talked about. Any idea about that, Nina?"

Back in the kitchen I cut the cord of the espresso machine with a bread knife and took it and the other things I had placed on the counter to the living room. I dropped my kit on the armchair and took a few steps back.

"Alright. I want you to bring yourself to a sitting position," I said. "Then slowly, very slowly, I want you to get up and sit on the chair."

He did this in less that five seconds, dragging the table lamp behind him on the floor as he moved towards the chair. He was nimble alright, this American spy, and I realized I was lucky to have found a scarf to tie his feet.

He looked at the things I had placed on the armchair.

"What, you're going to try to make me talk? You're going to hurt me? I told you. The key is no longer here. I delivered it at the US consulate half an hour after you left."

I took the cord from the espresso machine and circled around him at a good distance as he sat on the chair, a wood model with four vertical spindles at the back.

"I want you to press your wrists against the back of the chair so that I can tie your hands to it," I said. "If you make any movement whatsoever while I'm doing it, I swear will shoot you."

"Knock yourself out," he said.

I lowered myself on one knee behind the chair, as far away from it as I could, and placed the Walther on the floor. I passed the cable of the espresso machine between the wooden rods and around the electrical cord that already held his wrists. I did this twice, then tied a knot around the spindles. As soon as I was done, I picked up the Walther and quickly moved away.

I went back to the armchair and faced him. He looked up at me. A half smile lifted the corners of his mouth.

"Fancy you tying me up like this," he said.

How could I not have fallen for him? I looked at the paraphernalia I had assembled and suddenly felt very tired. What was I supposed to do with it? Cut his fingers? Burn his toes? Getting into a fight was one thing, but the thought of torturing someone took the wind out of my sails. Literally, I felt deflated. And to be honest, I wasn't as angry as I had been a few minutes before.

My CIA friend sensed it immediately.

"You should have seen your face when I told you I was going to the G7 to take part in a protest," he said.

We stared at each other for a second and smiled, briefly. I took a few steps back and sat on the sofa. We stared at each other again, two professional liars taking a breather. I tried to hate him, but I couldn't.

"What was it like, growing up in an orphanage?" he said.

"Unremarkable."

"Listen, regardless of everything that's happened, I want you to know that I always liked you. As a person. And I wish you would think about the offer I made you earlier. To come over to our side."

I didn't say anything. My mind had shifted back to neutral. I was exhausted and I couldn't think straight.

"You know, those people you trusted, they could have

gotten rid of you as soon as you would have given them the key," he said.

"Are you implying that you saved my life a second time by stealing it?"

"I probably did."

The human heart is a sad excuse of a mystery. Was it possible I still had feelings for someone who had lied to me so thoroughly? If I did then, surely, I was in need of a good psychiatrist. I wasn't sure I wanted to leave anymore. I didn't know where I should go. A new life in North America? Surely there was a price attached to that. I hesitated, but the sound of a door being shut interrupted my thinking. Someone had opened and closed the front door of Theo's apartment and a second later I heard footsteps coming up the stairs. I rose to my feet and gestured to Theo, or whoever he was, to keep quiet, then hid behind the door.

"Dan, watch out!" he said.

Whoever was coming up the staircase violently pushed open the door and it swung back and hit me. I jumped out of my hiding place and came face to face with the man with the eye patch. My assailant of the other night stood there and stared at me, his face an expression of complete surprise. His right hand disappeared under his coat as he reached for his weapon, and I lifted my arm and shot him. I'm not sure I wanted to kill him, and I instinctively directed my shot at his shoulder. He screamed and twisted sideways but still managed to pull out his gun. I moved forward to try and kick him, but he was quicker this time. He lifted his right arm and shot me as my foot hit him in the groin. A searing pain travelled through the upper part of my left arm. I punched him in the shoulder with the butt of my handgun, right at the spot where blood had started to ooze on the outside of his coat, and he grunted and bent forward and tried to grab me.

A cold sweat washed over me for a second that seemed to last a very long time and my vision briefly turned to black and white. I was about to pass out but knew I couldn't let that happen. I had to get out of there, or at the very least try. I kicked and pushed the man away and hurtled down the staircase, almost tumbling down its lower end. I shoved the gun inside my coat pocket and ran outside of the house. The fresh air brought me back to life and I staggered onto the sidewalk then found my footing and started to walk away as fast as I could. I was bleeding and my left arm felt warm and wet inside the sleeve of my jacket.

I walked back to the Volvo, opened its rear door and sat on the back seat, where I closed my eyes for a moment and took a few deep breaths. I heard people talking and opened them up. A couple of students shuffled past the car. Someone else was coming. An older man walking his mongrel dog. People minding their own business on a late Friday afternoon. I moved across the leather seat to the street side of the car to avoid attracting the attention of the strollers and carefully slid off my jacket. I pulled out my left arm from the sleeve of my hoodie and took a look at it.

There was plenty of blood but no severe injury. The bullet had cut a gash in the muscle at the top of my arm, just below the shoulder. It seemed to have gone in and out, without touching a bone or any major blood vessel. A flesh wound, nothing more, but one that did a fair bit of bleeding. I reached inside the bag I had packed, which lay on the floor behind the driver's seat, and took out the t-shirt. I draped it around the top of my arm and held it tightly in place with my right hand. I needed something to keep it wrapped firmly around my arm. Some kind of bandage. Ideally, some medical tape.

I thought of the pharmacy at the corner of Sherbrooke and Avenue du Parc, a three-minute ride by car. A large mega-store open around the clock. I pulled my clothes down over my injured arm without passing it through the sleeve of my hoodie and got out of the car to change seats. I felt slightly nauseous and took a few deep breaths then started the engine and signaled my way out of my parking place.

I lowered my window to get some fresh air. Beyond getting some much-needed medical supplies I wasn't sure what to do next. I didn't have the flash drive. It was gone. But I could still try to contact Uncle Ivan for help and the best way to do it was probably through the Russian consulate. It was my very last hope, regardless of what Theo had said earlier about him in his apartment. If I reached out to Uncle Ivan, I would perhaps have a chance at being rescued. And if that failed, as had pretty much everything else over the past forty-eight hours, I would have no alternative than to go back to the Americans and cut a deal with them.

I drove down Avenue du Parc and turned left at a green light at the corner of Sherbrooke. The pharmacy was immediately around the corner. I knew there was an alley behind it used by delivery trucks, and I went there and parked the car. I walked to the front of the pharmacy as I held my jacket tightly over my arm, and went in.

Past the turnstile a garish display of gift boxes and a giant sparkling Mother's Day banner greeted me in all sorts of pink tones. Thankfully the store was almost empty, and I started to amble up and down the aisles under ambient Muzak and unnatural white light.

Boxes of chocolates were in the first aisle, with all kinds of assorted nuts and chips, wish cards and stationery. Toothbrushes and toothpaste were in aisle number three. Medicinal products in aisle number five and halfway up the next one, in aisle number six, I finally found what I was looking for. A roll of flesh-coloured elastic band, a thick packet of gauze, a bottle of peroxide and some medical tape. I assembled my wound-nursing kit and returned to aisle number four to pick a box of hair dye. Natural black, nothing fancy.

"Carte de points?"

The woman at the cash register wanted to know if I had a points card.

"No," I said.

She started to scan my purchases without giving me the time of day.

"Twenty-two fifty-three."

The cashier didn't give a damn about my blood-stained jacket, my puffy lip and the purple spot on my cheek where the foundation had long faded away. In truth, she probably cared about very little, something I would have done myself if I had spent my days as she did, behind a cash register with a name tag that proclaimed she was '*votre ami(e)*' pinned to her uniform.

I took out my debit card and tapped it on the terminal.

"Need a bag?" she said.

I felt dizzy and wanted some fresh air. I grabbed the plastic bag with my purchases in it and headed towards the door, then hurried around the corner and into the alley. I suddenly felt exhausted, as if my legs could no longer support me. I stopped and rested for a moment against the brick wall of a building. My body had been drained of its last reserve of fuel.

I looked at the Volvo, parked at the end of the alley. It seemed incredibly far but I managed to walk to it, then opened the driver's door and sat behind the wheel. I closed the door and turned on the engine. The alley veered right, ten meters ahead of my parking spot, and continued all the way to Milton. I drove the car past a series of spray-painted concrete and brick walls and turned left on Milton. Where was I supposed to go now? The Russian consulate? I didn't feel well at all, and I also needed a change of clothes. Perhaps I could call Markus and ask him and Jacques to help me and take me there. It didn't matter anymore if they understood who I really was. Or maybe I just needed to rest for a while, inside the car. One way or another I couldn't drive any further.

I parked the car on a section of Durocher reserved for permit holders, fifty meters down the street from my apartment, and sat there and closed my eyes. I tried calling Markus but got his voice mail. I looked up the street. There seemed to be no one lurking about my home. I waited some more and after about ten minutes, I saw Jacques walk down the staircase of their house. He reached the sidewalk and started to walk away from where I was parked. I couldn't let that happen. I needed to speak to him. I opened the door of the Volvo.

"Jacques!"

He didn't hear me. I stepped out of the car to try and follow him. I took a few steps and realized I felt dizzy again and couldn't go on. I leaned against a parked car next to me. I looked down on the sidewalk and a cold sweat broke on my forehead and at the back of my neck. I lifted my eyes and saw that the street and everything around me had gone to black and white again, like an old photograph. A high-pitched noise started to ring inside my ears. It grew louder and I knew I was about to lose consciousness, alone, on the sidewalk. I tried to take a step forward, but I couldn't, and I leaned against the parked car again.

There was a man on the sidewalk ahead of me who started to walk quickly towards me. He wore a baseball cap and a short black coat. I rested my head against the roof of the car, and he started to run. His silhouette became a growing blur. I felt my knees buckle and I closed my eyes. My body started to crumple but someone caught a hold of me. I opened my eyes again and peered under a baseball cap at eyes the color of the bluest sky. For a moment, I thought I was looking into a mirror. These eyes. They were my own.

CHAPTER 19

"Is she okay? Do you need any help?"

I regained consciousness and instinctively felt for the Walther inside the side pocket of my coat. I was sitting on the sidewalk, propped up against the front tire of a parked car. I placed my hands back on the ground. There were small rocks underneath them, some minute gravel that pressed against the skin of my palms. My legs lay stretched out in front of me, inert, like the limbs of a mannequin. A man I didn't know had lowered himself to my right on a bent knee. I looked up at the voice. It belonged to a woman who stood to my left against the rainy sky. A well-dressed woman in a fitted beige raincoat, with brown hair and red lipstick. She held a briefcase in her hand and stared at me with an air of concern.

"It's alright. Thank you. She'll be fine."

The man next to me had spoken in a calm baritone voice. I turned my head to look at him. Small wrinkles creased the skin at the corners of his eyes. Deeper lines rose vertically between his brows which were only slightly arched, almost horizontal. His hair was light brown, mixed with some grey, from what I could see under his baseball cap. His lips were average in size. The mouth of a man, with folds that marked his age and descended on the sides of his chin.

He smiled a reassuring smile at the woman and my heart started to beat faster. Whoever this man was, I could tell he was putting on a show to try to reassure the woman in the raincoat. He wasn't just a passerby. I could see him thinking as he looked at her and measured her reactions. Pieces of my brain started to click back into place, and I knew all of a sudden that he was the man I had chased down the street a few nights before. The man who had left me the article of The New York Times, the scribbled note and the birth certificate.

"Are you sure?" the woman said.

"Absolutely. My daughter's diabetic. I got this," he said.

My daughter? He gave her an even warmer smile. The woman hesitated. She waved her manicured hand and pointed a red-fingered nail at me.

"She's obviously injured. She's bleeding."

If I wanted to let the woman know I needed help, now was the time. But then what? Was I going to ask her to call the police?

"I'm actually taking her to the hospital," the man said. "We're going right away."

I dragged my right foot closer to me and used my right hand to try to lift my body off the ground. The man rose and stuck a hand under my right arm to assist me. I placed one foot on the ground, then the other. The woman looked on as I steadied myself.

"Alright," the woman said. "You do that."

The man held me up in a firm grip. I could feel the strength of his muscles against my right side. He was taller than I was, about the same size as Theo. I took a few tentative steps. The woman looked at us then started to walk away in the opposite direction, towards downtown. I wasn't strong enough to push the man off me and I couldn't run either, not in the condition I was in. But more than that, I wasn't sure I even wanted to. But I firmly pulled my right shoulder from his grasp. He took a step back and stared at me. He must have been around fifty years old.

"Don't be afraid," he said. "I'm not going to hurt you."

Another one. I had never met this man before yet something about his voice, the way he stood and looked at me, felt oddly familiar. I tried to think about where I could have seen him before, other than the other night but my head felt light-headed, as if my brain had been replaced by a helium gas balloon.

"Who are you?" I said.

"Most people know me as Michael Ellis. And before that I was known as David Jankowski. But my real name is Nikolaï Grigorievitch Belinski."

I stopped breathing for a moment then gasped for air as if I had swum underwater and finally reached the surface of a pool. Nikolaï Belinski. The man mentioned in the article of The New York Times. And Jankowski, the name found on the birth certificate of a little girl born in Bethesda, twenty-five years earlier. A girl my age. Possibly me.

"What do you want?" I said.

"I wanted to find you. And I have. I've found you."

"You're Russian?"

"Yes," he said.

"They talked about you in that article in The New York Times, a long time ago. In 1995."

"Yes, they did."

"It was you who left me the article in the restaurant?"

"It was me."

"And the note and the birth certificate that you gave to Markus, my neighbour?"

"Yes. That was also me."

"Why are you doing this?"

"Because I wanted you to understand," he said.

"To understand what?"

"That I've been looking for you for the past twenty-four years."

The entire universe came to a halt. As did time, which stopped. And I stood there, caught up in a moment that didn't seem to have an end nor a beginning. I knew what he was going to say next. Different emotions rose inside me and fought one another. Fear, elation, suspiciousness. His lips moved and he said the words I had been secretly waiting for.

"And that I'm your father," the man said.

His words hit me almost physically. I was shaken but I didn't cry. I was too washed-out, too tired. The man looked up the street behind me and I did the same. The woman in the beige raincoat had returned, probably unconvinced I would be taken care of and suspicious I was in some kind of danger. She was standing about thirty meters away from us, her cell phone glued to her ear.

"We have to go," the man said.

He took hold of my arm again and we walked towards the Volvo.

"Give me the key," he said.

I reached inside my pocket and gave it to him. He unlocked the car and sat me on the passenger seat.

"Where are we going?" I said.

"To my place."

Nikolaï Belinski drove the Volvo up Durocher and across Prince-Arthur Street, over a distance of no more than a block and a half, then turned right into a narrow lane a few meters before the next street corner. I stared at him in disbelief. We had been in Dmitry's car for less than five minutes. If this was really where he lived, it was a mere ten-minute walk from my place. No wonder he had been able to follow me around and stroll by my living room windows so often and so easily.

Nikolaï parked the car behind a tall unkept fence of wood planks and pointed to a large apartment building to our left, a six storeys high beaux-arts style property in limestone and bricks the colour of sand.

"This is it", he said. "Airbnb. I moved in four weeks ago."

He reached for the door handle.

"Wait," I said.

He looked at me. I wasn't absolutely certain if I should trust this man who said he was my father. But then again, I didn't have much of a choice.

"How did you find me? And when you did find me, why didn't you just come and talk to me?"

"I was told that you were in Montreal by another Russian, a defector who lives in the United States. Not someone I know very well, and not someone I trust. And the way he contacted me was very suspicious. But he showed me your photograph and I knew right away that it had to be you. So, even though I suspected this could be some kind of trap, I had no choice but to come and find you. That's why I couldn't simply ring your doorbell or meet you for coffee in a restaurant. I may be in danger here. And from what I understand, so are you."

"What was his name, the defector?"

"Oleg Kozlov."

I bristled.

"Oleg Kozlov? That's the man Yuri met with when he went to the United States a few weeks ago."

"Is Yuri the big blond guy I saw sneak into your apartment the other night?"

"Yes."

"And you're saying he met with Kozlov *before* Kozlov told me about you? So, he was the one who told Kozlov where I could find you. How do you know about this?"

"I didn't. Not until about an hour ago."

"Was it Yuri who told you?"

"No. A CIA guy. But he never mentioned you. He said they weren't sure why Yuri had met with Kozlov."

"You met with the CIA?"

"I didn't know he was CIA until about two hours ago."

"So, it's true the Agency really is after you."

"Why do you say that?"

"Almost immediately after I arrived here, I realized you were being followed. And then someone in Montreal, someone I trust, told me the CIA had probably been keeping a tab on you for some time. He couldn't say why they were doing it. Just that you'd been under surveillance since last September, when you went back to university. Your adoptive parents, they're SVR agents, aren't they?"

"Yes."

"That's what I thought. Listen, we really shouldn't stay in the car. Let's go inside."

I didn't say anything.

"Look," he said. "I understand this is a lot to digest and you're right about being careful. But I swear I'm not going to hurt you."

"Okay."

I grabbed the plastic bag with the hair dye and the first-aid supplies, and we got out of the car and walked around the big apartment block to its front entrance on Avenue des Pins. The building, a pre-war high-end property, sat across the street from McGill's Molson Stadium and the university's athletic facilities. Immediately behind the stadium, the forested slopes of Mount Royal gently rolled uphill towards its low summit.

Nikolaï opened a first set of doors with thick rectangular windows to let me through, and I staggered inside the entry-way, completely spent. It was risky for me to follow him inside his apartment even though I had decided to trust him, but I had most definitely run out of gas, and of any better options. I was injured, exhausted and badly needed a place to stay. I was willing to roll the dice and quietly hope for the best.

My would-be father typed a code on a numbered keypad and a lock on a second set of doors started to buzz and clicked open. I followed him across a marbled-floor lobby and into a corridor to the right, at ground level, where he stopped in front of a door almost at the end of it. Number seven. Perhaps a harbinger of good luck. He pulled a key from his pocket and opened it, then dropped it on a small table in the entrance and shut us in.

"You must be hungry. Let's go sit in the kitchen," he said.

The apartment was tastefully decorated in clean, Scandistyle furniture. The layout of the place surprised me. It looked like the inside of a real house, with a living room, a dining room and what I guessed were two bedrooms, set at different angles along a narrow corridor. There was a lot of extra space in the apartment that served no specific purposes, something today's real estate developers would never consider, and every room seemed to have its own set of windows. The kitchen was at the back of the apartment. It wasn't particularly large but was big enough to accommodate a table and four chairs. All of it painted white, as was the kitchen itself.

I sat at the table with my hand resting instinctively on the Walther inside my coat pocket.

"Here," he said. "Have some orange juice."

He poured me a glass and placed it on the table. It dawned on me that it must have been dinner time and that I was famished. I drank the entire glass and realized I must have been dehydrated as well. My host opened the fridge again and placed some bread, some liver *pâté* and a jug of filtered water on the table. I started to eat while he looked on, his blue eyes full of curiosity and restrained tenderness. If this man was an actor pretending to be my father, he was a damn good one.

"I should look at your arm," he said.

He rose from his chair and came closer to me. I pulled the gun from my blood-stained jacket and held it on my lap. He saw it but said nothing then helped me take off my jacket and lifted the left side of my hoodie. He carefully removed the t-shirt I had wrapped around my wound, which was crusted with dried blood, and looked at the torn flesh at the top of my arm.

"It's not that bad," he said.

I reached for the plastic bag that lay at my feet and placed it on the table.

"I bought some stuff for it."

He opened a drawer and took out a pair of scissors and for the next few minutes wiped my wound clean and bandaged it tightly, using the medical tape and the gauze I had purchased at the pharmacy. He finished the job by wrapping the elastic band tightly around it.

"There," he said.

He turned away to wash his hands at the sink, then filled an electric kettle and put it on.

"I'll make us some tea. Then you should take a shower and get some rest."

There was no question I looked like a scruffy alley cat. My hair was dirty and my armpits smelled. Nikolaï opened a cupboard. He held out a box of tea bags and looked at me.

"Darjeeling," he said. "Marina's favourite."

The color of his eyes seemed to have changed for an instant, like the ocean does when clouds momentarily race across the sun. He came back to the table with two cups and sat down again, across from me.

"Marina, she was my mother?" I said.

I already knew the answer to that question, and he knew that I knew it, too. My would-be father took a small sip of his burning tea.

"I'm going to tell you everything," he said.

He hesitated.

"Katyusha," I said.

He nodded and placed both hands around his cup, sat back on his chair and lifted his eyes at me.

"I was sent by the Service to the United States in 1992. To New York. At the time, it was the easiest place to pass through customs. I'd never been to the West before. They had sent me to Kiev, to Berlin and to Prague. I'd also been to Kabul for a few weeks when they were pulling out the troops. But never across the iron curtain, or what was left of it. It was a big deal. I had to prepare for that trip. In Moscow, they had us act these little scenes where we would interact with agents pretending to be Americans."

He smiled.

"They were absolutely terrible," he said.

He took another sip of tea.

"But nothing can really prepare you for New York when you've lived all your life in the Soviet Union. The shock of it. The noise, the crowds, the yellow cabs. All these different people from all over the world. As if every nationality on the entire planet had at least one representative there, in that city. It blew me away."

"How old were you?" I said.

"Twenty-five. But when my plane landed at Kennedy Airport, I felt like a ten-year-old kid. You know, growing up in Moscow, in the seventies, it was a different world. Comrade Brezhnev never got the supply chains to work properly. We had to wait in line for everything. To buy some meat, some vegetables. A piece of cheese. The lines started at five in the morning. In winter, people would relay one another so that they wouldn't freeze their feet waiting for what they needed to buy."

"You waited in line too?"

"Sure. I waited with my mother or my father. And yet at the same time the country fought costly proxy wars in faraway places, as did the United States. In Central America, in Afghanistan. The Soviet government presented the world to its citizens as a simple dichotomy. Us versus them. A duality that worked just as well on the American side."

"But you decided to join the Service."

"I wanted to be a translator. The KGB recruited me when

227

I was a student at Moscow's State University. Back then, the KGB was prestigious. The most successful organization in the world at collecting foreign intelligence. What the country lacked in tanks and planes it made up for with its spy network. I was excited to work for them. I thought I was lucky to have been chosen."

"That was how many years before they sent you to New York?"

"Three years. They recruited me when I was twenty-two. And almost right away they sent me to Kiev. It was a short assignment. Things were getting pretty crazy in Eastern Europe. The entire region was unstable. Everything was changing so fast. The year before, East and West Germany had reunited. And now Gorbachev was in power, and the people had started to get a taste for freedom."

"And you didn't?"

"I wanted to serve my country. You see, what the West focused on at the time and what was really happening in the Soviet Union were two different things."

"What do you mean?"

"The people in the West saw the Berlin wall tumble, they saw the German people celebrate the reunification of Germany. Then Gorbachev started to talk about *perestroïka* and they saw delirious crowds into the streets of Moscow. All at once, everyone thought that the Cold War was over and that the West had won. But that's not really what happened. The structure of power remained largely intact in the Soviet Union, even though it was officially dissolved in 1991. The Russian secret service kept a low profile and waited for the right moment to get back into business. And then, it realized that this period of change presented perhaps the greatest opportunity of all time to stick it to the Americans."

"Because they no longer cared?"

"They still cared. But they got busy some other places. They relaxed their focus on Eastern Europe and went all in on

Saddam Hussein. The greater concerns of the CIA shifted to the Middle East and to South America. *Perestroïka* created an illusion of peace with the Russian state, an eye in the center of a hurricane. The KGB disappeared and the Foreign Intelligence Service was created in its place."

"And that's when they sent you to the US?"

"Exactly. That's when they sent me to *Amerika*."

Nikolaï took a sip of tea.

"I arrived in the U.S. in September and my instructions were to go straight to Brooklyn, as soon as I landed, to meet with a contact there. Another agent named Carlos. So, I left the airport and took the A Train. It was packed with people, and I was stuck at the end of a compartment with my back pressed against the wall. The train started to move and then these kids started to play some music on an enormous radio, this huge ghetto-blaster. And then they started to breakdance on the cabin's floor. And I just stood there, completely mesmerized. I'd never seen anything like it."

He chuckled.

"So, I finally made it to the right station, and I bolted outside with my suitcase, up the narrow staircase and onto the street. And then I was in Brooklyn. Another big shock. Because at the time, it really wasn't the prime real estate location it's become today. It wasn't as *nice*. You didn't see all these nannies crossing the streets with little kids. It was a melting pot of the amazing and the terrible. Everything humanity had to offer, stuck together in a heap, from the striving to the desperate. And of course, I'd never seen so many shops so close to one another. There was a shop that sold mattresses, next to another one that sold jewelry, and then another one that sold clothes. And then there was a doughnut shop with all these different doughnuts in the window. A shop that sold only doughnuts. I didn't even know such a thing existed."

"Was Carlos not supposed to come and meet you?"

"I met him at his apartment. He lived there, in Bedford-

Stuyvesant. He was a super-friendly guy. His father was Polish and his mother Salvadoran. As soon as I came in, he brought out two shot glasses of vodka. I'll never forget what he said to me. He lifted his glass and said 'Amigo, welcome to the kingdom of imperialism.'"

The image of it made me smile.

"Spoken like a true *guerrillero*," I said.

"Absolutely."

"And then what happened?"

"Carlos gave me my new identity papers. An American passport, my social security number, and a driving licence. My new name was David Jankowski, a NYU graduate. He then explained to me that I was leaving by train the next day to go to Washington D.C., to meet with another agent there. A woman. And that I was supposed to move in with her as if we were a couple."

"You didn't know any of this when you left Moscow?"

"No. It was like that on purpose. So that if I ever got caught, I wouldn't have anything interesting to say."

"And you took the train?"

"The next morning as I was supposed to. I went to Pennsylvania Station and I took a train to Washington D.C. On the train, I looked through the documents Carlos had given me more carefully. There was a map and some additional information about who I was and about my background. Stuff I was supposed to learn by heart. There was also a photograph of the woman I was supposed to meet. Marina Serov. She looked very serious on the photograph. She had pale skin and dark hair. I thought she looked pretty but nothing more. Do you want some more tea?"

"No thanks. I'm fine."

"In Washington, I took the Metro to Bethesda station. And again, it was a completely different experience. Bethesda was this quaint suburb with nice trees and beautiful houses with lawns and flowers. Completely different from Brooklyn. I pulled out the instructions Carlos had given me, and I walked to her place, which was close to the station. I found the right address and rung the doorbell. And your mother answered."

"And?"

"She didn't say anything at first, she just looked at me, because I just stood there with my mouth open. Have you ever seen the movie The Godfather?"

"I don't think so."

"Well, there's a scene in that movie when Michael Corleone, the central character, goes to Italy and falls in love with a girl in Sicily."

"Okay."

"He sees her one day, by chance, and he's thunderstruck and immediately wants to marry her. That's what happened to me with Marina. She opened that door and I fell in love with her, right off the bat."

"But you'd seen her photograph. On the train."

"I had. But when I saw her in person it was completely different. Her eyes were like two pieces of grey ice with some blue in it. She was ten times more beautiful than on the photo. She looked at me and it was like an electric jolt hit the inside of my head."

"And what about her? Did she like you?"

"She obviously thought I was some kind of idiot at first. I managed to say that I was David Jankowski and I put out my hand for a handshake. And she grabbed me and my suitcase and pulled me inside. Because she and I were supposed to be a couple and couples don't shake hands at the door, obviously."

"That's funny."

"Yeah. A couple of days later we were able to laugh about it."

"When she started to like you?"

"That took a while longer, but it was fine. It gave us time to get to know each other. We started visiting Washington together, by bus and metro. Marina's American name was

Carolyn Brown and we had to get used to calling each other Carolyn and David."

"I know. Name changes are tricky."

"They really are. So, Carolyn took David to the Air and Space Museum and to the Museum of Natural History, right across the Mall. And to Georgetown, to the Lincoln Memorial and the National Zoo."

"She liked museums?"

"She *loved* museums. You see, part of her job was to help me get used to my new life in the United States. To understand what Americans like to do and what food they like to eat. She took me shopping so that I would get comfortable interacting with people. And at night we watched Seinfeld together and Monday Night Football. We had the best of time."

"How old was she, Marina?"

"She was twenty-six at the time. A year older than me. She'd been in Washington for nine months, which is plenty of time to get used to it. She was originally from Novossibirsk, in Siberia. She grew up there and went to the local university."

"Didn't the two of you do any work? Surely the Service must have had a reason for sending you there."

"Oh, sure. I had my first meeting with our handler, Vladimir Politchev, two weeks after my arrival in D.C. Politchev was the officer in charge of the Service in Washington. He was a director at the Eurasia Center on Massachusetts Avenue, which meant that he didn't have to hide his Russian nationality. He was a big man with a bad temper. Ten years older than I was. Carlos had warned me about his bad reputation, so I knew what to expect. We met for the first time in a room at the back of a store, a dry cleaner. And right away I knew that something had happened between him and Marina."

"How did you know?"

"By the way he looked at her when she turned her back to

him. Also the way he would touch her, for just a bit too long, when he would be near her. I pretended not to see anything. I figured that it was over and that I had to accept the situation as it was. Everyone has a past, I did too."

"But then you and Marina started being together, as a real couple."

"We did. We became a real couple in November, on Thanksgiving."

He paused.

"But yeah, I started to work for Politchev. We both did."

"Doing what?"

"Surveillance work almost exclusively. We met with Politchev regularly, usually twice a month, so he could give us our instructions. For the most part, we took photographs of certain people and certain places and mapped out routes that could be used by other agents for purposes we were never told about. During the week, Marina and I worked at a small company that offered conference-room booking services in and around D.C. Of course, it was a front business. We were the only two employees."

"Did Politchev know that you and Marina had developed feelings for each other?"

"Yes. At a certain point, he knew. The man was no fool. Our meetings with him were never pleasant but once he knew that we liked each other, he became even more abrupt, even with Marina. He was rude to her and berated her over nothing. What I failed to see, at the time, was how angry and jealous he was. And then one day he requested that Marina come to a meeting alone. When she came home later that day, I realized that we were in trouble. Politchev had told her that she belonged to him only and to the Service, regardless of her feelings for me. He said that if he wanted, he could send her away to another posting almost immediately. All he needed was to make a phone call."

"What did you do?"

"I was angry. And worried. And I was right to be worried because the following week Politchev tried to have me killed."

"He did? How?"

"He sent me on a mission to Annapolis, to meet with an instructor from the Naval Academy. The meeting was in a parking lot and the man was waiting for me in his car. I pulled up next to him and rolled down my window and saw that he'd been drinking. The guy just sat there and looked at me and the next thing I knew he was aiming a gun at me. He had it with him, on his lap. He fired his gun at me, but he was drunk and he missed. I stomped on the gas pedal. A second later he shot himself in the face. There was blood all over the inside of his car."

"You think Politchev did this on purpose?"

"I'm sure he did. He must have known the meeting was risky and he sent me there anyway."

"What did you do about it?"

"Nothing. There was nothing I could do. But then we got lucky."

"What do you mean?"

"Politchev suddenly lost interest in us. From one week to the next, his focus was gone. The meetings got shorter. He barely gave us any work. What I learnt later was that he had become involved with another agent. A woman we never met. And for a while, he no longer cared about Marina and me."

"How long did it last?"

He smiled.

"Long enough for you to be born. When we told him that Marina was pregnant, he was pissed off, obviously, but the Service reacted favourably overall. They figured that us having a child would reinforce our cover. That it would allow us to develop friendships with other parents and eventually take part in play dates, sleepovers and parents-teacher meetings. They saw it as a golden opportunity for us to anchor ourselves in the community. They even bought us a house, not far from the apartment. A nice bungalow, all clean and proper. We moved in four months after you were born, and immediately became friends with our neighbours. We became Americans."

"And then what happened?"

Nikolaï inhaled deeply.

"I guess our luck ran out."

He took a sip of tea.

"Not long after your first birthday, Politchev asked Marina to come and meet him alone one night, during the week. It was highly unusual, and we didn't know what to make of it. Marina didn't want to go. She didn't trust Politchev and knew he was up to something. But in the end, she had no choice but to go and meet with him. So, I stayed home with you, and I waited for her. And then she came back much sooner than I expected. And the minute she walked in I knew something terrible had happened. She had marks on her face and her shirt buttons were ripped. She told me that Politchev had tried to rape her. That he was drunk when she showed up at their meeting place and almost immediately made a pass at her. She resisted him and he grew more insistent. They fought. She told me she'd scratched him on the cheeks and used one of her shoes to hit him in the face. I knew right away that we were in danger and that we had to run. If we stayed put, we would probably be dead in the next twenty-four hours. Or we would be separated, forever."

"What a sick motherfucker."

"Sure, you can say that. But then again, the world is full of awful people. It's when they have power that you see them for who they really are. So, that night after Marina came home, I took the car and I drove to a phone booth at the Metro station. And I called the FBI."

"You didn't think you could make it on your own?"

"No. They would have found us eventually. We needed protection. The FBI told me to pack my things and to meet them with my family in two hours at the indoor parking garage at Union Station. I drove back home and Marina and I got out of the house as fast as we could. We arrived at the parking lot ten minutes early and I parked the car on level four, as we'd agreed on the telephone. When the two cars with the FBI agents showed up, I thought we were finally safe. I thought we had made it. But as soon as they got out, a van came speeding up the ramp and everyone took cover. Three men got out of the van and started to shoot. One of the FBI agents was hit, and I ran up to him and took his gun, to try to help the others. Another car came circling around the floor of the garage and caught us from behind. Marina saw it and she tried to run out of our car with you in her arms. Some shots were fired. I saw her fall face down on the pavement. The way she fell, up to the last moment, she protected you. I screamed and I tried to get to her, but the men in the van were still shooting at us. And then this woman got out of the second car and took you. And then everything was over. The van and the car left. They took you with them in the car and left."

Outside the apartment, daylight had started to dim. Nikolaï rose from his chair and poured more water in the electric kettle. He leaned against the faux-marble counter of his rental's kitchen and stared at the window. His eyes were as dark as I imagined his thoughts to be.

"Is that when she died, Marina?"

He looked at me with the sad gaze of the broken-hearted.

"Yes. That's when they killed her. In the parking garage."

"What happened to Politchev?"

"They got him. I told the FBI where to find him and they arrested him. He was getting ready to leave the country."

"And then what happened?"

"I became Michael Ellis."

"You started working for the Americans?"

"I did, at first. I don't anymore. I'm a university professor. I teach eastern European history at the University of California. In Santa Barbara. They check on me once a month. To see that I'm alright. And right at this moment, I imagine they must be looking for me."

"Why do you think Yuri wanted you to come to Montreal?"

"I don't know. Revenge, maybe? I really don't know but it can't be something good. The Russians never forget. And Kozlov is one of the weird ones. Always looking for an edge to walk on. Guys like that are addicted to living dangerously."

He poured himself another cup of tea.

"So, let me guess. They trained you, didn't they? The Service? All this time you were with them?" he said.

"Yes. They did."

"And your adoptive parents, they got you involved in what happened at the G7?"

"Yes."

"I feared they would be using you."

He looked at the bruises on my face.

"Is that how you got beaten up, at the G7?"

"In part," I said. "By the way, it was you wasn't it, who came to my rescue on the street the other night?"

He chuckled.

"Yeah. That was me. How's that for paternal instinct?"

I smiled but then thought about Theo and about my assailant.

"The man you punched in the face works for the CIA. He was at the G7," I said.

"Really? Then they must have known you were coming."

"They did."

"What did you do exactly, at the G7?" my father said.

"Yuri and I were sent there to collect a flash drive from a member of the U.S. delegation."

"What was on the flash drive?"

"Photographs of the American president having sex with young girls."

"Mitchell Baker? The president of the United States?"

237

My father's eyes grew larger and he let out a long whistle.

"It happened thirty years ago," I said.

"And you got it? The flash drive?"

"Yes. It didn't go exactly according to plan. But I got it. And then it was stolen from me."

"By who?"

"The same CIA guy I told you about earlier. Not the one you punched in the face."

My father raised his eyebrows and took a sip of tea.

"But why the explosion?" he said.

"I don't know. I wasn't told anything about it before it happened. Yuri said it was to make my escape more difficult. I don't understand why he said that. All I know is that it was him who gave the explosives to Alford, the American with the flash drive. And then Alford blew himself up. At this point, I'm not even sure who Yuri is working for."

My father looked at me intently, put his cup on the counter and came back to the table.

"Katyusha," he said. "I think you're being set up. I don't know by who and I don't know why but sending you to the G7 and not telling you about a bomb is completely wrong. The Service may be using you for something you know nothing about, something they haven't told you. They may have wanted you there to take the fall. And being my daughter, you could be considered expendable. Perhaps this is part of a trap. For both of us."

His eyes locked themselves into mine.

"I can arrange for you to come with me and be safe. You shouldn't trust the Service anymore. Now is the time for you to run and save yourself," he said.

There it was. The offer of sanctuary, part two. Nikolaï rose from his chair.

"Give me an hour, alright? Screw these CIA guys and whatever games they're playing. I'll get in touch with my contacts at the FBI to see if they can arrange for you to travel back to California with me as soon as possible. Then I'll come back to get you."

"I haven't said yes to your offer," I said.

"At the very least think about it. Who do you still trust on the Russian side? I promise I won't force you to come with me. But please don't go anywhere while I'm gone. Get some rest. I won't tell anyone you're here."

I nodded.

"Alright," I said.

He paused.

"I don't ever want to lose you again," he said.

My would-be father left the kitchen and I heard the door of the apartment open and close. Did happy endings actually exist in the real world? Or was someone playing with me like a cat would with a wounded mouse? My brain didn't work anymore. And I was too exhausted to try to think it through.

CHAPTER 20

woke up on the sofa in the living room and reached for my phone. It was twenty minutes past eight, almost two hours since Nikolaï had left the apartment. I sat up and looked through the windows. Night had fallen. It was dark and damp outside.

I felt better after getting some sleep, but my body still ached in various places. What I needed was a few days of rest, or perhaps to hibernate for a week or two. To allow time, and the hurricane that had been chasing after me, to pass me by. I turned on a lamp and started to look around the apartment.

Who was he, this man who was my father? In the bedroom he was using I found his carry-on and looked inside of it. There was nothing in there that told me much about anything, except what he liked to read. A book by Elmore Leonard and another by Michael Lewis. There was a bottle of Lacoste *eau de toilette* for men on a chest of drawers. Some bills left crumpled on a side table. No ID documents or personal mementos of any kind. And he had obviously taken his wallet with him.

I went to the kitchen where I found the plastic bag from the pharmacy, with the hair dye in it. In the bathroom, I took off my clothes and mixed the foul-smelling ingredients of the hair dye in the plastic bottle included in the kit. I smeared the mixture all over my head, sat on the toilet and waited.

I couldn't take a shower with the bandage wrapped around my arm, so I sat in the bathtub to wash my hair. I used the body soap I found on the bathtub ledge, Nivea for men, and rinsed it all off. The bathroom was a sauna when I was done, and I wiped a circle in the center of the mirror above the sink and started to examine my face. Black hair looked good on me. It made my eyes stand out, in contrast to the pallor of my skin. My lower lip was back to its normal size, but my cheek was still bluish. I also still had bruises all over my body, starting with the nice round one over my hip bone that had started to fade. As for the gash on my knee, it was healing nicely. A scab had formed over the wound, and I used some of the leftover bandage in the plastic bag to wrap it up. When I bent down, a sharp pain shot through my lower left side that on a scale of ten I would have ranked a four. Probably a cracked rib. About that, there was nothing I could do.

I put on my underwear and my bra and slipped on my pair of jeans. In Nikolaï's bedroom I picked up a clean t-shirt, too large for me, and a blue University of California sweatshirt. I put on the t-shirt and strapped the Walther over it, then threw on the sweatshirt. I went back to the kitchen and ate a piece of bread with peanut butter and drank a glass of milk. I returned to the living room and found my shoes on the floor next to the sofa.

It was thirty minutes past nine. Something unexpected had likely happened to Nikolaï. He wasn't coming back as he had said he would and I knew I had to leave his apartment, to avoid any unpleasant surprises of my own. I thought the best thing would be to go out for a while and come back later, to see if he was there. But first I needed to find a jacket, something to keep me warm. I couldn't wear my windbreaker anymore. It was covered in dried blood. I looked around the apartment for some kind of coat but couldn't find any. Then I remembered the down feather vest I had taken from my apartment. In the sports bag I had left inside the Volvo.

I didn't have a key to Nikolaï's apartment and left the door unlocked, then quickly walked through the lobby and the double doorways. The freshness of the outside air revived me. It had rained some more, and the sidewalks were wet and the air filled with a chilled humidity. I walked around the apartment building and turned into the back alley. The Volvo was there, as we had left it. Parked alongside the fence. I approached it and opened the rear door on the driver's side. The sports bag was on the floor behind the passenger's seat, and as I bent inside the car to reach it, I heard the scraping of a shoe behind me. I knew right away that I was in trouble, and that it was too late for me to do anything. I felt the butt of a gun on my left side and the weight of a man pressing himself against me. Every muscle in my body hardened and my heart started to pound. I pulled my head out of the car and stood straight.

"*Privyet.*"

Yuri had whispered in my ear as a lover would. I turned around slowly as he kept his body close to mine, trapping me between Dmitry's car and his giant frame. To any passersby, we must have looked like a young couple about to kiss passionately. I noticed that the suede jacket was gone and that he had put on his old leather coat. He also wore a clean pair of jeans. Yuri had changed since we had last seen each other at the blood fest. He smelled nice, too. The light scent of an aftershave lotion. He looked at my newly black hair and at the contour of my face.

"Nice hair," he said.

"What do you want?"

"The same thing I wanted earlier in the day. That you come with me."

My partner held the tip of his Beretta stuck against my belly. He meant business this time. There was no smile edging its way onto his face.

"How did you find me?" I said.

"Dmitry's car has a beacon on it. The Service located it."

So much for thinking I could lose him with a few quick turns. But at least I knew he had been in touch with the Service, which meant he hadn't gone completely rogue.

"Where were you since I last saw you?" he said.

"At Stacey's apartment."

"Really? Is that where you left the flash drive?"

There was sarcasm in his voice. Yuri knew I was lying. He slipped his hand under Nikolaï's university shirt and pulled out the Walther from its holster, then dropped it on the floor of the car. That was the end of my SPVQ handgun. Unless I managed to come back to the Volvo on my own, I could kiss it goodbye.

"I need the vest that's inside my bag. It's freezing," I said.

"Move."

I took a step away from the car and Yuri reached inside the bag while keeping the gun and his eyes on me. He threw me the vest.

"Hurry up," he said.

I zipped it up as Yuri shut the door of the Volvo then pulled a tightly folded piece of paper from inside his jacket and placed it on the windshield under one of the wipers.

"What's this?"

"Nothing that should concern you. For now."

He came close to me and wrapped his left arm around my waist. His right hand, and the gun he held with it, he shoved inside the side pocket of his coat.

"You and I are going to walk together," he said.

I felt the heaviness of his hand over the side of my hip and the grip of his fingers as they found a comfortable resting place. There would be no slipping away this time.

"Let's go," he said.

We walked to the end of the alley and turned left on Durocher.

"Where are we going?" I said.

"You'll see. Put your arm around my waist."

I wrapped my arm around his back and stuck my fingers inside the right pocket of his coat, where he held the Beretta. A thin smile lifted the corners of his mouth.

"Don't even think about it," he said.

A flicker of affection shone for an instant in Yuri's eyes, and I knew he had allowed himself to like me again for a fleeting moment. We turned right on Prince-Arthur, a slow climb towards the McGill campus, walking side by side on the wet cement slabs.

"Why did you go to the United States when you were gone for two months?" I said.

"Who told you, Irina? Actually, it may be better for her if you don't answer that."

"And why did you meet with Kozlov, the Russian defector?"

"You're catching up pretty quickly. It really was time I got a hold of you, Katyusha."

"Who do you work for Yuri?"

"You'll see."

A couple passed us on our left, holding each other tight.

"Seriously. Don't you think I should know at this point?" I said.

"Alright. For now, let's just say that I work for the only person worth working for."

"Because of what, money? So you can buy yourself expensive things?"

We stopped at the corner of University and waited for a car to pass. Across the street faculty buildings, old and new, marked the eastern limit of the McGill campus.

"This way," Yuri said.

We crossed the street to a short flight of stairs that connected to a pedestrian alley between the Physics Building and my old playground, the Trottier Building. The school of computer science I knew like the back of my hand. As our footsteps echoed against the smooth facades of the buildings, I looked at the top windows of the building and said a silent goodbye to my desk on the third floor and to my former self.

At the back of the Trottier we turned right and continued walking, this time towards the old Strathcona Building, a neo-Tudor beauty where anatomy students cut open dead bodies. And then we turned again, this time to the left, and climbed another set of stairs nudged between the Strathcona and the much newer Genome Center, that led us to the top of Doctor Penfield Avenue.

Rutherford Park waited across the street, with its sprawling sports field. The park was located on top of the McTavish Reservoir, a gigantic municipal tank hidden inside the rocky flank of the mountain and filled with millions of gallons of drinking water. In the summer, students flocked to its pleasant, grass-covered top that overlooked the city. But the park was anything but pleasant that night. It was deserted, dark and muddy.

"Come," Yuri said.

We crossed the street and entered it. A light drizzle had started to fall, covering our hair in a misty dew.

"Where are we going?" I said. "To Thomson House?"

The old mansion was right across the park.

"No. Not to Thomson House."

Yuri led us onto a gravel path that circled around the sports field and ended at the reservoir's pumping station, a Château style construction located at the edge of the park on the city side.

"We're going in there?" I said.

I didn't like the thought of it. My guess was that no one ever went inside the station, except city employees once in a blue moon to check on the pumps. We stopped in front of a massive wood door that from the look of it could have withstood the assaults of the *milices* during the French Revolution. Yuri pulled out a key from his jacket, a very modern key he inserted into a very modern lock and opened the door.

It was completely dark inside the pumping station and Yuri turned on the flashlight of his mobile telephone. He pushed me forward and as he closed the heavy door behind us, I took out my phone and turned on my flashlight as well. The room we were in was a windowless vestibule, a long rectangular space that served no specific purpose, designed in the style of a grand manorial hall. The ceiling was surprisingly high with brown wooden beams crossing it. Heraldic shields were molded in plaster high above the doors. We had entered a miniature castle, built by the city of Montreal at a time it had money to spare.

We walked across the room to a metal door. Yuri knocked on it three times and opened it. Behind it was another rectangular room that stretched sideways to our left and right, with windows facing the illuminated skyscrapers of downtown on one side, and the grassy field of Rutherford Park on the other. A long time ago, it had probably been an office for the engineers who worked at the station, but the room was now completely empty. The windows on the city side were located just above Doctor Penfield, as it curved up the mountain, and the glare of a tall streetlight shone inside the room and made it bright enough for us to see half of it. The other side of the room, the one facing the park, was almost completely dark.

Yuri stopped and looked to his right. I did the same. There was a man leaning against the wall next to one of the windows that overlooked the park.

"Apologies for the delay. It took a while before *mademoiselle* showed up," Yuri said.

"I figured," the man said.

He took a few steps towards the center of the room and stopped and stood there, right in front of us. I could see that he was a big man with a heavy frame. The light coming from the windows on the city side of the room reached the tip of his shoes and bathed his body in a dim semidarkness that allowed me to determine he wore some kind of high-end waxed jacket. A Barbour, most likely. I couldn't see his face.

"*Dobriy vecher, Ekaterina Yegorova.*"

I flinched. The voice had stirred powerful memories and hit me at my core. It had jolted me. Was it even possible its owner stood right there before me? I couldn't believe it. The man took a few steps to the left and stopped, this time in a rectangle of light that illuminated his face. And there he was. With his enormous mustache and his black hair, now mixed with an equal amount of grey. Uncle Ivan.

"How are you my sweet child?" he said. "The black hair, it suits you."

He smiled. Joy swelled inside my chest. I was elated, relieved. The nightmarish roller coaster ride of the past forty-eight hours was coming to an end. I was safe, at last. Uncle Ivan had come all the way from Moscow to rescue me. I took a deep breath and realized how good it felt, to finally be able to breathe freely, something I hadn't done in days. Uncle Ivan smiled some more, and the glow of the streetlight caught the side of his gleaming white teeth.

"Ivan Iegorovitch, you came for me," I said. "All the way to Montreal."

I couldn't think of anything else to say.

"Yes, I came here for you."

I suddenly remembered the mission and the lost USB key, and felt an invisible hand squeeze the pit of my stomach.

"I lost the flash drive," I said. "The one I got from Alford. I'm so sorry. It was stolen from me."

I hardly recognized my voice. It sounded like that of a child apologizing to a neighbour for a broken window.

"I know, my sweet. It was delivered this morning to the American consulate. These things happen."

His answer startled me. Uncle Ivan knew about Theo. It was embarrassing. Did Yuri know about him as well? I couldn't look at him.

"But you don't need to worry about any of that anymore," Uncle Ivan said. "We already have plenty of *kompromat* on the American president. A little extra would have been nice but really, we don't need it."

He took a step forward and looked at us with eyes that shone like glistening black beads, then lifted his right hand as if to pick an imaginary fruit on a tree branch. Golden cufflinks shimmered below his wrist.

"The balls of the Commander in Chief are ripe for the picking," he said.

A full-throated laugh shook his entire torso. A Santa Claus kind of laugh, filled with benevolent goodwill, by a Father Christmas who seemingly held the testicles of the leader of the free world in a tight, steely grip. His black eyes never left us as he chortled and then he stopped and became serious again.

"And you, my sweet child. You have no idea. No idea whatsoever how precious you are to me. A unique young woman. The only one of your kind in the entire world," he said.

He put his hands in the pockets of his jacket, took a few steps towards the windows and stared at the illuminated skyline. I noticed the shoes on his feet were shiny loafers ornated with prominent tassels. Not the kind of shoes I remembered him wearing.

"You were such a smart child, Ekaterina," he said. "The director at the orphanage told me so the first time I asked about you. She wrote it in the report cards she delivered to me once a month. From the very first time you sat in a classroom. And we were lucky with regards to your health. No major illnesses, no accidents. Of course, if any of that had happened, I would have arranged for you to be treated immediately."

Something he said surprised me. Why had Uncle Ivan received monthly report cards during my early days of school? I had been a small child then and he had only appeared in my life when I was eleven, at the time he had recruited me for the Service.

"You were quick, quick to learn everything, my sweet. Which really wasn't much of a surprise considering the natural aptitudes of your parents."

I stopped breathing for a second. Uncle Ivan stared at me, watching my reactions after this last sentence he had offhandedly dropped. I didn't budge. I wasn't sure what he meant to say anymore. He continued.

"The director of the orphanage, that poor woman, was devoted to me. She agreed to release you in my care when you were eleven years old. And I got Irina and Dmitry to look after you. In exchange for a fair compensation, of course. I had to clear it all internally with Central Control at first, needless to say. But they quickly saw the advantages of having a child move to Canada with two of their agents as part of the Program, at no cost to them."

Yuri let out a brief noise of appreciation. I looked at him sideways. He didn't look back.

"What are you saying, Ivan Iegorovitch? Are you not part of the Service yourself? Did you not recruit me?" I said.

My heart had started to beat faster. I remembered the things Theo had said to me. That I wasn't a real agent. That I had been lied to. That my work for the Service was nothing but a charade, a cover-up for something Uncle Ivan wasn't telling me.

"I did recruit you, Ekaterina," he said. "For something

very special. A special project of mine. And Irina and Dmitry trained you well. You're more of an agent today than many people on the Service's payroll."

I turned to Yuri.

"Did you know any of this?" I said.

"Don't put poor Yuri on the spot," Uncle Ivan said. "He's an amazing asset and a very good agent. But he never was an orphan. He's a graduate of the Moscow Higher Military Command School. Aren't you, Yuri? And now he also works for me."

My partner gave me a sheepish look. My cheeks started to burn. I was angry and I was hurt. To say that I felt used was an understatement. I had been manipulated for years by the people I trusted, kept in the dark. Lied to. I looked at Uncle Ivan again and I wasn't so sure I liked him anymore. All I saw in him was deceit. And something more sombre.

"You're my special project, Katyusha," he said.

His smile was gone and so was mine.

"Where's Irina? Where's Dmitry?" I said.

Uncle Ivan raised his eyebrows.

"They've been returned," he said.

"To where?" I said.

"To Russia, for now. Until the Service decides to re-activate them and send them some place else. Or not. They grew very attached to you, my sweet. Especially Irina. It was becoming a problem."

"What do you want from me?"

"Nothing. I want you to be yourself, that's all," Uncle Ivan said.

He gestured with his head to Yuri, who grabbed my arm.

"He's here," Uncle Ivan said.

"Really?" Yuri said. "That was fast."

"Yes. Just as we had hoped. You must have missed each other by no more than a few minutes. The sensors caught him below the windows."

"Who is here? My father?" I said.

I tried to pull my arm out of Yuri's grip but couldn't. Then I thought of something.

"Ivan Iegorovitch, do you know that Yuri killed Anton? He must have been working for you as well."

"I know he did, my sweet. Anton was capable of anything. That's what made him so precious to me. But in the end, he was damaged goods. A ticking time bomb. And I couldn't trust his loyalty. Unfortunately for him, his heart never left the camaraderie of the Service."

"And did you know it was Yuri who brought the explosives to the G7 and gave them to Alford? Surely that wasn't part of the plan," I said. "It could have killed me and destroyed the key."

"It *was* part of the plan. And Yuri did it because I asked him to. I couldn't pass on the chance to stick it to the Americans, could I? But that idiot Alford wasn't supposed to blow himself up with all these people around. He was supposed to commit suicide later in the day like a good boy. Alone. In a corner of the hotel park somewhere. We wanted to create chaos but not that much."

"You wanted me to get caught?"

"No. Not at all. But I wanted you to run, my sweet. To be in danger. So that someone I've been wanting to have a word with for many years would come out of his hiding place. Now of course, because of what happened there is a bit of cleaning up to do. But in the end, nothing will come out of it. The president of the U.S.A. will publicly disavow the findings of his own intelligence agencies and will rely on the public declaration of complete innocence of our president. Alford will be branded a lone terrorist and that will be the end of it."

He looked at Yuri.

"It's time," he said.

Uncle Ivan moved towards a door next to the one we had used to enter the room. He opened it and started to climb down a staircase. Yuri pushed me forward and he and I followed. Two floors below the staircase ended and Uncle Ivan opened a metal door painted red that had a small rectangular window cut in its center. He flicked a light switch and fixtures on the ceiling came to life. We followed him inside a basement room where the pumps for the reservoir were located. Enormous pipes rose from the concrete floor and returned underground after having passed through the pumping machines, a series of giant metal boxes that stood taller than Yuri. There were dials attached to the side of the pumps and on the walls next to them more recent electronic panels with red and green pin lights. A constant humming filled the room. At the end of it a plywood table with grey metal legs and four matching chairs awaited no one in particular.

"Have a seat, Ekaterina," Uncle Ivan said.

Yuri took me by the arm to a chair and I sat on it.

"Tie her up," Uncle Ivan said. "With her hands at the front."

Yuri let go of my arm and reached inside the pocket of his jeans. I stood up, ready to bolt.

"Tut tut, my dear," Uncle Ivan said.

He pointed a black, squarish handgun at me. A Glock from the look of it, as preferred by the Service, that he'd quickly pulled from under his vest.

"Sit," he said.

I sat on the chair and Yuri proceeded to tie my wrists with plastic tie-wraps.

"How could you?" I said to him.

"Just stay calm," he said.

Uncle Ivan came closer and placed his gun on the table, far enough from my reach. He slid his hand inside his vest and pulled out a small rectangular plastic box that looked like a pencil case. He opened it delicately with his thick fingers and took out a syringe, which he placed on the table next to his handgun. He then took out a small glass bottle from the plastic case and placed it on the table as well. The bottle was filled with a translucent liquid. A cold shiver ran down my spine.

"What's this?" I said.

"You're wondering what this is about, aren't you? Of course, you are," Uncle Ivan said.

He placed the plastic case on the table as he spoke to me, then picked up the syringe in one hand, the bottle in the other, and plunged the needle through the soft rubber cap that sealed it.

"You were surprised earlier when I mentioned your parents, weren't you?" he said.

He looked at the syringe as he spoke, slowly filling it with the liquid in the bottle.

"Nikolaï Belinski and Marina Serov. Your father and your mother. Extremely smart, both of them. Just like you. Top of their classes. They used to work for me, in Washington. At the time, I was in charge of running a network there for the Service. I'd been in the city for two years when your father arrived and in that short period, we'd already far exceeded the expectations of Central Control."

He looked at me.

"I was about to be promoted. Moscow had decided to put me in charge of our special measures program. I would have been responsible for planning and implementing the actions that accelerated the slow crumbling from the inside of the United States. The disinformation campaigns, the financial support of rogue domestic political groups, the sowing of anger and confusion in the public domain. I was very much looking forward to it. Three more weeks and I would have been on my way back to Russia to start my new job."

I wasn't sure I understood what Uncle Ivan had said. Had he been in Washington at the same time as my father? Nikolaï hadn't mentioned him when he and I had sat together in his apartment's kitchen. Uncle Ivan placed the glass bottle back on the table and held the syringe in front of his eyes with the needle pointed up. He pressed the plunger until a drop appeared at the tip of the thin metal prod. He then lowered the syringe and looked at me again.

"But it all came crashing down on me before any of it happened. Because your parents betrayed me, Katyusha. They betrayed the Service. They betrayed their country. They went to the FBI and the FBI arrested me."

I swallowed hard.

"Politchev," I said.

"Yes, my sweet. Vladimir Ivan Iegorovitch Politchev. That is who I am."

I felt sick to my stomach and all of a sudden very weak. Politchev was my father's sworn enemy. The man responsible for my mother's death. His interest in me, his years of grooming, had been intentional from the start.

"For almost three years the Americans tried to break me. They kept me alone in a cell. They prevented me from sleeping. They blasted flashing lights and horrible sounds at me for hours until I thought my head was going to explode. And then they would take me outside in a special yard for a walk, so that I would feel reborn. But that was only to make it even more painful when they would lock me up again. They tortured me, plain and simple. And then one day, when I was ready to die, they told me that I was going home. An exchange of agents had been agreed to between Russia and the United States and I was put on a plane back to Moscow."

"Ivan Iegorovitch, you know I had nothing to do with any of this."

"I know my sweet. It was your father who did this to me. Your mother, she was a good agent before he came to Washington. She died because of him. She paid a price for her betrayal, but he never did. Your father got to ride into the sunset with his new American friends. He threw me to the wolves like a piece of meat and walked away. For three years it was my desire for revenge that kept me alive in that cell they kept me. And I swore to myself that if I ever got out, I would make him pay."

The red metal door clicked open at the other end of the room and Yuri pulled out his handgun. Uncle Ivan grabbed the Glock he had placed on the table and pushed the tip of it against the side of my head. He positioned himself behind me, using me as a shield as much as he could.

"And speaking of the devil," he said.

The door opened wider, and my father walked in, holding the Walther Yuri had dropped behind the seat of the Volvo. He held it with both hands and aimed it in turn at Yuri and at Uncle Ivan.

"Nikolaï Grigorievitch, what a pleasant surprise," Uncle Ivan said.

"Let her go, Politchev," my father said. "It's me you want, not her."

"I'm afraid that won't be possible. Now you let go of your gun unless you want Katyusha to be shot."

I felt the hard tip of the Glock slide to the back of my head, just below my hairline.

"Put your gun down," Yuri said.

He was aiming his Beretta at my father, he too holding it with both hands.

"I'm going to count to three," Uncle Ivan said.

My father slowly moved his gun to the side and lowered himself to deposit it on the ground.

"*Bystreye*," Yuri said. "Now place your hands over your head."

Nikolaï looked at me as he obeyed his orders. Yuri approached him and picked up the handgun on the floor, then retreated to his initial position. He shoved the Walther inside the back of his jeans.

"Now that's what I call a loving father," Uncle Ivan said.

"It's very touching to see you look at Katyusha that way. Now come, come closer."

My father walked towards us until he was about four meters from the plywood table. Behind me Uncle Ivan breathed heavily.

"Stop right there," Yuri said.

Ivan Iegorovitch Politchev placed a hand on my shoulder and I recoiled at the touch. His fat manicured fingers curled downward towards my breast and I felt an uncontrollable urge to rip them away.

"It took me years to find you, Nikolaï Grigorievitch. Until I was finally told a year ago that you were alive and well and living somewhere warm and sunny on the West coast. At last, the time had come to lure you to your daughter. But first I needed a plan. You see, I wanted to be certain that once you were here, in Montreal, you would come out of your hiding place and expose yourself. And that was only going to happen if your daughter was in great danger, and you had to come to her rescue. So, as the G7 summit was set to take place in Quebec this year, I sold the Service on a mission to retrieve some *kompromat* from an American attaché who would be attending it. Not that they really needed it, but who can say no to an additional piece of blackmail, huh?"

He chuckled, then continued.

"I told them I would cover the costs of the operation and that all I needed was for them to allow it. A complete no-brainer for Central Control and they agreed to it. But then you also had to learn of Katyusha's existence. So, I sent Yuri on a tour, to see who would be willing to sell one of their own. And Kozlov was the one who agreed. That crazy son of a bitch was always a gambler. Never to be trusted but always open for business. The perfect man for the job. Isn't it right, Yuri?"

He continued.

"After Alford's suicide, the plan was to leak Katyusha's

photograph to the news network for you to see it. But things became a little more complicated than we had anticipated. First there was the incident with the police and Irina's first instinct was to remove Katyusha from the mission which, to her knowledge, was entirely about the *kompromat*. Anton wanted to replace her with someone else and we had to fix that. Then there was the mishap with Alford and the explosion. And finally, we realized that the CIA was already in town, hot on the trail of Alford and probably keeping a tab on Katyusha too. And next thing we knew they had decided to hide her existence from the press."

My father didn't say anything. He blinked, once, but otherwise didn't move.

"You're not feeling well? That's quite alright. Everything will be over soon. Now get down on your knees," Uncle Ivan said.

He placed the Glock on the table and picked up the syringe.

"Before I kill you, Nikolaï Grigorievitch, I want you to experience the ultimate suffering. But not the physical kind. That would be messy and barbarian, don't you think? Now, do you know anything about heroin? In particular liquid heroin? That's how it was legally sold to people at the end of the nineteenth century by Bayer, the great pharmaceutical profiteer. A pure form of it that looked like water. This is what we have here, in this needle. But much more potent."

"If you hurt my daughter, Politchev, I swear I'll kill you," my father said.

"Oh don't worry. She won't feel a thing. That's the beauty of an overdose," Uncle Ivan said.

Yuri turned to look at my captor. He seemed surprised. My father noticed his reaction and put one foot on the ground, ready to pounce forward. His face was red with barely contained fury. Yuri saw him move.

"Stay right there," he said.

I jumped upright and kicked Uncle Ivan in the shins as hard as I could. He let out a scream.

"You little whore," he said.

He grabbed my arm and I twisted sideways to try to unclasp his grip, but his enormous paw wouldn't let go of me. He dropped the syringe on the table and grabbed my throat with his right hand.

"You want to play games, don't you?" he said.

His sausage fingers locked themselves around my throat in a tightening grip. I couldn't breathe and felt my eyes bulging out of my skull. My head started to spin, and my legs grew weak. I fell back on the chair, no longer able to resist and he finally let go of me. Uncle Ivan took a step back and passed his hand through his salt and pepper hair.

"A wild animal," he said. "Just like her mother."

I wanted to pounce on him and tear his eyes out. He grabbed my left arm and rolled up the sleeve of my jacket, then picked up the syringe again. Yuri looked at him. He suddenly seemed terrified.

"Ivan Iegorovitch, you never said you would be killing her," he said.

"Keep your mouth shut," Uncle Ivan said.

"You said we would take her back. That's what we told Central Control. The boat is ready for her transport. I've made all the arrangements, just as you said. The captain is waiting," Yuri said.

"The day I stop paying you, feel free to give me your opinion," Uncle Ivan said.

He quickly lifted my arm, aimed at my vein and jabbed the needle into it.

"No!" Yuri said.

He jumped forward to try to stop the injection, but it was too late. Uncle Ivan pressed the plunger and a cold shot of venom flowed inside my arm. He then picked up the Glock on the table with his left hand and shot Yuri in the face with it, almost at point blank. Yuri's head exploded and his giant frame crumpled backward to the ground. A pool of thick, red blood oozed from under what remained of his head. Pieces of skull scattered on the floor next to him. My father jumped to his feet. Uncle Ivan shot at him twice, but Nikolaï managed to throw himself behind one of the pumping machines. Ivan Iegorovitch grabbed the collar of my jacket and pulled me up. He breathed heavily, holding me close to him as a shield as he pulled me towards the door.

"You're not getting her, Nikolaï Grigorievitch."

Uncle Ivan opened the red metal door and took me up the staircase with him, his big brutish hand squeezing the collar of my jacket. I started to feel lightheaded. I could hear my heart pound inside of me like a distant drum lost in a deep forest. Under my feet, the stairs seemed to be changing texture. They were becoming soft, almost organic. I suddenly felt nauseous. Bright flashes lit up the staircase like a galaxy of twinkling stars as Uncle Ivan forcefully dragged me upstairs. I stumbled backward, my feet no longer understanding where they should go. We careened across the room where I had met him with Yuri and started to walk backward across the vestibule towards the exit. I couldn't tell if my shoes touched the ground or not.

Outside, a gush of fresh air swirled around me and stroke the side of my face. It was the most soothing and pleasant feeling I had ever experienced, and I closed my eyes for a second then opened them up again. We were moving. The sports field was pitch black, as if it swallowed any light that came close to it like a black hole would in a distant corner of the universe. I looked up and saw the sky roll over our heads in slow, moving waves, like a thick, dark curtain that undulated smoothly. I knew I was standing but I could as well have been lying down. The vertical had merged with the horizontal. My legs had become independent entities that carried me forward on their own volition. I could hear Uncle Ivan breathe close to me even louder than before, like wind being quickly forced in and out of a tunnel. Or was it my own breathing I heard?

A shot was fired, then another. It was Uncle Ivan who had fired his gun. He and I stumbled across the field. I tripped and he gripped my arm and pulled me forward. I tripped again, with my hands tied together by the plastic cuffs. The field seemed to go on forever and we carried forward for an hour or perhaps less than a minute. I stumbled one more time and my hands landed on a rough cement surface. We had reached a sidewalk. Uncle Ivan pulled me up and we started to clamber uphill. The climb was steep, and Uncle Ivan held me up firmly under the arm as my legs moved awkwardly up and down like the legs of a puppet whose strings were being pinched by a mischievous child. Multicolored twinkling lights blinked around me like a cloud of fluorescent lightning bugs.

Ahead of us the looming darkness of the mountain drew us forward, even though I felt I could no longer walk. We crossed a street and entered a forest. The trees moved and whispered around me, with leafless branches reaching towards me with their long black fingers. We followed a path of wet, stony slabs, quickly moving forward with Uncle Ivan holding my arm. I put one foot on a flagstone step I could barely see, then onto another, and a third. And then my body ceased to function. It shut itself down. My legs folded and I collapsed onto the cold surface beneath me. Uncle Ivan grabbed my collar and tried to lift me up, but I couldn't do it. I couldn't rise to my feet. Not anymore. A shot was fired, and he let go of me. He fired his gun above my head as I slipped to the side of the steps and rolled on the ground. The cold soil smelled of moss and of rotten leaves. I lay there, motionless. I was ready to stay there forever. To melt into the organic wetness beneath me. To disappear.

Footsteps moved away from me, up the stairs. Then new ones came closer and stopped. A hand touched the side of my face. I opened my eyes and saw my own eyes looking intensely at me. Then I heard a voice, anxious, talking to someone. The words cascading out. Explaining and asking. I closed my eyes and felt I was being dragged backward, by a person whose arms had locked themselves under my armpits. And then the footsteps echoed away, and I was alone again, with my back resting against the base of a tree. Every breath required an effort as if my lungs wanted to fall asleep. A drop of water fell on one of my hands, then another. It started to rain, and I let go of everything. I surrendered and the ground started to swallow me. I became one with the earth.

How long was it before my torso lifted itself towards the sky? Before my entire body jerked upward, as if electrified by lightning? The sudden breath that filled my lungs hurt me and greatly soothed me at the same time. Perhaps I was dead already, but I couldn't tell. I suppose that's what being dead is like. I didn't feel the needle as it was thrusted into my arm, I didn't feel the Naloxone rush to my heart and convince it to start beating again. I didn't know these hands that prodded me and cut the plastic tie-wraps that bounded my wrists. I opened my eyes and those eyes that peered into mine were not those of my father. They were brown. And kind. And I remembered that I knew their owner, with the grey hair.

"Ibrahim?"

"You mustn't talk, miss Nina. You must rest."

I let go of any intention I had to hold myself up. Around me silhouettes of men were rushing past. Men with long white shirts that ran lower that the short coats they wore. A light beam brushed the ground next to my feet.

"*Il est parti par-là.*"

"*Aintazar.* Ismael, you go with him."

"*Eajal! Eajal!*"

The ghosts with the flashlights disappeared up the stairs and into the forest. I was left alone with Ibrahim and a young woman with black hair, who wore a uniform as dark as the wet branches that floated above me. I lifted my head to try to look around. We were at the edge of the forest in Mount Royal park, thirty meters away from its entrance at the top of Peel street. I shivered. The cold had established its home inside my bones. My clothes were wet. I was exhausted. The young woman placed a blanket over me. I closed my eyes and lost consciousness once again.

CHAPTER 21

I regained consciousness for a fleeting moment as I lay on the back seat of a car. Through the windows a series of lampposts flew by, one after the other, as the car charged ahead on a highway. It seemed as if we were driving through space into a sea of shooting stars. I wasn't sure what was real. Perhaps reality itself was no more than an illusion. Such as my own, which I now knew had been smoke and mirrors. I closed my eyes and fell asleep, then woke up again when Ibrahim and the young woman with the black hair gently lifted me up.

"Sana, put your arm behind her back."

"Where are we?" I said.

My voice had morphed into a croaking whisper. My throat was parched, and I could hardly speak.

"Somewhere safe. This is my daughter, Sana," Ibrahim said.

The young woman stared at me with worried eyes, then tried to reassure me with a smile. I noticed her uniform with the STM badge, the *Société des transports de Montréal* three-letter logo, sewn on the right shoulder.

Ibrahim and his daughter had parked the car in front of a discreet one-storey building, a brick bungalow set on a quiet residential street. From the look of it, it could have been a small municipal library or a day care center. The double doors opened and a man with white hair dressed in a white djellaba came out to greet us.

"*As-salaam-alaikum*," he said.

"*Wa-alaikum-salaam*," Ibrahim said.

Ibrahim and the man carried me inside, with each of them holding my back with one arm and lifting one of my legs with the other, as if I sat on an invisible chair. Inside, they dropped me on a bench and Sana quickly removed my shoes. I was too tired to look around, to tired to think. I lowered myself sideways on the bench and rested my head against the seat. I closed my eyes and allowed my mind to drift away, one more time.

I woke up the next morning in a narrow bed, in my t-shirt and underwear, under clean sheets that smelled of freshly washed laundry. I was in a small room with a view of a court-yard, which I thought must have been at the back of the house. A glass of water had been left for me on a bedside table. I emptied it then tried to put it back in its place and dropped it on the floor instead. I closed my eyes and heard the shuffling of feet approaching my room. I opened them and saw a woman dressed in a bright blue tunic and black pants. Her black hair flowed under a turquoise headscarf loosely wrapped around her neck.

"*Bonjour*," she said. "I'm Amina, Ibrahim's wife."

She bent down and picked up the empty glass.

"Where am I?" I said.

"In a mosque."

She pointed to her head.

"I don't usually wear this," she said.

"What happened?"

"Ibrahim and our daughter, Sana, brought you here last night. In Dollard-des-Ormeaux"

A suburb on the West Island. I remembered the drive at high speed.

"You were dying when they found you. Sana injected you with Naxolone to counter the effect of the heroin. Ibrahim knew she would have some with her, at work."

I didn't understand and Amina saw it.

"Last night your father called Ibrahim in a panic. He said he needed help, that you were dying because someone had given you an overdose of heroin. Sana works in the Metro. All the security guards in the Metro carry an overdose rescue kit with them since two men died last summer at a Metro station. Ibrahim called her immediately."

As told by Amina, a decision taken by a quick-thinking municipal civil servant nine months before was the reason I was still alive.

"Sana drove directly to where your father had said they would find you. She met Ibrahim there and they gave you the Naxolone, then they brought you here."

"There was a man here last night. In a white djellaba."

"That was the Iman. He and his wife set you up in this room after you passed out."

Other images were coming back to me. Men running past me as I lay on the ground. The beams of flashlights disappearing into the night.

"I remember there was a group of men when they found me," I said.

"Ibrahim was at the community center when your father called. The people he was with all came along to help."

She paused and examined my face.

"You should eat something," she said.

"How did my father and Ibrahim know each other?"

She smiled.

"You'll have to ask your father yourself. He shouldn't be very long."

Amina was graceful and self-assured, with large green eyes and perfectly formed eyebrows. When she turned her head sideways, I recognized the fine aquiline nose she had given her security agent daughter. She brought me some toasts and a bowl of broth from the mosque's kitchen, which was adjacent to my room, and helped me with my pillows so that I could sit.

"Thank you," I said.

It was raining outside and after I finished my bowl of *bouillon*, I spent the rest of the morning listening to the rain with my eyes closed, as the drops hit the windowsill in a soothing rhythm. I thought about Yuri and how, in the last minutes of his life, he had tried to save me. I cried and regretted he was dead. I missed him. And I realized how much he had meant to me.

In the afternoon Ibrahim came to the mosque for a visit. He took one look at me and understood I was sad. He brought a kitchen chair inside my room and sat at the foot of the bed.

"You're getting better, miss Nina," he said.

"You know, Nina's not my real name."

"I know."

"Where's Nikolaï?" I said.

"He's meeting with the Americans."

"And Uncle Ivan?"

"He's dead."

"What happened?"

"Your father shot him."

I waited for him to continue.

"When we found you, you were lying against the base of a tree, alone. Nikolaï had ran into the park after Politchev. The men I came with went looking for him while Sana and I took care of you. Eventually, three of the men found your father and they continued looking for Politchev in a group. They found one of his shoes and knew he couldn't be very far, but they still couldn't find him. And then Politchev fired his gun at your father and almost killed him. He'd been hiding behind a big rock, waiting. Your father said that Politchev had twisted his ankle and couldn't go any further. An ambush was his only way out."

"And then what happened?"

"Your father ran straight to Politchev, even though he could have been killed. He got to him and shot him in the head at point blank. More than once. I don't know if you realize the level of hatred your father had for Politchev. That man killed your mother, the woman he loved, and then tried to kill you, his only child, after he'd been looking for you for more than twenty years."

I nodded.

"How did you meet him, my father?"

Ibrahim smiled.

"That's a long story," he said.

"I'd like you to tell me. If you have time."

"I have plenty of time and I suppose we should start at the beginning. I was born in Tunis, the capital of Tunisia. I grew up there. It's also where I went to university. And when I was in my twenties, I was recruited by the local KGB."

"When was that?"

"In 1983. Or maybe 1982. I don't remember the exact year. I was a member of the Movement of Socialist Democrats when I was a student at the university, *le MDS*. But after I graduated, there wasn't much to do in Tunis. The economy was terrible. The cultural attaché at the Soviet embassy used to organize a *soirée* once a month, usually the screening of a film or a documentary followed by a discussion panel. And I used to go there with a group of friends. That's how they recruited me."

"What did you do for them?"

"Not much, really. They would call me once in a while and give me a photograph, then ask me to establish contact on their behalf with that person in Tunis they had targeted. Sometimes it was a foreigner, even an American on a couple of occasions. But more often it was a member of the government. Anyone they thought they could establish a mutually profitable friendship with."

"Did it work?"

"It did. Very often. You'd be surprised how easily people can be bought, for the right price. Once we knew the person was interested, I would set up a real meeting with someone from the KGB who worked at the embassy. It was easy, steady work. And in those days, I truly believed what I was doing was for the greater good. But then Oleg Agraniants happened."

"Who?"

"Oleg Agraniants. The chief of operations for the KGB in North Africa. In 1986, he defected to the United States. One morning he packed his wife and his three children into his Lada and drove across the city, straight to the American embassy. His betrayal had a catastrophic effect on the espionage network of the Soviets in the Middle East. It changed everything."

"What do you mean?"

"After he defected, everyone in Tunis became suspicious of everyone else. A culture of paranoia spread all over the network. Moscow sent a new team to the embassy. They took over the people I knew and issued new guidelines. Everyone was required to report regularly on their coworkers to the new resident KGB chief, to denounce any unusual or questionable behaviour. Most of the time, people had nothing to say. But the pressure was intense. So, people started to invent things."

"Really?"

"Yes. Some people made false accusations against one another, to settle personal disputes or to be promoted. The more zealous you were, the better you looked in the eyes of the higher brass. And I knew that sooner or later someone would use me as a scapegoat. Because I was expendable. I was just a local *arabe*. And then one day a man came up to me as I was buying fruits at an outdoor market. A short, round man in a short-sleeved shirt. He asked me to take a walk with him and I did. He worked for the CIA."

"So you switched sides?"

"I did. I no longer trusted anyone among the Russians. And I was fearful of what was going to happen to me. I even thought they would get rid of me. The CIA promised me a new life in North America if I was ever in danger. So, I became a double agent. It went on for almost three years. Then Aldrich Ames happened."

"Who's Aldrich Ames?"

"Aldrich Ames was a CIA officer who worked in the United States. In 1990, he sold to the KGB the complete list of all the assets the Agency had recruited among the Soviets' secret service. All the double agents, including the ones in Tunis."

"Including you?"

"I didn't wait to see if I was on the list. I got a call from the Americans who told me to go to the airport as quickly as I could. There was a plane there, waiting. I left Tunis that day and I never went back."

"And you came to Montreal?"

"I stayed in the U.S. for a couple of years. But I missed speaking French and I decided to move to Montreal for a while. And then I met Amina and I decided to stay."

"But how did you meet my father?"

"In 1995, when your father defected, I was asked by the CIA to come to D.C. for his debriefing. I never got to speak to him. They made me watch for a couple of hours from behind a one-way mirror. The Agency wanted to know if I knew him. They also wanted to be certain that they weren't being played again by the Russians and that your father wasn't a double agent pretending he wanted to defect.

I didn't know your father and I'd never heard of him. At the time of the interview everybody at the Agency knew his child had just been abducted and his wife killed. His suffering was gut-wrenching to watch, and it made a deep impression on me. I thought the agents interviewing him were going overboard with their precautions and I told them so. And then I didn't see your father again until three weeks ago."

"How did it happen?"

"I recognized him. On the street. But first you should know that last September, not long after the beginning of the fall semester, I was approached by a CIA agent. An undercover guy who said he lived in Montreal. He came up to me after I finished work one day at McGill and said he knew who I was and asked if we could talk. He showed me a picture of you and told me you were a graduate student in computer science. He also told me that the Agency strongly suspected you were an agent working for the Russians. Based on my past affiliation with the CIA, he asked me to keep my eyes open and to report back to him anything I thought was worth mentioning. And lo and behold soon after that meeting, you started stealing research papers from the professors at the faculty."

He chuckled.

"You knew about me stealing the files?" I said.

"I did. And I started watching you when you began to break into their offices. You were good. Always timing your break-ins with my rounds, never getting caught. You knew what you were doing. And I wondered why someone like you was working for the Russians."

"Did you report me to the CIA?"

"Not really, no. I just kept watching you and I had a bit of fun, too. Like that night I walked in an office you were in, and you had to hide under a desk."

So much for thinking I was doing a stellar job. Ibrahim chuckled again, then gave me a big smile, and I smiled, too.

"In a way, you reminded me of my younger self. Doing what you were being told. Not really questioning the reasoning behind it. You see, on my end of things and after all these years, I've come to the conclusion that God doesn't look more kindly upon one side or the other."

"But what about my father?"

"Well, one day, when I was on my way to work, I saw you walking on the sidewalk. And there was this guy I spotted, walking behind you. You went inside the Trottier and he pretended to continue past it, but then he turned around and came back towards me. And I looked at him as he came closer and at first, I thought he was a CIA guy, following you. But then I looked at him more attentively and something clicked. I remembered him from the debriefing, years ago. And I remembered about his wife being shot and about his daughter being abducted by the Russians. And I suddenly realized that daughter could be you."

"What did you do?"

"I followed your father for a couple of blocks and then I called after him. In Russian. He stopped right there. I told him I knew who he was from the debriefing, and I explained to him who I was. We went inside this pizza place around the corner, and I told him everything I knew about you. About the stealing at night of the research and the CIA man who wanted me to keep watch over you. He told me the reason he was here and how it had happened. And to me, his was the higher purpose. That was the work of God. A man looking for his daughter. That's how I met your father and I decided to help him."

Ibrahim left for work at the end of the afternoon. At dinner time, I sat in the kitchen and Amina fed me some couscous in a big ceramic bowl. She told me she would be sleeping at the mosque that night, as would one of their friends, for security reasons. The friend was an enormous young man called Habib who showed up shortly after nine.

"I will keep you safe," Habib said, after being introduced by Amina. "Nothing will happen to you."

He set up a folding bed in a corner of the kitchen and slept all dressed-up in his Adidas tracksuit under a couple of blankets. Where Amina slept, I never figured out. She went to bed after I had fallen asleep and reappeared in the kitchen early in the morning before I even opened my eyes.

"The doctor is coming to see you this morning," she said, as I momentarily left my room to use the washroom.

And a doctor did come to see me that morning.

"Multiple bruises, a couple of cracked ribs, probably a slight concussion. Also, your larynx seems to have suffered some kind of violent mistreatment. You're lucky to be young and in good health. In your weakened physical condition, the heroin you were injected with could have been fatal," he said.

The doctor was nonplussed about my situation. He seemed to be the kind of medical professional who was used to seeing patients in unorthodox settings, and I wondered if perhaps he had also treated Theo and his one-eyed friend.

Later, as I rested in bed after lunch, I heard my father's voice in the kitchen as he spoke to Amina. He knocked on my doorframe and I opened my eyes. Joy lit up his entire face. He looked tired, but very happy.

"*Privyet*," he said.

I thought of Yuri and it made me sad again. My father saw it and came in and sat at the end of the bed, careful not to take more space than what was necessary. I was happy to see him. I didn't know if he and I would ever become close, but he was the only person I had left, and I was willing to give it a try.

"I spoke with the Americans. They will arrange for you to have a passport so that you can leave with me to the United States. In exchange, once you're in California, you'll have to meet with them and answer their questions. You have to agree to tell them everything you know about the Service, Politchev and the people you lived with. What they did. Everything. That is the price of your freedom," he said.

I thought for a moment about Irina and Dmitry and what would become of them.

"Alright," I said. "I'll do it."

He leaned forward and squeezed one of my hands.

"I'll take your photograph and your passport will be ready tomorrow morning. We'll catch a flight home in the evening."

Home. It was a strange concept. But the offer was the best I had received so far, and the only one I would get. The next morning, I hugged Amina as I prepared to leave. She had cleaned up my clothes and handed them to me neatly folded as if they were new. My father told me I could return to my apartment one last time before we left. There would be some people watching over me. I would be safe. He drove me back to town in a rental car he had parked in front of the mosque. He stopped in front of my apartment and told me he would pick me up at six.

I went in and called Stacey a short time after. We met for coffee an hour later.

"I can't believe you were hit by a car," she said over an *allongé* with milk.

It was the only way I could explain to my friend my battered physical state and my days of silence.

"And now you're leaving for Paris *tonight*. I mean, wow."

My friend wore a black miniskirt, opaque black stockings and black motorcycle boots. Her hair had been piled high into a loosely clipped chignon that fell over the back of her head in a disorderly but alluring heap.

"It's only for a week. I'll be back," I said.

"And what about Theo? Is it still on?"

"Not really."

"Yeah. Same here. With Jules, I mean. He's super nice but I don't know. We had fun but then I don't think that we care about the same things."

"What do you mean?"

"He's very *corporate*. You don't really see it at first, but he is."

"Why? Because he's a law student?"

"Yeah, I guess."

She took a sip of her coffee and looked at me. I saw her lips curl up at the corner and recognized that smile immediately. I knew precisely what was next.

"And there's this other guy I met," she said.

"Oh my God, Stacey."

"I know, I know, I *know*."

Before we left, she showed me a photograph of her new love interest on Instagram. Fabien, a graduate student in anthropology and a yoga instructor. Longish hair, sustainably appropriate clothes. And apparently, a wicked body. I kissed my friend goodbye with a lump in my chest.

"I'll see you soon," I said.

"Sure. Unless you fall in love with a Frenchman and never come back."

She sauntered up the street while I turned around and walked in the opposite direction. I would probably never see Stacey again and I missed her already. But I knew she would be fine. Staceys of the world always are.

At six o'clock my father came to pick me up in a limo car.

"You're okay?" he said.

"Yeah. As much as possible."

Later, as we waited in the airport lounge, we talked about Yuri and Uncle Ivan.

"How did you know I was at the pumping station?" I said.

"There was a written note left on the windshield of the Volvo."

I remembered Yuri leaving it. That was how they had lured Nikolaï Belinski to Rutherford Park.

"I couldn't tell if it was your handwriting or not. I suspected it was a setup, but I knew you were probably in danger, and I had to find you," he said.

"What happened to the bodies?"

"They've been taken care of."

I flew to California with my father on May 1st, the Spring and Labour Day as it is known in Russia. That day, Nina

Palester disappeared forever, as did her doppelgänger, Ekaterina Yegorova, the child born of unknown parents. In the following days, I read the Montreal news every morning on the Internet. There was never any mention of any murderous activity at the McTavish pumping station or on Mount Royal. No article about shots being fired or a body being found. Nor was my face or my name ever associated with the horrors of the G7 summit. I simply vanished.

CHAPTER 22

The sand had gotten cooler under my feet. I grabbed my running shoes and put them on. Above the horizon the sky had turned pink and orange. I had never seen the Pacific Ocean before I'd landed in California with my father. And I was mesmerized the first time I saw it. It spoke to me, the ocean, as I took long walks along the beach. It convinced me of the possibility of a fresh start and of a brand-new life. Because of the ocean, I looked around my new home and decided I liked it. I got used to Santa Barbara and its quaint colonial charm, and to Nikolaï's townhouse in Sycamore Creek. All of it auditioned to be my new existence and because of the ocean, won the part. And because of my father, too.

I tied my shoes as I watched the last lights of the sun disappear behind the horizontal line at the end of the Earth. Officer Jenkins had called again this morning and left a message, but I hadn't returned his call. He'd said he wanted to know how things were going. It had been three months since my first debriefing, and I supposed it was fair game. We had agreed that it would be okay for him to call me once in a while, to see if I hadn't changed my mind about working for them.

I started to walk back along East Beach towards the volley-ball courts, with the roaring waves to my right and the tall coconut trees of East Cabrillo Boulevard to my left. My father and I live in a gated community. A small village of pristine white houses with red-tiled roofs and well-tended gardens. There are flowers and bushes. Some very tall trees. Friendly people walking their dogs. From my bedroom window, I can see the ocean and its long rolling waves. There's a fireplace in our living room and, connected to the kitchen, a large patio where we can sit in the morning and eat our breakfast.

We've settled nicely, the two of us. We live together yet somehow manage to give each other plenty of space. I often go for a run on the beach before dinner while my father sits in our living room with his readings or a TV show. I called him *papa* in Russian, three weeks ago, for the first time. He made a point of not overreacting and of pretending everything was fine, but I saw the tears in the corner of his eyes. In return, he started calling me Sosha, a made-up diminutive he concocted out of my two previous Russian names, Sofia and Katyusha. He also calls me sweetie.

Nikolaï sometimes talks to me about my mother, Maria. How smart and beautiful she was, and what a good agent she was known to be. And he tells me about my family, in Russia, where I supposedly have a pair of grandparents still alive and uncles and aunts and a small group of cousins. According to my father, almost all of them live in Moscow. It's funny to think I once lived so close to them and didn't even know they existed. He hasn't seen any member of his family since he defected to the U.S. and I know he misses them, perhaps more so now, as he gets older.

I crossed the street at a red light and entered the gated compound I call home.

"Hi Rose."

Mrs. Coppola, our next-door neighbour, greeted me from the sidewalk with her dog, a one-eyed poodle named Jojo.

"Hi Mrs. Coppola. How are you? How's Jojo doing?"

"He's been better for the past two days. But he's such a finicky little eater. Worse than my late husband. Aren't you, you bad little boy?"

Rose Ellis. That was my new name. The grown daughter of Michael Ellis who until recently lived with her mother in France. "A *daughter*? You never even said you had any *children*!" Mrs. Coppola had said to Nikolaï, the day we had been introduced.

I like Mrs. Coppola a lot. Seventy-five years old and always wearing her pink running shoes with thick fluorescent soles and her Nike track pants. She reminds me of a holiday card. Sparkly, cheerful and always wishing you the best.

I pulled out the key to our front door and opened it.

"Is that you sweetie?"

"Yes *papa*. It's me."

My father sat outside on our garden terrace. I slid open the patio door and joined him.

"That was a good run," he said.

"Not bad. The usual."

There was a printed page of paper on the outdoor table.

"What's this?"

"It's an email I received. I printed it for you," he said.

Officer Jenkins had written to my father this time, instead of me.

"He called again this morning. I already told them no," I said.

"I know. He said he left you a message. The way he's presenting it, it's an open-ended invitation. If you ever change your mind."

"Why would I ever want to work for them?"

My father crossed his arms and looked at me.

"I don't know Sosha. It's your decision."

"That's not very helpful."

"Alright. Then I'll tell you what I think."

He paused.

"Sweetie, for years you thought you were working for Russia and in the end you realized you weren't. You were being used by Politchev as a decoy to get to me. The SVR isn't what you think it is. It enabled Politchev to keep you in a cage just as he wanted. And I don't think anyone at Central Control ever cared about what happened to you."

"I know. But what does it have to do with me working for the Americans? If anything, their side, or anybody else's side, isn't much different. And I don't believe in that moral superiority bullshit either."

"I get it. And you're right. But one thing I've come to value after living away from Russia for so many years is the idea of a democratic society, at least in principle. The trolling they had you do on the Internet is them chipping away at it, bit by bit. In the U.S. and also in Europe. They're making people lose faith in the free press. In the judicial system and the electoral system."

"I know. I understand the implications of what I did, and I can't say I'm happy about it. But what exactly are you getting at?"

"What did Jenkins tell you, the last time you saw him?"

"He came in to see me after they were done asking me all their questions. It was just me and him. That's when he mentioned the offer again. To work for them. He said I was a special person with a rare set of knowledge and a very special set of skills. And he said that if I ever wanted to use that knowledge and those skills for the greater good, that I should give him a call. He said he would be very happy if that ever happened."

"Yeah. Jenkins is a recruiter for the National Counterintelligence and Security Center."

"I know. He told me."

"The NCSC is a special place. It attracts people from all the other intelligence agencies. Most of the work they do is counterintelligence at the highest level. Including fighting against the cyber threats, the disinformation and the meddling other nations do to undermine stable, democratic societies"

"I know and I understand why I'd be interesting to them."

"You may not have been a real SVR agent, sweetie, but Irina and Dmitry trained you well. And you're also some kind of computer science genius, from what I understand. Don't underestimate your value."

I smiled. I loved my *papa* a little more every day.

"I'm not a genius and you know it."

"Well, to me what you were doing at McGill is pretty impressive. And if that's the kind of work they would have you do at the NCSC then all I'm saying is that maybe you should think about it. A free society is one of the few things humanity as a whole should be fighting for."

"Sure. But surely that's not the only kind of work they would have me do, right? These guys have their own set of dirty tricks and I'm done with being used, *papa*. By anyone."

"I understand. But you'd be free to leave at any time."

"What, just like that?"

"Absolutely."

Above the palm trees a couple of pelicans flew across the sky. My father rose from his chair.

"Do you want something to drink? Some lemonade?"

"Sure. Thank you."

He went inside and closed the screen of the patio door behind him. The evening air was breezy and pleasant. I picked up the piece of paper again to look at it.

"So what exactly would you do in my place?" I called to Nikolaï through the screen door.

He came back with two glasses in his hands, and I rose to slide the door open.

"I would probably say yes, with some conditions. You're twenty-five years old, sweetie. Sooner or later, you're going to want to do something. Have a life. Maybe even finish your graduate studies."

"I couldn't do that if I said yes to Jenkins. And I can't apply for any kind of graduate studies without a student's record. The student I was no longer exists."

"But here you are, Sosha. And you're a brilliant young woman. If you were to work for Jenkins, you could make it a condition of your employment. You could ask him to do only part-time work for the NCSC, some specific work related to your field, and the rest of the time go to university. How would like to go to Stanford? Or Berkeley?"

"Stanford?"

"Sure. All you have to do is ask the NCSC to make it happen."

"And you think they would say yes?"

"I do. They can do anything. And by the way, you have nothing to lose. Jenkins called me after he wrote to me. He said that you'd been highly recommended by that CIA agent you met in Montreal. The one who tried to turn you over."

Theo. My cheeks started to burn and I took a sip of lemonade.

"I think they will agree to any conditions that allow you to pursue your studies. But that being said, there's no reason to rush things. Take your time," my father said. "Don't say yes to Jenkins until you're ready for it, *if* you decide to accept their offer."

"And if I don't like it, I just quit?"

"You just quit."

He stood up.

"I'll go make dinner. Spaghetti carbonara? Quick and dirty."

"Sure."

He smiled.

"Thanks *papa*," I said.

I looked away, to where I knew the ocean was. Dusk had

fallen on Santa Barbara and a couple of stars already shone above us, towards the east. I had never felt as free as I had over the past three months. As liberated. But I knew I needed to find my path forward. I would have to think about it for a while longer. Take my time, as my father said. And it would come to me. As surely as I knew who I was. Rose Ellis, for now.

ABOUT THE AUTHOR

There is never a good time to quit. But after 25 years in private practice at top tier law firms, Chloé Archambault said goodbye to the office and the partnership and started a new life as a sole practitioner, a writer and an amateur photographer. Now, instead of talking all day to clients, she has coffee in the morning with imaginary friends, one of them Ekaterina Yegorova, a Russian agent roaming the streets of Montreal.

Chloé writes with the visual in mind and a strong imagery is a defining facet of her writing style. The reader is the camera; observing, getting close and falling down hard.

A born and bred Montrealer, Chloé lives with her family in her beloved city, where she studied literature, then law, and earned her degrees. She complains about the extreme cold of its winter and the suffocating heat of its summer but wouldn't move anywhere else.

ALSO BY
CHLOÉ ARCHAMBAULT

The Decoy

A Valuable Asset

Made in United States
Orlando, FL
18 December 2023

41112074R10171